# Waiting for Autumn

Neesha E. Oliver

Little Flower Publishing

This book is a work of fiction. Names, characters, places, and incidents are the product of the author's imagination or are used fictitiously. Any resemblance to actual events, locales, or persons, living or dead, is coincidental.

Little Flower Publishing

ISBN: 0692559000
ISBN-13: 978-0692559000

*Cover design/photos by David M. Oliver*

*To Autumn, the daughter we have loved and cherished so much but never had the chance to meet*

*To the couples who know and understand what it means to have loved and lost someone who only ever existed in your dreams*

*To the childless mothers who need someone to understand the heart wrenching feeling of what it means to be infertile. You are not alone.*

# *Acknowledgements*

I would not have been able to write this without inspiration from our Lord. My deepest gratitude to Him for giving me the strength to complete this novel through all the tears and heartache that were poured into each word.

A huge thank you to my husband, who not only encouraged me to complete this and helped by formatting the book and designing the cover but also who cradled me through the despair that is infertility. I love you forever and always!

To my family and friends who supported me throughout this process. I am grateful for your encouragement and prayers.

Thank you to all our doctors and nurses in NaProTechnology who cared for us and prayed for us through our infertility journey. Your kindness was unsurpassed, and you truly exemplified the tenderness and care of our Lord. Thank you for being so attentive and caring in such an intimate and sensitive matter.

# Waiting
## for Autumn

# IF ONLY

Amelia Bayberry sat quietly and listened intently in the midst of the ornate Anglican church while the pastor referenced the Genesis passage in the Bible to "Be fruitful and multiply" during his sermon the inner turmoil in her heart pulled at her eyes, and she kept her tears from bursting forth. It was a normal day for anyone else listening, but for Amelia, the torture ate at her since her body denied her the ability to obey the command God gave to the first couple on earth. She and her husband, Jake, had been trying to conceive a child since they were married – over six years ago.

Amelia and Jake were married when he was a junior in college, and she was in the last semester of her senior year. She remembered that Jake had taken a class on ethics at their Christian college, and Jake had mentioned to her that the professor said birth control creates a hostile environment in the uterus meaning that the egg and sperm could still join for conception but not for implantation into the uterine lining. She remembered crying because she couldn't reconcile the fact that they may have destroyed a pregnancy by using the birth control.

She had stopped using birth control shortly after they were married, but her intent for using it was never to avoid pregnancy as most women had but only to regulate her cycles so she could make sure she wouldn't have an unexpected monthly visitor on their wedding day or honeymoon. She continued using it for a couple months after the wedding only because she liked knowing the exact day her cycle would start, but when Jake told her the information from his ethics class she was devastated that she ever used it at all and stopped using it immediately.

Even if her and Jake had conceived during the time she was on the birth control, her uterus would have rejected the baby trying to implant. When Amelia wondered if their only baby could have been conceived during that time, she wanted to scream and burst out in crying from the agony of her naivety. *Why aren't people educated about what birth control really does?* The thought of it all made her chest feel heavy as if it was going to collapse on her.

Now she felt cursed – not fully woman; not fully human - because every month she experienced the unpleasant part of being a woman but wondered if she would ever experience the wonderful life-giving excitement of being a woman. *Why is it taking us so long to get pregnant?* She thought to herself and secretly hoped that God had heard her question.

"It will happen when it happens," Jake would say to her and smile while he kissed her on the forehead when she would bring up her impatience about not being pregnant. She would agree with him and try not to let her frustration eat at her.

One of the children in front of her who was wiggling around paused to look at Amelia and smiled. Amelia smiled back and blinked back the tears that wanted to follow. She always felt that she had a gift with children; they seemed naturally attracted to her. She thought it was a sign from God that she would have children someday, but sometimes the gift tormented her like a curse since the thing she wanted most and seemed to have a gift for was kept her out of her reach. She was locked in a tower as she watched all the other girls attend the ball to catch the prince's attention. But where was her fairy godmother who with a single wave of her wand could give her a glass slipper that she could cherish until the prince came to free her?

Every Sunday was like this for her – painfully emotional. She noticed all the little children in the church while she hoped someday she and Jake would have one of their own. She studied how each child and parent interacted. It was all foreign to her – yet she wanted to learn it all first hand. She had always been a hands-on kind of learner. Having to sit back and watch everyone else was so difficult for her.

Every child in her presence became like her child, though she restrained herself from acting like a mother. Times when she wanted to put her hand behind a child who had been standing on the church pew in front of her so they wouldn't fall since they looked a little unsteady on their feet, she paused and kept her hand on her lap. Even though the child wasn't in any real danger, her motherly instincts wanted to take action, but every time she had to hush them, and a little part of herself would die as she realized that she wasn't the mother - and may never be one. She knew the parent would be grateful for her help if the child almost fell, but if they didn't, she was sure they would probably glare at her. *Who wants someone hovering around their child? I know I wouldn't.* Amelia condemned herself for trying to be helpful.

Amelia and Jake determined that this year they wanted to be active about seeking answers to their baby "situation." Amelia hated thinking of it that way since the word "situation" had so many negative connotations, but there was no other word she could find to use. Amelia loathed the word infertility, so baby stuff or baby situation were the only alternative phrases she could use, but either way still sounded like a precarious way to hide the truth that they were dealing with infertility. Since they had been married for awhile and still didn't have children, it was becoming very difficult to hide the reality of their infertility because people would automatically assume that they didn't want children or that they were purposely holding off on having children to experience the lavishness of life. Others that didn't hold that opinion would question them about having children, but Amelia didn't want to invite the world into their personal struggle.

"Look what I found," Amelia thought back on their conversation from a few days earlier. "There is way we can figure out our infertility without going through the regular fertility clinics." She pointed to a link that showed on the computer screen after some searching about a Catholic approach to infertility. Even though they weren't Catholic, they believed in the Catholic Church's opinion on human life and approach to infertility.

"Naprotechnology, what's that?" Jake put his hand on her shoulder.

"Apparently, this is the Catholic Church's way of dealing with infertility; it stands for Natural Procreative Technology. They have trained Catholic doctors that help women with their infertility issues from a disease perspective." Jake gave her a puzzled look. "In other words, they view infertility almost like a side effect from something else that is going on the body. So they find out what that is, treat it, and then hopefully the infertility is resolved." She smiled.

She reached down to grab Jake's hand and squeezed it gently. She realized she hadn't even heard the rest of the sermon or how the Bible verse that caused her initial distraction even related to anything else the pastor talked about. Lately, it seemed that either babies or pregnant women bombarded her everywhere she turned. She couldn't turn on a show or movie without somehow miraculously choosing one that involved babies or women getting pregnant. She and Jake would glance at each other as to say, "*Really? How did we manage to pick something like this again?*"

Some days, Amelia wished she would wake up to realize this was only a bad dream. She loved Jake more than anyone and wished more than anything that she could give him a child -that they could share in that joy together. She desperately wanted to find answers to their inability to conceive, but at the same time, she was terrified to find out that it may not be a bad dream at all and, in fact, be a reality she needed to face. If they were permanently infertile, that seemed a harder reality to bear than the dealing with the uncertainty of it all. Could she handle that kind of disappointment if that ended up being the truth? She wasn't so sure, but she also knew that she couldn't live in the misery she carried by the mystery of not knowing anymore either, as awkwardly comfortable as it had become for her. She needed the answers like she needed the air for her next breath.

Their first appointment at a Catholic fertility center to start their process with Naprotechnology was scheduled for next month. They chose the Catholic fertility center over the mainstream method of fertility clinics as their avenue of treatment because they were opposed to supporting the modern day practices that were offered such as IVF (in vitro-fertilization). IVF would involve a doctor fertilizing several eggs in a laboratory by using the male's sperm and then inserting several of the embryos into the woman while she is hyped up on hormones in hopes that one of them will take while the rest of the embryos are stored frozen. The bond of creating a child together the way God had intended was very special to Amelia and Jake, and they couldn't imagine telling their child someday that he or she was created in a lab or that their frozen siblings had been terminated or lost in an epic battle to conceive them.

They wanted to preserve the conception of a child as an intimate process between man and woman the way God created it to be, not between doctor and woman. They wanted a clinic that would not only understand their beliefs, but also agree with them and with the sanctity of life. Yes, they *may* be able to achieve pregnancy faster if they had chosen a regular clinic, but the Catholic fertility center's goal is not only to help women achieve a healthy pregnancy, but also to investigate if there is a potential medical problem as the root cause that could be contributing to the infertility.

A few days earlier, they received their first call from the nurse and doctor of the facility in regards to their application. They answered a bunch of questions, and the doctor said he would send them an informational packet along with a prescription for blood work that Amelia would need to have done before their first visit with him. The fertility center was located in Gardner, Massachusetts, leaving Amelia and Jake with a two hour commute since they lived in Ipswich, Massachusetts; it was a little over halfway across the state.

The doctor also instructed them to connect with a nurse who was registered with the same Catholic program and certified in the Creighton Model charting method because the nurse would need to facilitate them in charting Amelia's cycles by showing them how to use a series of numbers and letters. The data on the charts recorded from Amelia's cervical mucus observations would be computed into metadata that would output results for the doctor to examine scientifically and better determine the cause of infertility.

Amelia and Jake decided they weren't going to let their families know about their infertility since they weren't completely sure they couldn't have children yet and didn't have a confirmed diagnosis either. They only told their parents but asked them not to tell anyone else in the family. They also shared it with a few friends at church, so they could have people praying for them. And since there would be days they would have to be late for work so Amelia could have blood tests done on certain days of her cycle and times they would need to take half days off in order to make it to an afternoon appointment in Gardner, they informed their direct managers at work so their frequent absences wouldn't become an issue of concern. All the coordination involved with finding the answers to their infertility began to overwhelm Amelia, but she would rather feel overwhelmed and receive some answers than perpetually wonder if this was ever going to be an option for them.

After work on Monday, Amelia opened her journal and wrote:

*Today at work I found myself gazing at the photo of Jake and me at Christmas time that we used as our Christmas photo with our cat held tightly between the two of us; however, my mind constantly replaces our cat with a baby. I wonder if maybe this Christmas or next – at latest – if our little one will be here? I let my mind begin to wonder if the baby would be old enough to be baptized at Christmas like I was. I can't help but picture our little girl – my fantasies always seem to see a little girl - in the cutest little white dress with a white crocheted blanket given to her by the church ladies who make them for the baptized infants. I can't wait to parade proudly around the church with Jake's arm around her showing off our little white angel from above. I can't wait to hold the tiny candle given to the parents that would be lit from the Christ candle. I feel like I can't wait anymore... I feel more ready than ever.*

*I know the Bible says to "Be fruitful and multiply" – does God know that we're trying? Why can't He or why won't He help us? It's been six years with nothing preventing us from getting pregnant and yet still no baby. Sometimes it feels like some women just look at a baby and get pregnant, yet I try to do everything right for my health by being vegetarian and try to figure out the best days to get pregnant by tracking my ovulation schedule, and I still can't conceive. I don't understand. Sometimes I'm so embarrassed that our cat is like our child. Everyone has stories and photos of their children, but all I have are stories of my cat, and the only photos on my cell phone are of her. It hurts more than anyone can ever imagine or understand. The longing.... the pain... the un-fulfillment. I sure hope that this journey with the fertility doctor will have a happy ending for us. I don't think I could bear it any other way, though I know I will have to ...*

Later that night, Amelia made a visit to Lane. They had been roommates in college and best friends ever since. Lane was one of Amelia's maids of honor, and Amelia assisted Lane in buying her first home. They were practically like sisters because they always instinctively knew what the other needed to hear even if it was difficult to say, and they were never easily offended by the other's honesty because they respected the other's courage in their truthfulness.

"How was your anniversary in Vermont?" Lane sipped some hot cocoa as Amelia stirred hers and sat down on one of Lane's cushioned kitchen table chairs. Amelia and Jake honeymooned in Manchester Center, Vermont and returned there for their anniversary every January as often as they could.

"It was perfect – as always. There's just *something* about Vermont. I can't wait until we have children and can bring them there every year. There's different air up there – it's magical." Amelia's enthusiastically wide smile warmed Lane's heart as she liked to see her friend so happy especially during the trials she knew Amelia and Jake were facing. "Remember how Jake and I went to the Hideaway Cottage for our honeymoon?" Lane nodded and stirred a peppermint stick into her cocoa. "Well, we've decided that next year we're going to splurge and rent the place again for a week in celebration of the next phase in our life – having children. It'll be like a book end to each section of life we go through. Hopefully we'll have some answers by the end of this year and be able to move forward with having our own children or possibly adopting."

Secretly Amelia hoped that she would either be pregnant before then or have news to tell Jake while at the cottage that she was pregnant ... if only she could be.

# CHARTS & GONGS

A month passed, and Amelia and Jake stared at the large mill looking building before them through their rainy windshield. The hospital was in Manchester, New Hampshire. The car clock turned 7:10pm, and they were moments from meeting their nurse for the first time that would train them on how to use the specific charting method that Dr. Carter mentioned. Amelia couldn't believe it was already February, and in one more week, they would be at the doors of the fertility clinic for their first time as well. Everything was happening so fast but still not fast enough since she still wasn't pregnant.

Amelia grabbed her purse and peered at the dark and dreary building while she put away the GPS. As they rushed to the door in the pouring rain, she expanded her umbrella with a click of a button and nearly slipped on the stone slab stairs leading from the parking lot since the rain began to freeze.

Once they located the suite in the hospital from the directory board, Jake tried to open the door, but it was locked. He jiggled the handle again and tried knocking loudly. They waited a couple of minutes hoping she would appear from any of the open doors they could see through the small rectangular window cutout in the door. Disappointment crossed both their faces, and Amelia's heart sank. *Is everything going to be this hard?* They had taken the last appointment of the day to allow them time to travel and even though the rain had made the commute a little difficult, they managed to arrive only ten minutes late after driving for an hour and a half. Amelia had called and left a message on their way to let the office know that they were running a little behind due to the weather.

"Try calling her again," Jake pointed to her purse obviously hopeful that they hadn't missed their opportunity to meet with the nurse. Amelia began to search for her cell phone while Jake tried knocking again. "Wait, here she comes."

Amelia saw a woman walking towards them waving. "Sorry, I lock this outer door once it's after hours since my office is in the back." Amelia and Jake were just relieved they didn't miss the appointment.

"So sorry we're late." Amelia apologized about the weather.

"Oh, no problem at all. No need to apologize. I received your voicemail." The woman smiled warmly at them. "Follow me, my office is this way." She began walking away, and they followed. "Oh!" she stopped quickly and turned back to them,

"I'm Nanette Mabrey." Amelia and Jake introduced themselves, and they shook hands before continuing to her office.

The first half hour of the appointment involved a PowerPoint presentation on Nanette's computer where she reviewed how women's fertility works, which seemed more like a where do babies come from talk with more scientific terms and graphics that Amelia and Jake would remember indefinitely. In the second half hour of the appointment, Nanette reviewed the charting process including an array of colorful stickers - some with babies and some without - along with the codes needed to record the level of Amelia's cervical mucus quality and different phases of her cycle, which they learned will help them identify the best days for conceiving as well as allow the doctor to better determine whether there were any problems with her cycle.

"Have you met with the doctor yet?" Nanette interrupted her own speech about how even though the appointments with her and the doctor are separate the whole process still works together as a whole unit.

"Not yet," Amelia answered quickly. "We meet with him next week."

"Typically, you're supposed to meet with the doctor before your appointment with me, but we can make it work this way as well."

*Great, I'm failing at this already*, Amelia condemned herself as she fiddled with her thumbs on her lap. "He said he had wanted us to meet with a nurse as soon as possible before our appointment with him."

"Oh, that's odd. Ok." Nanette continued her speech about the whole process.

*Are we really going to get any answers from these people? They can't even get their own process straight. How can I expect that they're going to be able to help us?* Amelia tried focusing on the loads of information that was being recited to them instead of her critical attitude that was clouding her judgment.

"Wow! That was entirely way too much information than I ever wanted to learn about a women's body," Jake said as they drove out of the parking lot. They both laughed. It felt good to laugh in the midst of all the serious information they had ingested, and they both knew the other was thinking the same thing.

"I appreciate that the husband is responsible for recording the information on the chart every night. Since I'll be doing all the observations of myself during the day every time I use the bathroom, it's nice to know that you'll be aware of these signs as well. It's not all on my shoulders. It's nice to know you'll be actively involved, you know?"

"I've always told you, Amelia, I'm here for you. We'll get through this together – no matter what happens, no matter the outcome. I love you, and I'm glad that I can do something to help in this since there's not much else for me to do."

The next week seemed to pass quickly, and before they knew it, Amelia and Jake were on their way to Gardner, Massachusetts for their first fertility appointment with the doctor. In her mind, Amelia had pictured they would arrive at a tiny facility and that the facility may even be in an older house since she couldn't imagine too many people would search out a Catholic fertility center. As they pulled into the parking lot of their destination, Amelia quickly realized that the practice was not at all what she was expecting.

*Another hospital*, Amelia gazed at the giant building before her, *I'm beginning to feel like a guinea pig in a test experiment, except that I'm a willing subject - not because I want to be but because I have no other choice. God - why do have to go through this?*

After they checked at the reception window of the office suite, they sat in the waiting room for a few minutes before a nurse came out and asked them to follow her down the hallway. "Hi, I'm Sandra." She said as they maneuvered around the hallways. She was pleasant by making small conversations about the weather and such. Once in an exam room, Amelia's weight and height were recorded, and then the nurse took Amelia's pulse and blood pressure. After she made some notes, she turned to Amelia and Jake, "What brings you here today?" as if she didn't know.

Amelia's her heart jumped into her throat. Was she really going to have to say all her fears out loud? Jake could tell by the unease on Amelia's face when she glanced at him that she was having a hard time gathering her words. He cleared his throat softly, "We've been trying to have children for a while now, and we want to check on everything to make sure there isn't another reason that could be preventing us from achieving pregnancy." Amelia loved Jake so much because he was always so smooth with his wording. He didn't allow emotions overtake him. He was her rock when she felt unsteady.

The nurse began writing again, and then looked up, "And how long have you been struggling with infertility?"

"Six years," Amelia quickly blurted out surprising herself. Once the words left her mouth, it sounded like such a long time. In her head, six years felt like yesterday. She could see herself walking down the aisle in her white wedding dress, but when she said six years out loud, it rang in her head like a gong being beaten over and over again by a very strong man. She held back the shutter that rang down her spine. *This is going to be impossible*, she thought as she watched the nurse make more notes on the papers sprawled on the desk in front of her.

"I'm sorry to hear that you have been struggling with this for that long," the nurse truly sounded sympathetic. "That's a long time to go without answers."

Amelia blinked back tears that threatened her composure, "Thank you." She looked at Jake, who smiled sympathetically at her. They knew they had come to the right place.

The questions continued for another ten minutes or so. Amelia didn't mind answering the questions. She was trying to stay hopeful that somehow these people would be able to help them. She had not trusted doctors much since she was a teenager when she had a cyst on her ovary, and it had been hard for Amelia to make the decision to trust any doctor again, especially now with such an intimate part of herself but also her life – her fertility.

"When I was a teenager, I had complained to my primary care physician of pain in my abdomen every time I would exercise, but my doctor passed it off saying that the pain was because I wasn't getting enough exercise. I didn't think it was that. I could tell there was something wrong." Amelia explained to the nurse when asked if she had any surgeries. "Then I went in for a physical for my application into a summer camp, and the doctor seemed really concerned when pressing on my abdomen. He brought in a nurse to feel it as well. Then the doctor took my mom in a separate room and the nurse stayed with me. She asked if I had any recent boyfriends, and as I tied my shoes, I realized what she was getting at. When I responded that I didn't have any recent boyfriends, she asked if I thought I could be pregnant. I was fourteen and never had intercourse because I was saving myself for marriage, of course I wasn't pregnant - unless there was another virgin birth like the Virgin Mary, but as far as I knew, the Bible didn't say anything about that." The nurse chuckled, and Amelia was relieved that the mood had lightened a bit. "What was worse was that at the same time I realized the doctor was saying the same thing to my mother in the next room!"

"Oh, no!" Sandra's mouth opened.

"Well, they had thought I was pregnant because he could feel a large mass in my abdomen. They did a blood test to confirm I wasn't pregnant because they wouldn't believe me - which obviously came back negative - before they took an ultrasound revealing that I had a cyst the size of a large grapefruit attached to my ovary. I ended up having surgery two weeks later because the pain had increased so much." Amelia paused as the nurse jotted down some notes. "So part of the reason coming here was to make sure that the surgery didn't have any ill effects on my fertility. I still have both ovaries. The cyst was only attached to an ovary by a very thin membrane, so they only needed to barely scrape the ovary to remove the cyst."

She continued explaining how her and Jake had tried for five years to conceive a child the natural way – no contraceptives, basically letting it happen whenever it would happen. After the first year, she started worrying that something was wrong, but she lived in denial about it for a while. After four and a half years of trying, she started reading up on infertility and picked up a book called *Take Charge of Your Fertility* by Toni Weschler. It had been very helpful in explaining trends in a woman's cycle from temperatures to cervical mucus and saliva changes.

Amelia used that method of achieving for about a year before she realized that something must really be wrong since they still weren't getting pregnant. She had figured she must not be ovulating, so she had purchased an ovulation kit every month consistently for six months. Without fail, the smiley face came up every month to mock her and indicate she was in fact ovulating giving her a 24-48 hour window of when the ovulation would happen, so they could plan intercourse accordingly. Even with narrowing down the days of ovulation and practically standing on her head after intercourse for half an hour, Amelia still wasn't getting pregnant.

She knew at that point something had to be extremely wrong, and she needed answers before she could consider adoption. She had to know what was wrong with her or Jake that was causing them trouble with conceiving. Granted, she had the surgery for a cyst on her ovary which may have caused scar tissue, and Jake had a low sperm count due to a misdiagnosis from his doctor when he was younger, but surely that couldn't be the sole reason to their dilemma.

Once the nurse had finished taking all the notes, she left the room to find the doctor. "Hello," they heard a voice from behind the door, "I'm Dr. Carter." He came into the room and shook both their hands. Amelia found herself reiterating everything to him, as he asked a lot of the same questions. He talked towards the end of their appointment about the options open to them through the clinic. There were medications Amelia could try to ramp up certain parts of her cycle that may not be working properly, which he would be able to determine from blood tests done over a couple months to check her hormone levels. He also mentioned that many women with unexplained infertility suffered from endometriosis but that there was no test that could be done to determine whether a woman had endometriosis or not. She would have to undergo a laparoscopy surgery for the doctor to completely make a diagnosis.

"What about my auto-immune problems? Can those cause complications with pregnancy? Or could it be causing the infertility?"

"Actually, if you were to get pregnant, the body should calm down all of your auto-immune reactions *because* of the baby, and you should be fine during the pregnancy," but he also mentioned how after the baby is born, she may have problems with her auto-immune stuff since the body wouldn't have a reason to stay calm anymore.

Dr. Carter explained that some couples want to move faster and start off with the surgery right away; whereas, other couples like trying the medications first. "Every couple is different; some want to do everything within the first couple of months, and other couples want to take their time in the different treatments. One way doesn't work better than the other, it's all in how much time you want to spend on this process. I know how hard it is for couples, so you have to decide what is comfortable for you two." Amelia was thinking that her and Jake were definitely more on the slow side of things - it took her six years to even step into a clinic. "And of course, there is no guarantee of a pregnancy, but we have better statistics of women not only getting pregnant but also actually sustaining the pregnancy successfully through birth than any of the alternative clinics out there."

Before the appointment ended, Dr. Carter said, "Oh, and don't forget to do your homework!" It seemed he wanted to end the appointment on a lighter note, so they chuckled with him as they knew what he meant. They didn't know it yet, but this was how he always ended his appointments. Though they had been so used to timing intercourse throughout the month, they didn't need to be reminded of making sure they were doing it. They knew he meant well but sometimes it was difficult to time intercourse when coming out of a stressful day and being completely exhausted yet having to plan intercourse because it was a fertile day.

The drive home was quite silent for a while as Amelia sat with her thoughts. Her thoughts swirled around in the car like fireflies – she desperately wanted to catch them but also felt it might be better to let them be free. Jake could tell something was bothering Amelia but wasn't sure what to say to console his wife, though he knew her well enough to know that her thoughts were getting the best of her. "What are you thinking about? Talk to me, Amelia."

"I won't do it." She breathed heavily trying to hold back her tears, "I can't have surgery! I don't believe I have endometriosis." Amelia had heard of endometriosis and read about it before as she did with all the diseases or complications that could cause infertility in a woman's body. She had researched all of those possibilities before ever thinking about coming to a clinic. She had ruled out endometriosis because the symptoms didn't match up with what she felt, and those she knew who had it or talked to women whose friends had it didn't sound like anything Amelia experienced. Dr. Carter said that the majority of his patients dealing with infertility have endometriosis. "How can he say that without even knowing for a fact that I have this…" she thought out loud, "and apparently the surgery is the only way to know… but I just don't believe that *I* have it. And I can't have surgery again…I don't want to…" she felt a breakdown creeping into her soul.

"That's only one of the options. I don't want you to have surgery either. That's not why we're doing this." He put his hand on her thigh. "Listen, we don't know for sure that you have it. Let's just take this whole process one step at a time. Right now, we'll monitor everything we need to and make the changes to our diets and such." Even though they were already vegetarians, which the doctor had assured them was to their benefit, it was recommended by Nanette that Amelia eat a higher fat dairy diet to help her boost her hormones and fat content in her body, which they confirmed with Dr. Carter.

"But what if I do have endometriosis?" She couldn't hold back her tears anymore. The car windows started to steam up a little. "My body… I just can't…" Amelia would never finish her sentences when she was really upset about something. She would have herself so frustrated that all the words looming in her head couldn't make it out of her mouth fast enough. Crying uncontrollably was usually the only solution at that point.

Her mind immediately flooded back to her experience with the cyst on her ovary. The doctors had told her it was benign, which was a great relief but her recovery from the surgery had been nothing but horrible. Once she endured the hours of vomiting after surgery from the anesthesia and pain medication, she suffered from a kidney infection followed by a stomach infection. Her recovery ended up being a full month instead of a couple of weeks. A lot of the complications with the surgery, Amelia felt, came from her having an auto-immune disease called lupus. She was only borderline lupus, which meant it can have times where it was more dormant and times where it would flare up. She gave blood once in college for the Red Cross and ended up sick for a whole month afterwards because her body over-reacted causing a flare up. It was so bad that she lost her voice for a whole week. The doctors didn't even know what she had; some doctors thought she had mono, and others thought she had AIDS, but all tests came back negative, of course. It was only her body overreacting to her giving blood just as it had overreacted when she had surgery for her ovarian cyst.

Amelia swore to herself that no surgery would be worth all the complications unless it was a matter of life or death. Though having a baby wasn't a matter of her life and death, she would have to let a part of herself die if she tried everything else the doctor suggested except for the surgery and still couldn't conceive. Was she really the only one in the way of her dream?

"Listen to me. I don't want you to have the surgery either. We're not doing this to put you, us, through more pain when we don't even know that is what you have or not." Jake gripped her hand tightly, "Remember, I have problems too. I couldn't let you go through that and then still not get pregnant because of my issues."

"I can still get pregnant with your low sperm count though. The doctor said he has seen couples get pregnant with a sperm count lower than one million, so the issue has to be with me. I'm the one that needs to get pregnant and carry the baby. If we don't have that ability, we have nothing."

It all suddenly felt impossible. Was she just giving herself false hope? This whole process was supposed to give her answers, not make her more confused. Surgery was not an option, and Amelia felt the stabbing reality deep in her gut that having children may actually not be an option as well. She wasn't ready to bear that reality yet. *It can't be– not yet- not so early in the process*, she thought to herself, *please God, don't let that be the reality.*

The rest of the car ride home was quiet as they each sat with their thoughts and listened to JJ Heller on the iPod they plugged into the jack on the console in their Jeep. Amelia couldn't help but feel bad for herself, though she hated feeling that way. As they drove by house after house that night, she wondered how many children were behind each door tucked into bed for the night. She thought about how her dreams of owning a home filled with lots of children might only be a figment of her imagination. Could she live with that? She had an awful feeling deep in her heart that the answer to her question wasn't going to have a favorable answer. She didn't want to accept the reality that was slowly revealing itself, but she may have to... and that scared her more than anything. Though nothing was for certain, the dreams she held so closely to her heart- the ones she longed for as a flower longs for the sun to rejuvenate its energy– started to watch the clouds settle in and act as if the sun had never existed; so too her energy would never return. She would have to find new dreams, but she didn't *want* to find new dreams. There was nothing wrong with the dreams she already had - just like everyone else dreams of and is granted. Why should she have to change her dreams? She wanted her dreams to come true like all the fairy tales she had ever heard and cherished. She wanted the happy ending.

That night Amelia couldn't fall asleep. She waited until Jake dozed off, and then quietly snuck out of bed and grabbed her journal and a pen on the way to the living room.

*Why? It's all I can seem to keep asking myself. Why does it hurt so much? Why can't we have children? Why does it seem that everyone else in the world can? Why? Why? Why? God – why? Yet there never seems to be an answer. Why?! Why can't I have an answer? This was my biggest fear – still not having an answer – and even though we only just started this process; I have this horrible feeling that there's not going to be an answer. Why? What's worse – a question that has an unfavorable answer or a question that has no answer at all? The latter – as it leaves you with no closure. It leaves you to wander in some type of morphed reality that isn't really existence at all because there's nothing to grasp hold of; it's a bunch of unanswered questions floating around waiting for a resolution that may never exist.*

# SURPRISES AREN'T ALWAYS FUN

As Amelia held the baby in her arms, joy radiated throughout her whole body. The baby's gaze upon her almost brought tears to her eyes. Jake came up behind her and embraced them both. Amelia kissed Jake on the cheek, "Our girl is so adorable, isn't she?"

"You're both adorable," he kissed her on the forehead.

Amelia jolted awake only to find Chloe, their black and white tabby cat, sitting on her chest purring. The sun began to peek through cracks on either side of the shades. *No baby*, Amelia thought to herself as she held the empty, lonely room in her eyes. The dream had felt so incredibly real to her though. Sometimes she wondered if God was giving her some type of premonition, but she tried not to put too much hope in that. She didn't want to be presumptuous. She raised her hand and pet Chloe slowly, and the purring increased in volume. She glanced over to Jake, but he was still completely asleep. "Jake," she whispered. Nothing. She tapped his nose with the tip of her finger. He still did not stir. She shrugged her shoulders at Chloe.

It was days like these when Amelia wished she had some other reason to get out of bed other than just her sheer will. Should she let herself sleep in a little longer? It was Saturday and only seven-thirty, but she didn't feel tired anymore. If she did let herself fall back to sleep, would the wonderful alternate reality come back to her?

What would it be like if they had a baby right now? Amelia would probably have been up much earlier, maybe she would be tired wishing she could sleep in – remembering the good 'ole days when she didn't have to get out bed for anything or anyone. Would she rather be the frustrated mother looking back on what her life was like without kids, or be the woman who is constantly tortured of wanting the exact opposite? Sometimes Amelia's thoughts made her head hurt, and because she had been awake so long without sitting up, she actually began to have a headache.

Chloe jumped down as Amelia propped herself up with some of the pillows on the bed. *Would the wee hours of the morning be precious to me as long as I was holding my little one?* A tear started in her eye. How she longed to see a crib in the corner of their bedroom – would it be pink and lacy for a girl or blue with polka dots for a boy? Sometimes she wished her imagination wasn't so active. In the imaginary crib, she could see little fingers twirling in the air waiting for mother to grab hold of them.

Amelia shook her head. She couldn't let herself think about the child anymore.

*My God, why does it hurt so much? It feels like too much to handle.* She wrote in her prayer journal as she settled at the kitchen table. *I know I need to make You enough, but it's hard to know how… please, help me understand. I feel haunted by a world that I want to be a part of so badly, but what if it's a world I may never be a part of? How can I be proud of who I am, who You created me to be, when my body can't do what it was created to do? I feel broken in the worst way a woman could ever feel broken. Can You fix me? Will You fix me? Please, I'm begging You. Please…please….*

Amelia's face and lap filled with tears as her pen fell to the floor. She was thankful to have this time to grieve by herself. She needed this time – a sacred quiet place where she could let it all out. She felt that every moment of the day she would have to keep herself put together as if everything was normal, but inside she was always on the verge of a breakdown.

Amelia heard the phone ring and quickly ran to grab it before it woke Jake. The caller ID showed Claire Fitzpatrick, her older sister. "Hey, sis!" Claire spoke gingerly for so early in the morning. Claire had never been a morning person, so Amelia was thrown off a bit by her enthusiasm.

She quietly wiped her nose and tears from her face and tried to not sound stuffed up when greeting her back, "Hey, what's up?" She pretended to sound as enthusiastic as Claire had and as though nothing was wrong.

"I was wondering if you'd like to catch breakfast and a coffee with me at Starbucks this morning?" Amelia told Claire she wanted to check with Jake first to make sure he didn't have any plans for them, but that the idea sounded good. As she hung up with her sister, Jake slowly walked out of the bedroom rubbing his eyes. "Morning," she smiled, and he greeted her with a morning kiss.

She told him about Claire's plans of wanting to take Amelia out for breakfast. She hadn't spent time with her older sister in a while, so she figured she should make the effort. "Sorry we're not going to have breakfast together. I love Saturday morning breakfasts with you." She hugged him.

"I know. Me too! But it'll be good to spend time with your sister. Go have fun! We can do our breakfast next Saturday. I'll probably grab something small and go for a walk anyway."

The morning with Claire was a blur to Amelia as she drove home from Starbucks. She remembered her and Claire ordering and sitting down in booth, but she couldn't remember much of the conversation up until Claire declared, "I'm pregnant!" It was as if time paused in that moment. The coffee making noises and people chattering had become muffled in the background after Claire's declaration. Amelia kept replaying it in her mind. "I took a pregnancy test this morning, and the little stick showed two lines for positive. I had to tell someone else besides Seth because we have been trying for a few months, and I'm so excited that I'm finally pregnant! No one else knows yet. We're going to tell everyone officially at Easter in a couple of weeks, after we confirm with the doctor. You can tell Jake if you want, but no one else. Not even John."

John was their younger brother. Amelia had always been closer with John than Claire. Since Amelia was the middle child, she liked being the older sister than the younger one. Though Amelia admired her older sister in the way every a younger sister does, she did find Claire annoying at times and a bit overwhelming, but Amelia and John always seemed to have a stronger connection. Other than the occasional teasing, Amelia and John had this mutual understanding of each other. They never really fought at all growing up. Even though Amelia was only a few years older than him, she never made him feel inferior, and he always appreciated that about her. As they matured, the respect for each other only grew stronger. They could go months and months without speaking, not because they were mad but because the busyness of life, especially after Amelia married Jake. But even with the lapse of time between when her and John spoke, the minute they talked again was as if no time had passed at all – as if they picked up right where they left off.

Amelia and Claire on the other hand were close because they were family, but Claire's presence could be spotty at times. She would pop up when she had news, but then could disappear without a word for weeks or even months. Even though Claire was only a couple of years older than Amelia, there were times when Amelia felt older than Claire – or at least more mature. Especially now with Claire being pregnant, Amelia thought that Claire had no idea how long was a long time to wait when trying to conceive. *A few months? She thinks that's long? Try six years!* Her throat began to tighten with sadness and anger, and her vision became blurry as her tears threatened to appear. She blinked several times to clear her vision and see the road in front of her more clearly.

Amelia suddenly decided to stop by Lane's house and was relieved to see Lane's car in the driveway. Sometimes Lane would spend her mornings painting at the beach or in the state park to catch the morning light, so she was glad Lane was either back from one of her excursions or didn't go out this morning because she desperately needed to talk to someone. She didn't want to be a total wreck for Jake when she got home. She needed a woman who could understand her and be a solid support for her emotional state right now. Lane had been that rock for her more times than Lane probably knew. She hated showing up without letting Lane know, but she knew Lane would understand.

Amelia knocked lightly as it was only nine in the morning and would knock louder in a few minutes if there was no response, since Lane was a morning person. She was the kind of person who when they were in college would be showered, dressed, make-up and hair done before their first morning class while Amelia crawled out of bed only a few minutes before class looking like she had survived a tornado.

The door opened slowly, "Amelia? Nice to see you." Lane hugged her. "Are you ok?" Lane always read Amelia's emotions so well.

They sat at Lane's kitchen table that overlooked her garden covered in a light layer of freshly fallen snow, while Amelia described the morning that she had. "I am happy for her, Lane. She's the older sister. She should be pregnant before I am, but now that she is, I feel like there's going to be more pressure on me and Jake from the family. I'm the next oldest, and I can't bring everyone into this yet. We still can't grasp it for ourselves yet."

"Honestly, Claire being pregnant might be a good thing if you think about it." Amelia looked puzzled at Lane's comment. "Maybe it will keep your family distracted for a bit. After the baby's born, everyone will want to spend time with the new baby. They won't look for you and Jake to have kids until Claire and Seth's child is a couple of years old."

Amelia sipped her tea, "I doubt it." For the next twenty minutes, Amelia discussed how she was beginning to feel left behind in the game of life. "Everyone else seems to be collecting careers, houses, and children, while our car contains only two pegs for passengers - Jake and I. I want to experience it all at the same time everyone else is, but the dial isn't in our favor." Slowly she and Jake were becoming the minority, and she felt inferior to other women as if they knew better how to be a woman because their bodies could bear children and hers couldn't. Sure she would never gain weight or have stretch marks, but was a thin body that hadn't experienced the weight of motherhood really all that attractive? It wasn't to her. It was a constant reminder of her body's inability to develop and accomplish what it was made to do... of her failure.

As Amelia stood up to leave, Lane put her hand on Amelia's arm, "I'm praying for you, Amelia. I'm not sure why this is happening to you and Jake. You are both going to be wonderful parents someday though. I know that without a doubt." As they embraced each other, a tear trickled down Amelia's cheek.

"Thank you, Lane. I really appreciate it."

Sometimes Amelia felt bad venting to Lane about all her insecurities. Here Amelia was married and wanting children and a house, and Lane wasn't even married yet. However, Lane explained many times to Amelia that she didn't feel a relationship was in her future. She was perfectly content with the way her life was. It wasn't as if she would reject love if it happened to her, but she wasn't trying to seek it out either. She was content with just *being*, and Amelia felt she had so much she could learn from the way Lane lived her life. Lane had a more calm peaceful way about her; it was almost nun-like. Amelia really respected her for that and wished she could be more calm and peaceful.

On her way home, she decided to make a stop at the supermarket to pick up a pack of the ready-made cookies that she could pull out of the package and plop onto a baking sheet. All she wanted to do was curl up with Jake and watch a movie while eating some warm chocolate chip cookies right out of the oven. As she turned the corner to leave the cold aisle in the store, she bumped into John. "Hey, Amelia!" Before she knew it, he had his arms in a big bear hug around her.

"Hey, John," her voice muffled in his sweater, "how's your job going?" She was unsure how she was going to keep Claire's news from him. Amelia wasn't the type of person that could hide her feelings well when something was bothering her, and John knew her too well. She needed to make the conversation short and make a quick exit.

John had worked with a landscaping business as soon as he was old enough to start working because of his fond memories of working outside with their father. Amelia sometimes made faces at him through the front window as though she were taunting him, but he never cared because he preferred to be outside spending time with their father than in the kitchen baking cookies with their mom like her and Claire did. Just as the sun set on a Saturday evening, he and their father would sniff the air; "Ah, chocolate chip!" his father would say – their father's favorite cookie. The times spent in the yard with their father were some of his favorite pastime memories, and his love of the outdoors grew from these cherished memories.

"Business is a little slow right now," the landscaping business did plowing in the winter, but this winter had been particularly mild, which in New England was odd. "I'd like us to have a couple of Nor'easter's, but I think it's a little late in the season for that."

"Keep your fingers crossed!" Amelia smiled.

He pointed to the package in her hand, "Chocolate chip cookies – good choice! Cheating though." He shook is finger back and forth at her with as smirk on his face. "You have mom's recipe for her famous chocolate chip cookies, right?" She nodded. "We'll have to plan sometime to get together soon, and you can make a batch of them for me." He nudged her with his elbow. "Hey, have you heard from Claire at all? I haven't seen or heard from her since Christmas."

Amelia wasn't sure how to answer the question without having to lie in some way, "We'll see her at Easter in a couple of weeks, so I guess we'll see what she's been up to then." She needed an excuse to escape before any more questions came up that would make Amelia blurt out anything, "Well, I need to get going, Jake's expecting me home any minute, and I don't want him to worry." She quickly kissed John on the cheek and started walking toward the twelve items or less checkout line, "We'll definitely have to catch up sometime soon though."

# EASTER

The weeks had passed so quickly since her meeting with Claire, and now Easter had arrived, and Amelia had been dreading spending time with the family since Claire had revealed her plan to Amelia. Amelia was relieved that she wouldn't have to keep Claire's secret for much longer though. It was hard enough to keep her own secret about her and Jake's infertility. Amelia shuttered when she thought of how difficult it was going to be to receive Claire's news again while the family swooned over her and touched her belly.

Amelia retreated to the car after the church service, while she waited for Jake. He was part of the altar servers that served communion during service, so he was also responsible for cleaning up the altar and altar pieces after service. She brought her journal with her though knowing she would have some time to herself and wrote:

*Today church was filled with families. It is one of the two seasons when church is filled with more people than any other time of the year – the other being Christmas – and both being when baptisms could potentially happen. Sometimes I would rather crawl into a hole and hide from it all on those two days, which I always feel bad about because they are the most beautiful times of the year to attend church. They are both such significant days, and I really don't want to miss out on them, but it would be easier to ignore the fact that other people have lives filled with children; however, I know I cannot dwell on my feelings of despair too much. I know it would sink me completely, but it is also so incredibly difficult to face the smiles and laughter of the families in churches on those days. Every little giggle from a child drills a hole in my heart, and all I can do is sit and watch my life drain out onto the floor while I hold the tears in my throat hoping that no one will notice. Most days it feels like I am carrying a bunch of rocks in my pockets weighing me down, but the pressure is bearable; however when these situations arise, I am holding a boulder above my head hoping that my strength will be enough to stop it from crushing me.*

*God, how much longer will I have to carry this? I know You can help me. Why do You choose not to help? I know You care, but why are You so silent? I don't know how to carry this any longer, and honestly, I don't know how You can help. I know Your plans are better than any plans I could ever have for my life, and I'm trying to trust that everything in the end will be all right. But when is*

*the end? How much longer do I have to wait to see
what the end looks like? How many more couples
my age do I have to see pregnant and not only have
one, but two, three, and four children – yet year
after year I remain barren?*

*This season of fertility mocks me. Each year,
all the animals have their young, the flowers bloom
again with new life, and yet I'm stuck in the midst of
them all surrounded with all the new life that is
blooming. My life remains the same still. Is there
something wrong with my soil? Why is my ground
dry and barren? I care so tenderly for it, yet I see
others who till with less care and time and yet they
flourish. Do You know how painful that is? What is
wrong with me? Do You not trust I can handle this?
Do You think I would be a bad mother? I don't
understand. I'm not sure I ever will.*

Amelia quickly wiped the tears streaming down
her face as she noticed Jake exiting the church and
tucked her journal into her purse. She tried to be
strong for him as well – mostly because she didn't
want him to see her as an emotional wreck of a wife
all the time. She wanted to be remembered as the
strong woman who persevered through this time not
the wallowing woman who needed comfort
constantly; however, more times than not she
needed to be the former woman but yet she seemed
to always resort to the latter.

"Ready for this?" Jake put the car in park as
they both stared at her parents' house.

She wasn't sure what was harder to endure -
church with all the families or waiting for Claire's

news to be released. "As ready as I'll ever be." The truth was that she was not ready – ever. It was never easy to hear that another woman was pregnant. At least Claire's pregnancy would not shock her today, but seeing the joy on everyone's face would tear at Amelia because it was a joy she'll never see in their faces for herself. Then, inevitably, there would be the questions to her and Jake: she already knew how the day was going to unfold.

As they entered through the front door, everyone was gathered in the kitchen lending a helping hand with the meal in some way. John noticed them first, "Hey!" Everyone looked up from what they were doing, and there were hugs and greetings all around.

"About thirty more minutes until it's all ready," Janet, Amelia's mother, announced. Claire and Amelia joined her in the kitchen while the men settled into the living room. The time passed seamlessly before dinner; however Amelia felt on edge the whole time as she anticipated Claire's announcement.

"I'll set the table!" Claire quickly grabbed the stack of plates from the kitchen counter and hurried to the dining room. Amelia thought it strange how eager Claire was to set the table because she usually avoided anything that didn't bring attention to herself. She liked helping their mother more with the food because it was recognized and commented on, and she would be able to take some credit. Not many people comment on how nicely the table was set, so Claire never really minded with that task or with doing dishes after dinner. *Maybe this*

*pregnancy thing is making Claire mature a bit
more*, Amelia smirked as the thought crossed her
mind though she was still preoccupied with how to
handle Claire's news with the crowd of people
around, so she let Claire skip off to do whatever her
heart pleased. Should Amelia act surprised when
Claire announces the news? Amelia was never
really the type of person to have a giddy personality
and respond like she was on a women's network
show or anything. She really had no idea how to
gauge her reaction to the news.

A few minutes later, they all gathered at the
table each person standing behind their chair as they
had done before every meal. Their father gave a
blessing over the meal, and before everyone went to
pick up their plates to serve themselves from the
kitchen, Claire yelled out, "Wait!" Everyone froze
thinking that there was something wrong.

Amelia's heart began to race, *Here we go...*

"There is something under your plates," Claire
continued. "It's something that will give you a hint
about some news that Seth and I have to share." She
looked to Seth and they smiled lovingly at each
other. "Ok, pick up your plates." Claire gestured
with lifting her arms in the air.

There was a tiny bow under each setting – one
blue and one pink at every other place. Everyone
looked at each other a little confused – except
Amelia and Jake. They knew. Jake just shrugged
when people looked at him, and Amelia decided to
keep staring at the little bows. She didn't want to
look at anyone. Her eyes fixated on the bows, and
she could see the little pink one tied around the fine

hair on a child's tiny head. She began to blink quickly suppressing the tears that threatened to appear.

Their mother's gasp broke Amelia's bow fixation, "Are you … oh my gosh... pregnant?" Claire nodded, and they both started crying. Tears of joy, of course, but Amelia wanted to roll her eyes, though she resisted. She glanced over to John noticing he was looking at her – almost as if he was studying her. She furled her eyebrows at him and nodded her head in the direction of Claire hoping he would get the hint that he should go and congratulate their sister.

Dinner had been full of conversation about Seth, Claire, and the baby. There were many comments about the food as well such as, "Should you be eating that? I heard that certain cheeses are not good during pregnancy," and "I heard that eating spicy food will give your child curly hair." Not that there was anything spicy at the table, but anything to do with food and pregnancy was brought up. Laughs were heard around the table and everyone was participating in the merriment - except for Amelia. She tried to act like she wanted to participate in the conversation, but she really didn't have the energy to be part of it all. She wanted to be the center of attention in this area of life for once. She didn't want to be the cheerleader on the sidelines anymore. She was tired of being the bottom of the pyramid - the support system - she wanted to be the cheerleader on top that everyone looked at and received the attention. Part of her wondered if she was meant to always be the support and never be the supported.

Her throat began to grow tight, "I need to use the bathroom," she whispered to Jake as she laid her cloth napkin on the table.

"You ok?" He knew it was hard for her to bear.

"Yea, I'll be fine. Just need a minute." She whispered to avoid attention being drawn to herself.

She closed the bathroom door gently and pushed the button to lock the door. She turned to the mirror above the sink and took herself in for a moment. Who was the woman in the mirror? Who was she becoming? A person that was so jealous that she couldn't enjoy her own sister's joy? A tear began to form. The woman in the mirror looked so sad. The tiny creases near her eyes threatened to become wrinkles in another ten years. Amelia remembered what her face looked like ten years ago – hopeful, full of life and dreams, happy. Now her face showed spent and tired. It was worn and more weathered. *I know what would make my skin look better... pregnancy! Apparently your skin radiates when you're pregnant – you get this beautiful hue to your face. My face should have that beautiful hue to it right now, not this pitiful existence – what is this?*

She hung her head down and watched as tear after tear fell into the sink. She knew she shouldn't condemn herself, but the deep pit in her heart felt too vast to hold herself above it today. *Oh Lord, I need You to hold me!* She looked to the ceiling with its popcorn nubs hoping that they would open to heaven's glory and for a moment she would see a glimpse of heaven. Instead she remained alone –

utterly alone – and sat down on the fluffy toilet seat cover. The shower curtain was covered in a flower print full of tiny blue and yellow flowers. Immediately her mind thought of how it would be a cute print for crib sheets. Why is it that everything she looked at always reverted to baby things? Before all the infertility stuff had crept into her life, she thought it was her biological clock ticking, but now she felt haunted by the thoughts.

She remembered how it was only a few days earlier her and Jake sat in their dark apartment picking out baby names. Because it had been Earth Day, the sat in the candlelight and dreamed of first and middle names that they thought sounded good together for boys and girls. Now all she could think about was how impossible that whole dream felt.

Amelia and Jake waved to everyone through the car windows as they drove away. Amelia took in a depth breath and exhaled loudly glad to finally have the day over with. How horrible was it that she was happy that Easter was over? The day the Lord rose from the dead, and all she thought of was *her* misery.

"What are you thinking about?" Jake interrupted her thoughts.

She was hesitant to answer as there were so many things running through her mind. Where to start? She had always been a thinker, and most times, it would get the best of her. She decided to go with the most predominant thought that was pretty much the theme for the whole day, "You know, just … baby stuff."

"What about the baby stuff? Talk to me." He put his hand on her leg. "I don't think today went as badly as you thought it was going to. No one asked us about having children yet or anything."

"No, I know. Regardless of whether people ask or not, it's still always on my mind. Sometimes I feel like it consumes me. I can't do anything, look at anything, or even enjoy anything because I'm always reminded of children and how we don't have any …" she took a breath, "… can't have any. It's still so hard to believe that she's pregnant. It makes me want to be pregnant even more than I already do."

"Why can't you be happy for your sister?" Jake's voice sounded a little barky, and she knew that meant he was starting to get irritated. "You'd want her to be happy for us if you were pregnant."

"Jake, it's not that I'm not happy for her." Amelia defended herself though she didn't think she should have to. He should understand that it's hard for a woman to be the one on the outside looking in on the life she wishes for her and her husband.

"Then what is it, Amelia? You can't go around and sulk every time you find out someone is pregnant, and it's not you."

"Why are you so upset?" She blinked back tears. "Don't you understand that it's hard for me?" She took in a deep breath.

"It's hard for me to, Amelia, but I don't let it stop me from living life. I love you, and I love our lives even if we can never have children – not because I don't want children – but because my happiness isn't based on whether we have children or not."

Amelia wasn't so sure she could say the same. She loved Jake more than anyone, of course, but she couldn't help but feel that there was someone always missing in their family. For years, she pushed it to the back of her mind thinking that a child would come into their lives when God would bless them with a child at the right time. Now that years passed and there still was no child, she began to question why God would bring them together only to bring them through this agony of being barren. "I just want our love to be able to create something that's as special as our love is to each other. I want to physically feel that love growing inside of me." The sobbing started, "and I …" she tried to breathe in between the sobs, "feel like … every day that dream … moves further from my grasp." She searched for a tissue in her purse. "Do you know how painful it is to watch, what feels like, everyone else in the entire world getting pregnant and yet live in my broken body that cannot do what it was made to do! It's not a matter of not being happy for others, Jake. I think I have a right to feel bad for myself sometimes."

"Amelia," he sighed, "I don't want this to ruin you though."

"Well, it is going to ruin me for a little bit! I am ruined right now!" She didn't want to be angry with him, but she wanted him to understand her feeling of broken-ness the way that she was experiencing it - not the way he wanted her to feel it.

He tried to calm her down by speaking softer, "We don't even know that we can't have our own children yet, Amelia."

"And you don't know that we can!" She chimed back.

"Listen," he squeezed her hand gently, "We've only just begun this process. You have to give this whole thing a chance. You can't throw your hands up and give up on it and assume nothing is going to work already. They said it can be awhile before they figure out what could be causing our infertility. In the meantime, I don't want you always to be depressed."

She blew her nose with her dampened tissue from her tears. "I'm sorry if I can't be as strong as you need me to be. I'm trying. I can't guarantee that I'm not going to cry and break down at times. It hurts, Jake, more than you can imagine."

"Amelia, it hurts me too. Don't forget that I'm going through this with you." But it wasn't the same to her. He wasn't a woman and didn't have all the emotions running through his veins the way women do. He also didn't have the monthly visitor as a physical sign of her failure. He may be hurting too, but he would never fully understand the depth of pain and sorrow that she felt deep inside of her … the longing that may never be fulfilled.

# MAY SHOWERS

Amelia stepped off the scale in the bathroom. *A few more pounds...* Amelia gained a few pounds since they had started the high-fat diary diet a month ago recommended to them by Nanette. Apparently eating more diary was supposed to increase their fertility, so they drank whole milk from Appleton Farms and bought pints of ice cream from White Farms Ice Cream, which was only a few minutes down the street from them. Though neither were organic, they liked supporting local small businesses. Along with being vegetarian, they tried to buy everything organic, but if they couldn't buy organic than they purchased through local companies. The grocery store had organic milk and ice cream, but Appleton Farms' milk came in a glass jar like in the old days, and they would return the jar to their farm stand for the deposit return. For the ice cream, they couldn't pass up the flavor of White

Farms Ice Cream. It was so rich and creamy making it exactly what they needed for the high-fat.

Though Amelia didn't like gaining weight, she felt like she was doing it for the health of their future baby, so that made her feel a little better about it and made it all worth it. She stared at herself in the mirror in the bathroom, lifted up her shirt just above her belly, and turned sideways. She could definitely tell she gained some weight, and though most women would probably freak out at this point, Amelia liked seeing the extra weight. She felt more womanly as her body began to look fuller, even her chest felt larger.

As she turned to face the mirror again, she noticed a spot in her hair a few inches above her forehead. It looked slightly red but she figured it was the color of her scalp in that spot, though she never noticed it being like that before. She moved her hair around a bit to see if her scalp looked the same in other spots, and it didn't. She found the spot again and tried to see anything, but because of the placement of it, she couldn't really get a close look.

"Jake, can you take a look at this? I'm not sure what this is?" Amelia walked into the bedroom where Jake was on the bed waiting for her to finish getting ready. They were planning on heading out for a walk on the beach. It was the first day in May that was slightly warm, and Jake was excited to get out to the beach. He always claimed he could "smell" when the seasons were changing and just around the corner, and this morning Jake smelled that summer was on its way.

Amelia leaned over so he could see the top front part of her head where she pointed that was to the right of her where she parted her hair. "Move your finger, I can't see anything." He moved her hand aside.

She waited, and he remained silent. "What is it? If anything.... I thought I might have sunburn or something. Not sure how, but I noticed that it looked different."

"There's nothing there."

Of course there was nothing there. Whenever she thought there was something wrong with her, there never ended up being any evidence of what she felt or saw – ever. She felt like she sounded insane or like some kind of hypochondriac. In the pit of her stomach, she had this horrible premonition that their infertility was going to end up the same way – inconclusive with no evidence as to why they couldn't get pregnant. "Ok, well thanks for checking. Just thought it looked weird."

"No, I mean there is nothing there." He said frankly.

"I heard you." She pulled away from him. He didn't need to mock her.

"No, Amelia. There is nothing there as in nothing at all." The look of concern on his face began to worry her.

"What do you mean?" She tried not to panic. Maybe she would rather be a hypochondriac and have nothing wrong than actually *have* something happen.

"There is no hair or anything on that spot. There's nothing there at all."

"No hair at all!?" She ran into the bathroom to examine further. She was so close to the mirror that it began to fog up as she separated her hair to find the "bald" spot. She put her finger on it. It felt completely smooth as though there had never been hair there. She couldn't believe her eyes. Jake walked in. "Why isn't there any hair in that spot?" She turned to him, and he shrugged.

Amelia immediately connected this to her autoimmune problems. She was only borderline lupus though, and her mother had always been borderline lupus as well with no major problems. Her mother never lost hair either; however, being borderline meant that you could live symptom free for a while and then have flare-ups that caused autoimmune side effects. She had not been feeling that well lately, but she figured she was stressed about everything with Claire and all the stress with their infertility.

On the way to the beach, Amelia voiced her concern to Jake about how maybe her autoimmune issues were a bigger problem than they realized and may be the cause of their infertility - maybe her lupus was stopping her from getting pregnant. She couldn't stand the thought that her body could kill off something that was so precious to her. The body that she needed to work in harmony was now her enemy secretly fighting her all along.

"I hate autoimmune issues. They fell like a cancer to me – killing off any hope I have of the future we want." Though she couldn't be certain that this was the cause of everything, she had a very strong suspicion that it had something to do with it all.

"You can't be so worried about everything, Amelia." Jake climbed out of the Jeep once they arrived in the parking lot at the beach.

"Jake, I'm losing my hair! I think I have a valid reason to be concerned!" She slammed her door. Sometimes it really irritated her how much he would push things aside like they weren't a big deal. She knew that he cared, but she couldn't understand why he would make light of things sometimes that should really be of concern to him.

They walked the beach hand in hand in silence – both wrestling with their own thoughts. They passed people with their dogs and families with their children. Only people in New England were out on the beach in the middle of May before the heat and beach season started. Though it wasn't extremely warm out, Amelia began to feel a little warm. She figured it was due to them walking fast. Since Jake was much taller than her by a foot, he tended to walk a little faster than her. "Can we slow down for a bit?" She took in a deep breath hoping that would help cool her down a bit.

"Sure. You ok?"

"Just feeling a little warm is all." She took off the light jacket she had on. The cool ocean breeze cooled her skin though internally she still felt warm. It was as if she was burning up from the inside out. She had never experienced anything like this before. She was always usually cold; even on a humid summer day her hands would be like ice.

After walking slower and keeping her jacket off, Amelia eventually cooled down. She definitely never experienced anything like that before and prayed to God that she would never experience it ever again, but she had a feeling that this was only the beginning of the unknown things that were going to happen to her body. She tried not to think about it, but being a chronic worrier didn't help the matter.

A few nights later, Amelia woke in the middle of the night extremely hot, dizzy, and nauseous. She thought maybe she was getting the flu or something. The minute she stood on her feet to head to the bathroom, her heart started pounding as though she ran a marathon. Her perspiring increased, and she knew that she needed to cool herself down immediately. She made her way to the living room as fast as she could and turned on the floor fan aiming it towards the couch and turned on the ceiling fan that was above the couch. She slowly laid down and propped a pillow behind her back and head. She lay there feeling so helpless and unsure what her heart and body were going to do next. She then realized she hadn't even thought to wake Jake. *Oh God, please don't let me die this way.* She had been so concerned about trying to figure out solutions that waking Jake hadn't even crossed her mind.

Eventually, her body cooled down after what seemed like an hour. Her dizziness and nauseousness subsided, so she decided to get back into bed. She made sure to turn on the fan in the bedroom hoping that she wouldn't get warm again.

Though waking in the night really hot had been happening more frequently lately, she had never experienced it in this manner.

Another week passed before another incident happened. It was a Saturday morning and was their first scheduled day to pick up their farm share at Green Meadows - their local organic farm located in Hamilton. The heat wave for May continued, and that morning Amelia woke up with her clothes damp. Upon waking, she felt as though she was being suffocated by her body. Her temperature was normal, but the heat coming from her body was as if a volcano was being held back from erupting. Her stomach turned a little, but she forced herself to continue with her morning. She fed Chloe and then changed so that they could get to the farm stand to have their breakfast. She loved getting an iced coffee and croissant from the farm. She decided to dress in shorts and a tank top to make sure she wouldn't overheat. Since she sometimes had issues with her blood sugar getting low, she thought she should eat a little something before the farm but figuring they would be there shortly, she decided to hold off and save room for the croissant and coffee that awaited her.

Once they arrived at the farm, Jake checked their name off the pickup list. The farm seemed more packed than usual for a Saturday, but it was probably because it was the first week and everyone was excited to be outside and back at the farm. Jake kept asking her questions about the share items, "Do you want beets or potatoes?" as they worked their way around the little store. She was having a hard time concentrating on his questions for some reason; it was almost as if she was having an out of body experience where though she was present, she didn't feel like she was actually able to participate in all that was happening - almost like a dream.

"You choose," she said quickly. Suddenly the commotion of all the people began to make her dizzy, and she could feel her temperature rising. A weak feeling started plaguing her limbs like when her blood sugar would drop, but this was different in that it almost felt as though her body was physically shutting down. She found it was a struggle just to stay on her feet, and then she started to become nauseous. She looked to Jake, but he was focused on gathering the share items. Amelia placed her hand on the table next to her for support. She wasn't sure what to expect next, but she was beginning to expect the worse. Her heart began to beat faster which didn't help her situation.

She needed to breathe some fresh air, but at the same time her feet were like bricks and the rest of her body was boycotting any movement she wanted to make. She knew she needed to do something soon though because the last thing she wanted to do was collapse in the middle of the farm stand store. Since Jake had made his way halfway around the center table, she would have to yell to him but even to speak above a whisper was a task she didn't have the energy for, and she couldn't muster the strength to walk over to him either. Her stomach clenched and the nauseousness was not relenting. She forced one foot in front of the other like a child learning to walk for the first time, and the movement of her feet felt foreign to her as their heaviness made it difficult to move. When she was within a few feet of Jake, she managed to say, "I need the keys. I need to get out of here."

"Are you ok?" Up to this point, Jake hadn't noticed she wasn't feeling well. "Do you want me to go with you?" He was at the counter about to check out with the items not included in their share.

"No, I'm not ok. I don't know what's wrong. Please I need to get out of here now." She put out her hand motioning for him to give her the keys. "Please finish up in here, but I need to go outside." He handed her the keys, and she rushed outside as quickly as her feet would carry her to the car.

She opened the door to the Jeep, and the heat that had collected while they were in the store, though not much, poured out of the car making it feel like she opened the door to a sauna and not helping her situation at all. At this point, she was too weak to pull herself into the Jeep, and she didn't want to sit in the hot vehicle, so she sat on the door sill with the door propped open. She hung her head down hoping the door would block her from the heat and sun. All of her pores completely opened and yet they were still struggling to cool her body. Sweat poured from her head as though she had finished a marathon. Her breathing became shallow, and Amelia really thought this was the end. *Oh God, please help me!* She thought and prayed to herself.

A slight breeze blew by as she wondered if she would ever see Jake again. *What is taking him so long?* She breathed in slowly and out slowly trying not to panic. She hated being so vulnerable and out of control. She felt so completely and utterly helpless. She sympathized with what elderly people feel like when their bodies start giving out on them in old age, but she was only in her twenties. *This shouldn't be happening to me.* After a few minutes, the symptoms started to lessen, and she could hear Jake's voice in the distance, "Are you ok?" He came over to her side of the car.

"I'm so scared, Jake." She looked up into his eyes with tears in her eyes. "I thought I was going to die. What's wrong with me?" He scooped her up in his arms and held her sweating trembling body. She explained everything that happened.

"When do you have your annual physical? It's coming up soon, right?"

"Yes, this week actually." Even though it was this week, it seemed like years away after what she had just experienced. She wanted answers now, especially since these incidences were happening more and more frequently. She knew now that this had to be directly related to her autoimmune issues, but she couldn't understand why she was having such a problem with them.

Later that night, she lie awake in bed replaying what happened earlier in the day and the previous week. Jake rolled over and noticed her still wake, "You're still up?"

"Yea," she whispered.

"Why? Are you ok?"

"I'm fine… just thinking is all."

"About what?"

"Jake, I can barely take care of myself right now in the state that I'm in - whatever it is I'm going through. What if we had a baby right now? I wouldn't even be able to take care of it. Maybe all of this was a bad idea. Maybe we should stop trying to have children."

He sighed. "Amelia, I could help. If you were sick when we have a baby, I would fill in where you couldn't. Remember we're a team? You're not in this alone. I'm right here."

"I know," but she didn't want him to have to worry about taking care of her and a baby all the time. She wanted to be the perfect 50's housewife and mother that could handle it all while baking a cake in a nice dress and apron.

In the following weeks as Amelia awaited the results from all the tests her primary doctor ran, she dealt with more hot flashes and near black-outs – sometimes in the middle of the night and sometimes during the day. There was no rhyme or reason to when, where, or why they would happen. Amelia began to feel that her life would be better lived in an air-conditioned bubble.

Finally the package came in the mail from her primary care doctor, and the letter read:

*Dear Mrs. Bayberry,*

*The test results came back negative for Lyme and thyroid dysfunction. Most of your results on everything we tested came back within their normal range. However, your auto-immune antibodies were high, and I recommend that you see a rheumatologist. I have included a list of my recommendations. If you would like assistance in scheduling an appointment, please feel free to contact the office to have a nurse schedule an appointment for you.*

She quickly rummaged through all the paperwork trying to find the page that showed the high results in the autoimmune areas. There were a lot of pages since they had taken five vials of blood, and then she spotted it. Her rheumatoid factor range should have been between 1 and 13 and hers ranked in at a 54. No wonder why she was losing her hair! She kept scanning the page and also found that her SS-A antibody should be less than 1, and hers came in at 8. Her heart sank. Why was her body doing this to her – especially now when they were trying to have children? It was as if her body was trying to sabotage any chance for her to experience happiness.

She dropped the papers on the table and looked up at Jake who had been standing next to her, "I hate my body!" He wrapped his arm around her as she sobbed. "Why does my body have to do this to me? Why can't I just be normal?" She wanted to scream at the top of her lungs and pound her fists on the table and have a full on tantrum like a three-year-old who didn't get their way, but she refrained and resulted to pouting on the couch with a box of tissues instead.

Jake sat next to her, "So, now what? You're going to schedule with the rheumatologist, right?" She could hear the concern in his voice.

"Yup," she was totally irritated that she had to even deal with this. What was worse was knowing that this was definitely going to delay any chance of pregnancy. "Should we even continue with this fertility clinic stuff?" She couldn't believe she was asking the question.

"Why wouldn't we?"

"Because, I'm sick Jake! I have to get better before we can keep trying. I can't get pregnant in the state I'm in right now. I can barely function like a normal person right now. I'm sure it wouldn't be healthy for me or the baby if I was to get pregnant in this state. And who knows? If I was to get pregnant, my body might choose to attack the fetus and kill it off! I wouldn't be able to live with myself knowing that any chance at pregnancy might be destroyed in an instant by my *stupid* body!" She was yelling now with tears running down her face, but she wasn't angry with him. She was yelling into the empty void in her heart.

"Well, we can't risk your health. We do need to get you better. I fully agree with that."

Were they actually giving up… already? Her heart sank. They had to though. Her body gave her no other choice. Only five months into the process, only one meeting with the clinic and charting nurse, and they had already hit the end of their road. How could that be? It was *so* completely unfair. She felt like such a failure. Having a baby felt more impossible now than when they started.

Amelia wrote in her journal that night before slipping into bed:

*I'm beginning to feel this was all a bad idea. Why did I have to know answers? Maybe it would have been better always wondering. Ignorance is bliss, right? Why couldn't I have just been content with being ignorant? Why? Now I've just made things worse. I feel like my journey has been cut short though. I was just barely in the race and someone pushed me down, and I've broken a leg. That's what it feels like.*

*God, why did You bring me this far only to end it here? It's not fair. What's the point in starting this process if I was just going to end up sick? I want to hope that there's a miracle around the corner for us. I want to believe everything is going to end up all right. But I'm beginning to wonder if I've been chasing someone else's happy ending. What could You possibly have for my life that would be more fulfilling than having children with my husband – the thing You created us to do?!*

*I've begged You more times than I can count to bless us with a child. I don't know why You won't. I don't know why You let women who do drugs and prostitute themselves get pregnant and have children that have to either grow up in horrible situations or be ripped from their homes to be placed in foster homes because their mother is unfit, when Jake and I would provide a loving home that would teach our children about You. Why is it that my only option to have a child is to adopt someone else's child who may not have even been cared for properly in the womb? I don't understand, and I'm not sure I ever will.*

She closed her journal and set it on her night stand. She snuggled under the sheets, and she immediately felt Chloe jump up on the bed. Amelia tapped the blankets, so Chloe would come over, but

Chloe was always a daddy's girl. She walked right over to Jake and laid on top of him even though he was dead to the world. Chloe began to purr loudly as though he was petting her. *I can't even have the love of my own cat!* She thought as she rolled over and tears began to run down her face and soak her pillow. She tried not to let herself get too worked up because she didn't want to wake up all stuffy and puffy-eyed.

When Amelia opened her eyes the next morning, they hurt slightly and felt a little swollen. *So much for keeping my eyes from looking puffy,* she thought to herself, *oh well.* She turned over expecting to give Jake a morning kiss on the cheek, but she was surprised to find him gone. Amelia sat up slightly and noticed a light pink envelope lay on his pillow with "To My Wife" written across the front of it. She picked it up curious to why he had bought her a card.

She slid her finger under the flap to open the envelope and pulled out the card. "Happy Mother's Day" was written across the front with pink and yellow rose bouquets tied with white ribbons in the background. She wasn't sure why he had bought her a mother's day card, and she began to feel a bit upset that he had. Jake was always so sensitive to her feelings, so she couldn't imagine why he did this. She flipped to the inside of the card. It was blank inside except for where Jake had handwritten a message:

*I love you, Amelia. I know that we don't have any children yet, but I wanted to celebrate you today because I know you're going to make a wonderful mother!*

*I bought this card that had a blank inside because it's like our story as parents. It's blank right now, but instead of losing hope, we should look at it the way a painter looks at a blank canvas or a writer looks at a blank page - full of potential and adventure. You can never plan for an adventure completely because no matter how prepared you think you are for it, something unexpected always happens - but that is also the beauty of the adventure and what makes it so special. If we could plan for everything in life, it wouldn't hold any excitement.*

*I'm happy to be on this adventure to parenthood with you, and I know right now that we're experiencing a detour that we weren't expecting, but we can either give up on the adventure altogether or keep painting and writing and see this through to the end. I want to see the final picture because I know it's going to be beautiful. I hope you'll continue on this adventure with me because I can't do it without you and the picture will not be beautiful without you in it.*

She could barely see his last few sentences as tears streamed down her face. She looked up from the card and saw Jake standing in the doorway with his hand stretched out. "You going to join me?" He smiled at her.

She jumped up from the bed and into his arms. "Forever and always!"

# LULLABIES

Amelia listened to the words of the JJ Heller song, "I Get To Be The One," play on the iPod in the bedroom  and she watched as tears formed in her eyes as she looked at herself in the bathroom mirror. The song talked about watching a little baby grow up and how lucky the mother was to be able to witness it all before her eyes.

They usually had music playing in the apartment when they were getting ready in the morning, but since her monthly visitor had started this morning, the song pierced her heart. Would she ever be able to hold a baby of her own? The pain in her abdomen suggested otherwise. She pictured what it would be like to hold a baby in her arms with their tiny fingers and toes that were formed from her and Jake. She wondered what it would be like to see the baby for the first time and watch the little eyelids open to take her in for the first time. The thought of that never happening made Amelia want to collapse on the floor into a little ball and cry forever.

The song continued on how such a small person could make the mother's heart burst with so much love, and how when the baby was still in the womb that the mother loved the baby without even knowing who he or she was.

She took a deep breath and slowly exhaled, grabbed her contact lens case, and decided to continue on her morning routine. *Just move on. You'll be ok. Don't think about it.* She told herself, but trying to put her contacts in proved more challenging than expected since her eyes were expelling so much water. She gave up and slowly walked into the bedroom to find Jake for consolation. He was making the bed and humming along to the song, when he noticed her standing in the doorway.

"Amelia, are you ok?" she couldn't even utter the words. He came over and embraced her. "What's the matter?"

"I started my period today, Jake." She grabbed his hands, "I'm sorry we're not pregnant this month."

"It's ok, hunny. I'm not upset with you."

"I know. I'm just disappointed." She took a deep breath in to catch herself from balling hysterically. "And this song… I just want a little baby for us to love and care for. Will that ever happen for us?" He pulled her closer.

"I hope it will. That's all we can do is hope that someday we will be able to hold our own little baby." He stroked her hair. "Hunny, if a song can make you this upset and you're also not feeling well from your autoimmune stuff, maybe we should talk about not going any further with this process with the fertility clinic?" Even though they had talked about stopping the process, they hadn't fully decided on it yet.

She pulled away from him, "Do you think this process is what is making me so upset? It's not. It's the fact that this may never be a reality for us. This process is the only thing that is giving me hope right now. If we stop, then it's all over. We're done. It's like a death sentence."

"Well, you don't seem to be very happy. I just want my happy wife back."

"Jake, believe me, I'm doing all I can to be happy right now. You don't understand how hard this all is for me. Each month I have my period feels like another month that's wasted. It's another month I've failed – that my body has failed. If I give up the clinic, what else do I have? I'm not ready for adoption yet. We haven't even explored the clinic stuff enough yet. We've only just started. I feel stuck though – maybe that's why I can't fully be happy. I don't want to stop the clinic stuff because that means it's all over – everything we've ever hoped for is all over, but I find it hard continuing as well because I don't want to keep getting my period and that being a physical reminder every month that none of this is working anyway. I want to be guaranteed that one of these months I *will* be pregnant, but nothing and no one can guarantee that for us. So I'm just left here – in this world between what life is for us right now and what it may never be for us in the future, and I'm not sure how to deal with it all. It feels completely unbearable at times – like right now."

"Amelia, I love our lives together whether we have children or not, and you know that. It will be sad if we can't, but I don't want you to think our lives will totally suck if we can never have kids."

"Jake, I love our lives too, and I know our lives won't suck if we don't have kids, but you have to give me time to wrap my head around that concept. It's just different for women. We have so many more emotions that we feel. It's too hard to explain." She walked out of the room and finished getting ready in the bathroom.

She felt like a zombie at work all day - doing her menial duties while wishing she was a stay at home mom spending morning after morning watching her little one grow up. She sniffed her hands after rubbing in her Johnson's & Johnson's lotion at her desk – how she wished to smell the lotion on her newborn's skin. It's the smell every mother loves after giving their baby a bath like the new car smell to a guy every time he opens the car door. The only difference between the two is that people are not usually fond of others sniffing their babies like they are when they have new cars. In fact, people usually invite others to smell their new cars but not their children. That would just be weird. So instead, Amelia held her hands close to her face while breathing in the only essence of a baby that she had like some pathetic loser. Things like this made her feel completely insane.

Amelia was glad she was going to spend some time together with Lane tonight. She was in much need of some quality girl time. She just had to hold herself together for the rest of the day. Some days were easier than others, but today being the first day of her period made it particularly difficult.

Lane already had the water boiled for tea when Amelia arrived and an assortment of biscuits, biscotti, and croissants arranged on a small three-tiered platter. This was exactly what Amelia needed she thought to herself as she sniffed the chai tea from her teacup. They made casual conversation about the day as they enjoyed the tea and baked goods. Lane told Amelia about the new painting project she would begin work on shortly. Lane had an art gallery in a little shop downtown on Central Street.

Lane explained how the project was inspired by Amelia, "I want to capture a mood in the painting that portrays the times in our lives that can be dark – times where it's hard for us to see the next step to take – but in the distance I want the light to be captured in such a way that it draws the eyes beyond the dark sections, which will be the majority of the painting. I want the light to be so pure and intoxicating that the person almost doesn't even notice the darkness. I want it to bring them up out of the darkness."

Amelia smiled as she pictured it in her head. "That sounds so beautiful." Amelia secretly wished that she could do that exact thing - look up out of the darkness she felt closing in on her all the time.

She asked Lane what objects she was going to put in the painting.

"I'm not that far yet. I have this light and dark contrast idea, but the objects haven't been clear yet. I keep praying about it and am trying to be patient as I wait for the answer from the Lord. I know it will come in the right time, but I wanted you to know that you've inspired it." Lane smiled and nudged Amelia's hand, "See, sometimes good things can come out of unfortunate circumstances."

Amelia stirred some cinnamon and cream into her tea and then looked her friend in the eye, "I wish something good could come to me out of my unfortunate circumstance. I'm glad that it has inspired you." She could feel her emotions welling up behind her eyes, "Lane, is it wrong to want a happy ending? I'm so afraid that I'm in the fairy tale where Sleeping Beauty never wakes up to meet her prince, where Snow White is cursed forever, and Cinderella never gets freed from her tower. I feel completely trapped inside this body of mine. It's so unpredictable, and it's suffocating me. It's cutting me off from everything I want. I don't know whether to keep pushing on and risk my body completely collapsing with the possibility that maybe there would be something on the other side of all this pain, or if I should give up and try to save what I have left of myself while I sit back and stare in my cell at the soot stained walls realizing that my world is devoid of color, and the glass slipper was only a dream." She blinked back the tears that threatened to break her down again. "But then again, just to have one night free from all worry, to enjoy the ball and the fantasy, even though it was only a moment, would be better than not experiencing nothing at all..."

"I pray all the time for the Lord to bring you and Jake a child, Amelia. I don't know why He hasn't. You both will be wonderful parents. It's horrible that your autoimmune stuff is kicking up at the same time. You do know that you need to get yourself better though before you can worry about taking care of anyone else, right?"

"I don't think I can give up yet though."

"It's not giving up. You need to get your body back to normal before you can keep proceeding with anything the doctor wants you to do. When is your next appointment?"

"Not until next month. We were scheduled for March, but we had to reschedule because the doctor had a conference to attend, and the next available Friday afternoon appointment wasn't until June." Amelia knew that Lane was right about getting her body healthy again, but in a sense it did feel like giving up because it meant more waiting – waiting to get better so they can wait while they try to have a child again. It was two steps backward when she hadn't even taken a half a step forward.

They prayed together before Amelia left, and Lane gave Amelia some of the goodies to take home to Jake. Amelia was so emotionally and mentally exhausted from the day that all she could think about was a hot bath she wanted to soak in when she got home. She wanted to wash all her sadness away, though she knew it wasn't possible – if it were only that easy.

As she entered the door to their apartment, she called out, "Hey hun, I'm home," and Chloe came to greet her at the door. She walked into the living room only to be greeted by Jake and her brother, John, sitting on the couch chatting. The wonderful bath that she had been dreaming about became an unlikely possibility.

Jake stood up and walked over to Amelia, "I'll leave you two alone." He kissed her on the forehead and walked down the hallway to the bedroom. Obviously Jake knew something that she didn't.

"Hey sis, we need to talk." She had enough of her own problems to deal with, she wasn't really ready to hear about how lonely John was right now. She knew it was selfish to feel that way, but she didn't care about being selfish right now. She wanted to be in the bath soaking away her sorrows and tuning out the world.

"What's up John?" She plopped on the couch next to him still in her work clothes. "Not to be rude, but can you cut to the chase? This is the first time I've been home today, and I *really* need to have some time to relax." She could always tell John what she felt without risk of offending him. They understood each other that way.

"It's not what is up with me. It's what's up with you?" Her entire countenance tensed. "You've been different lately, Amelia. I noticed it in the grocery store when we bumped into each other, and then Easter confirmed my suspicions. I can tell something is up. You can't keep things from me. You know that. I know you too well." She couldn't believe she was going to have to reveal everything to him. They had only told their parents and didn't want everyone to know yet. "C'mon Mel," that is what he called her for short since they were kids, "you can tell me anything."

He grabbed her hand, and her walls came crashing down. "John... we can't have kids."

He looked puzzled, "What do you mean? A landlord can't tell you whether you can have kids or not."

"No, it's not that. It's nothing to do with that." Tears welled up in her eyes and began to spill over. She couldn't hold it together any longer, "We're infertile." The silence surrounded them for a few minutes while the tears dripped on her slacks and their hands. "The day I saw you in the store, Claire had just told me that she was pregnant, and Easter was completely unbearable for me."

"Why didn't you tell me sooner?"

"We weren't telling anyone but our parents. It's something that Jake and I have to work through and to include too many others in it makes it that much harder. I know I can tell you anything, but honestly I'm beginning to wonder what's true anymore. I'm not sure what to believe in anymore. I feel more and more lost every day. Please don't tell anyone else."

"I understand. I'm so sorry that you're dealing with this especially considering the circumstances with Claire." He hugged her and whispered, "Your secret is safe with me."

"Thank you, John." Amelia informed him of the fertility clinic and where they were at with her health and the decisions they needed to face.

As he was leaving, he said, "I won't ask you about this all the time because I want to give you your space but know that I'm always a listening ear if you ever need it." And that was why she loved her brother so much. He always gave her the space that she needed. Telling the rest of the family someday was going to be a difficult task because they *would* suffocate her. She loved and respected her brother now more than ever.

On Saturday, Amelia woke with mixed emotions; she was excited but also nervous and anxious. She pushed her spinach from the omelet Jake had made around her plate as she thought about the coming hours.

"Oh, I'd love to take go on this trip sometime!" Jake had been reading his Appalachian Mountain Club magazine since he was an avid hiker and loved the White Mountains of New Hampshire. "What's the matter? Don't like spinach?" He noticed her somber demeanor once he glanced up from his magazine.

"Oh! No, it's fine." She glanced at him from where her head rested on her hand. "Thinking about today, that's all."

Amelia danced at the Ipswich Moving Company, the local dance company. She usually attended the adult ballet class but she would also pop into some modern classes as well. Every year, there was a dance recital for the children's and teenager's dance classes. She had been asked to help out with one of the performances, which meant watching the smaller children until it was their class' turn to perform on stage. She genuinely wanted to help and figured it would be fun to see the children perform, but she was nervous as what to expect since this was her first year helping out.

"Do you not want to do go?" Jake was still trying to figure out what was bothering her about the day specifically, so he could offer suggestions to fix the situation that would make her happy.

"Well, yes ... and no." Jake gave her a puzzled look that most men give women when their complicated emotions bubble to the surface. "I do truly want to help, and I think it will be fun, but I'm feeling sad for myself, you know, because we don't have a child of our own to watch at the recital." She put some of the spinach in her mouth, "Just feeling bummy is all..."

Once she arrived at the Ipswich High School auditorium in the afternoon, her insecurity began to rise. She knew a handful of the adults that she had taken some classes with, but as each parent dropped their child off into her care, she realized that she had no idea how to interact with little children. She checked their names off from the list on her clipboard and pointed them in the direction of the coloring pages and crayons. She checked the clock, and there was twenty more minutes until the show started. She stood there and watched the children interact with each other and color the pages before them. All the other helpers seemed to know each other and were in conversations, so she awkwardly stood there all alone.

"I can't find pink," a little girl tugged at Amelia's shirt. Amelia looked down to the adorable blonde-haired five-year-old with pig tails and a pink tutu.

Amelia glanced around but all the only pink crayon was being used by another little girl. She reached into the basket on top of the table, "Here you go," she said with a smile as she handed the little girl a pink colored marker. She smiled back and rushed back to her coloring page on the floor. *Maybe I can do this mother thing. That wasn't so scary.* She thought to herself. Maybe it was a good idea to help out. It would help her feel more confident around children.

Amelia checked in a few more stragglers who were cutting it close to showtime as there was only seven more minutes before they had to bring the children into the auditorium. She reviewed her list and was glad to see that all her names were checked off. She looked around the room full of children and saw how fancy some children were dressed with makeup and hair done. She couldn't believe that parents went through such lengths to have their little girls dolled up like they were some kind of movie stars. Amelia was happy to see the little girls who parents had kept them looking like little girls with very simple hair styles and tutus.

She began thinking how she would keep her child with a simple style because little girls are cute in their own way. There was no reason to doll them up because she thought that took away from their cuteness and rushed them into adulthood. Though, she wouldn't want her child to feel like she wasn't special or something since the other little girls would have more sequined leotards and tutus, but she would teach her child to value simplicity as well.

"Oh, no, no," one of the other helpers interrupted Amelia's thoughts, "let me take those." The teenager collected the markers that the children were coloring with. "We don't let them color with the markers. One year a girl colored on her skin and then had a break down because she couldn't get it off before the show." The helper didn't seem to be speaking to Amelia specifically, as she didn't know who had given out the markers, and Amelia had only given one out, but she was speaking into the room generally.

Immediately Amelia began to condemn herself. *That hadn't even crossed my mind. Maybe I won't be a good mother... I can't believe I didn't think of that. What is even worse is that a teenager knows more about taking care of children than I do.* She blinked several times to keep the tears from rushing down her face.

"One minute!" Someone had come into the room and yelled, which meant they needed to gather the children in a line and hold hands. Amelia focused at the task at hand and tried to ignore her feelings of inadequacy.

As she sat in the pit, which was the area in front of the stage that was hidden from the audience where the orchestra would usually sit, she had to quiet the children between each classes turn. The little pig tailed girl scooted closer to Amelia. She was sucking her thumb but started to talk to Amelia at the same time during one of the performances. Amelia was just ready to tell her she needed to be quiet when she heard the little girl whisper, "Can I sit in your lap? I'm afraid of the dark." Amelia's heart softened as she nodded and the little girl snuggled into Amelia's crossed legs.

The little girl's pig tails swung back and forth as she watched the dancing on stage, and her hair tickled Amelia's nose but she could smell the Johnson and Johnson's baby shampoo with each swoosh. The warmth of the child on her lap made Amelia long for the closeness of her own child to love, hold, and cuddle with. A complete stranger's child trusted her enough to feel safe in her lap and to save her from her fear of the dark. Amelia wanted to be that refuge for her own child. Since her monthly visitor was still present even though it was towards the end of the cycle, she was reminded of how impossible the reality of having her own children felt.

Maybe she should adopt. She could have adopted the child in her lap in a heartbeat just to feel the love of a child and the child's complete trust in her ability to be a mother to her. As she watched each of the children dance across the stage in their own unique way, they danced their way into her heart. The tears she held at bay tickled her nose and tightened her throat, and she longed for a child to call her own more now than ever.

# AUTUMN'S JOY

"We have to get this plant, Jake!" Amelia
blurted with an enthusiastically wide smile that
made it impossible for him to deny her. She pointed
to a plant that had clusters of tiny flowers with a
pinkish purple hue.

They were out shopping for plants to decorate
their balcony with as they did every spring. The
plant surprised her with its beauty, but when she
grabbed the tag to check the price and noticed the
name of the plant was Autumn Joy, she felt that it
must be a sign from God that they would conceive
soon because it was the exact name they had
thought of for their first daughter.

As she placed it on the corner of their balcony,
she matter-of-factly stated, "Perfect!" She looked to
Jake for confirmation. He smiled. "What? You don't
like it?"

"No, it's not that, Amelia. I don't want you to get your hopes up too much. I can tell by the look on your face."

"I know, but it's really hard to *not* think that it's God trying to tell us something. Come on - think about it. I've never heard of this plant before or ever seen one. Then all of a sudden when we're going through all this difficult stuff with the infertility this plant shows up, and it's name happens to be the exact name we want to name our first daughter. That can't just be a coincidence, right?!"

"I know. I wouldn't think so, but I also don't want to be let down either." He hugged her. "But we can only hope, right?" He squeezed her tightly.

"Right." She exhaled.

She was so excited about the plant that she found herself sitting out on the balcony staring at it and imagining what their little girl would look like someday. She thought of the cute little outfits she would buy and all the fun things they would do together as a family. It all felt like it was so close that she could reach out and touch it. The anticipation of it all felt like it would burst out of her chest.

That night, she wrote in her journal:

*Today we found a plant called Autumn Joy. It's beautiful, and I'm still in shock of the name. It feels like having a baby is so close even though I'm still not feeling 100%. Maybe the doctor is right and getting pregnant will help all of my auto-immune symptoms.*

*God, is this a sign that we'll conceive soon? I feel like it is, but I don't want false hope either. I just don't think it could be a coincidence that we stumble upon a plant with the exact name that we want to use for a child. Well, I plan to care for this plant as I would a child. I want it to be the best version of its kind. It will be my baby until I can have one someday...*

A few days later, Amelia went to water the plant and noticed that one of the stems was looking particularly droopy and almost brown. Thinking that maybe she hadn't watered it enough, she made sure she to give it a good douse of water. The next day though showed another stem drooping, and the first stem was completely shriveled and had died. She wondered if maybe she watered it too much now.

"Hmm...," she leaned in close to the plant to investigate further. "Jake!" she screamed.

"Yeah," he shouted from inside the apartment.

"Come here, quick! You have to see this!" waving her hand for him to come join her, she was furious and sad all at the same time.

He opened the slider door and stepped outside. She pointed to the new drooping stem. "Aphids!" Jake wasn't understanding the look of complete devastation on her face.

"We can mix up some soap, water, and eucalyptus mixture to spray on it like we've done with our other plants in the past." He didn't seem too concerned with the issue.

"No!" She sat down in the chair beside the plant, "It's invested! It'll never work." She put her head in her hands. The plant wasn't a sign from God that they were going to conceive; it was just another reminder of the failure she was at life. Why had she ever fooled herself to think she could care for anything?

"Well, I think it's worth a try." He put his hand on her back.

"Whatever." She stood up and went inside.

"Amelia," he called to her, "where are you going?"

"I need some air," she closed the apartment door behind her. She wasn't sure where she was going, but she all she knew was that she needed to get out. She needed freedom from the failure that surrounded her all the time. She wanted to get in the car and drive to some place by herself in some lonely cottage on the shore of Maine, but she only got as far as Crane's Beach, which was only a ten minute drive from them.

The beach still wasn't in its busy season yet but it would be soon with June arriving in another week and the warmer weather around the corner, but for now she knew she would have some solace. She picked a spot on the sand only about twenty feet from the sand dunes. The seagulls soared above with some roaming the beach and a couple of them bobbing in the water. The plovers squeaked, which sounded more like a mouse than a bird, as they searched the beach for morsels of left over shell fish from the seagulls gorging.

Amelia listened as the waves slowly rolled in and went out. Something about the ocean always calmed her. It vastness could hold all her thoughts by bringing them to the depths of the ocean, and if she waited long enough, she hoped one day to see them return to her anew - the way broken glass returns as beautifully formed sea glass. Would the mess of the life she felt she was in ever become something beautiful? She grabbed a handful of sand and let it slowly sift through her fingers. It didn't matter how hard she squeezed, she couldn't keep the sand in her hand. That's the way her life felt right now like she was desperately trying to hold on to the hope that they would be able to conceive, but it didn't matter how hard she tried to hold onto it, the sand still left her hand leaving only a few granules. She flattened her palm and inspected the remaining granules. Each grain was a different size and slightly different color - *just as each child is unique the way that God made them*, she thought to herself. Somehow everything always related back to children with her. She quickly blew the sand off her palm.

"I sprayed the plant, so we'll have to wait and see," Jake said when she came through the door to the apartment.

She glanced from the plant to Jake, "I really don't think it's going to survive, and that's fine." She sat down and crossed her arms. "I'm more upset about the disappointment I'm experiencing because I let my hopes get so high that I was certain it was a sign." She sighed, "Now it's just a reminder of the death I already feel." Her eyes moistened. "Maybe it's a sign that I need to let our idea of having a baby shrivel and die too." The tears dropped one by one from each eye. "I don't know that I can though, or that if this longing will *ever* go away. It feels like it will eat at me forever like the aphids at the plant."

Jake wasn't sure what to say to comfort his wife, though he wished he could take all her sadness away. He blamed their infertility on himself even though he wouldn't admit that to Amelia. He wanted to be the strong rock for her. She needed that, but times like these made him feel so helpless. Sometimes he wished that they hadn't started this process because more times than not, he felt that it made Amelia more sad about their infertility, and it caused her auto-immune problems to kick up.

"Amelia, I know you may not want to hear this, but maybe we should think about giving up on this entire process and try to accept the fact that we're not able to have our own children." Jake seemed to mention giving up a lot, but she had always passed it off to him trying to make a quick fix. That was his personality - if there was a problem, he wanted to fix it as quickly and as painlessly as possible. Now she began to wonder if maybe he really did want to open the window and let their dreams drift away on the air - maybe he wasn't giving a quick solution but that his heart actually wanted this.

Her heart sank, "You want to give up?" The tears trickled more down her cheeks.

"Well, it's not giving up if we decide that it's not the best thing for us to do. I mean we haven't seen many results yet, and your health hasn't been great. I'm just saying that maybe we shouldn't keep going with this. We should start discussing sometime soon how much longer we're going to go through this process. Plus, it seems like the doctor keeps suggesting the surgery, and that's not really an option for us - so we may end up with no children in the end anyway. Why not stop all of this now?"

"I know I may be sick right now, but I'm never going to want to give up, Jake. I don't know how to make that decision. We've only been doing this for eight months. I don't know if I'll ever know when I'm ready to stop this process. I'll always wonder if I waited another month, if that would be the month we got pregnant. And part of me feels like I've been gipped because of my sickness. I didn't get a fair chance at it all. I know I need to get better first, but I want to wait until I get better before I make any commitment one way or the other. And once we've tried everything and the only thing left to do is the surgery, I can't say for sure that I wouldn't actually do it. If it meant having children or not, I don't think I could deny the surgery - even though I am absolutely against it - I would probably do it for the sake of our children. Do *you* really want to quit this process already?"

He grabbed her hand, "No, of course not, but it's so hard to see you go through this. I just want you to be happy again." She was relieved to hear that it wasn't really his heart's decision and that he was only trying to make her happy with a quick fix.

"I want to be happy again too, Jake, but giving up now isn't going to make me any more happy. I need to let myself work through this. I'm going to feel down at times, but if it's grief I have to go through then it's grief, and you need to let me grieve."

"I know." He wrapped his arms around her, and they held each other tightly for a few moments in silence.

*I don't like to quit and give up, but I feel like I have no choice.* Amelia nestled into the covers before bed that night and continued to write in her journal. *I don't want to tell the doctor that we're done with the process for now, but at the same time I need to get better, and if I'm honest with myself, it might be good to have a break from it all and not have to worry about trying to get pregnant. It feels like a burden being lifted from my shoulders, and yet at the same time, an emptiness moves into my soul that I don't want to feel. I'm scared of letting go of something I've yearned for so long. I know it's what I must do, and I have to face whatever I have to face even if it's dark, gloomy sadness that tries to overtake me. I must fight it all.*

As they drove to their appointment with the fertility clinic the next week, Amelia began to think how she was going to miss seeing Dr. Carter and his nurse, Sandra, even though this was only going to be their second appointment, she felt like they had been working with them forever. She also thought about their charting nurse, Nanette, and how they would also have to make an appointment with her to give her the news of them deciding to end the process. There was so much work to be done to cancel everything that it was beginning to seem easier to keep going with it all, since Amelia didn't want to deal with all the goodbyes.

"Nanette's such a sweet soul, and I do believe she really truly cares for us. It's sad to think we have to cancel this process with her as well." Amelia said sadly as she watched tree after tree pass by her window on the highway.

"I know. I really like Nanette as well, but if we're stopping this process then we can't keep seeing her either. We have to stop everything."

"Well, we don't *have* to, but I understand not seeing Nanette if we weren't doing the whole process."

"Exactly." The car was silent for a few minutes except for the humming of the road. Though they usually would play music from their iPod when driving on longer trips, a sadness hung in the air that didn't encourage the noise of any type of music. "We'll see what the doctor has to say today. Maybe he'll suggest us to continue with Nanette until we're ready to start the process with him again?"

"I don't know if I could start again after deciding to end this." Amelia couldn't believe she was admitting this out loud. Even though they were only supposed to be taking a break because of her health, it felt more permanent. "It's too much of an emotional roller coaster, and I can't keep riding it. I could get sick again, and we would have to end the process for a second time. Just seems silly to me... if we stop this, we have to completely stop." Amelia's eyes filled with tears and her voice cracked a little as she finished her sentence realizing that stopping meant they were never going to have a baby of their own. This fertility clinic was her last chance at having their own family. She blinked several times,

*I'm ok, I'm ok.... breathe, you just have to get through this appointment and then you can cry and grieve forever,* and she took a deep breath in and slowly let it escape from her lungs.

After they parked, Jake opened Amelia's car door and grabbed her hand as they walked into the hospital. *Is this really effecting him as much as it is me? I really wish I knew because I don't want to end this, but I'm doing it for him and my health because I know he wants me to be happy again. Though after stopping this, I still won't be happy for a while, at least I'll be able to rip my heart out, throw it into a box with lock and key, and store it away somewhere until I stop feeling the pain; whereas, if we continue, my heart remains in my chest ever hopeful and yet bleeding with emotion constantly at every sign of failure to conceive a child.* They entered the elevator in silence, and as the doors shut to carry them to the third floor, the morbidity of their situation rose with each ding of the floor indicator. She half expected to see a funeral processional when they reached their floor since that would be more fitting for the feelings that were flooding her soul. When the doors opened, she joined in line for the imaginary funeral processional for their child, and all she wanted to do was run back down the hallway and escape forever - she didn't care where, she wanted to leave and be anywhere else but where she was. If she left the processional, then her child wasn't really dead. *It's good we're ending this... then it can be over once and for all. I won't need to carry around this horrible hope anymore. I can chop it off and let it die instantly instead of watching it wither and die slowly.*

Sandra greeted them with her friendly white smile as she had before and ushered them into a room. She asked Amelia what her current medications were as she had in the previous appointment and said that Dr. Carter would review the results from her last blood tests with them. Then she took Amelia's weight, blood pressure, and heart rate. Sandra then asked for Amelia's charts and worked on calculations to figure out the overall score for each cycle based on the numbers and letters that were written down my Jake each month to track Amelia's cycle.

"How's everything been going?" She asked as she still worked on the last calculation and whispering to herself as she finished adding and multiplying.

"Actually, things haven't been going too well." Amelia explained how she had lost her hair in a spot on her head along with the night sweats and the serious episodes she had due to her auto-immune flare up because of the high fat dairy diet. "I need to schedule an appointment with a rheumatologist, but I'm still in the process of searching for one." Sandra inspected the bald spot that Amelia had referenced, and then made some notes in her file. "I think we're planning on adopting some day because apparently my body can't even handle the minor changes that are used with this more natural way of dealing with infertility."

"Oh, well adoption is a good option as well, and that's great that you are thinking about helping out in that way. There are a lot of children who need homes." Even with Sandra's enthusiasm, Amelia still didn't feel like they were making the right decision, and since they couldn't afford a house right now, their one bedroom apartment wasn't going to be the best housing option when written on an adoption application - nothing more says you don't have room in your life for children like a one bedroom apartment. Though it was only meant to be temporary until they bought a house, their finances didn't allow for them the flexibility to own a home because of their student loan debt - they practically paid a mortgage amount between both of their student loans.

Sandra moved Jake and Amelia to another room where they waited for Dr. Carter. *One down, one to go... for today anyway. Then we still have to tell Nanette...* Even though they only waited a few minutes, the time seemed to stop and Amelia thought it would never start again. She kept thinking how to word everything to Dr. Carter without breaking down hysterically.

Dr. Carter greeted them as he had before with a smile and a handshake. He sat down on his stool and reviewed the notes quickly. "Looks like there have a been a few blood tests since the last time we met, so we can take a look at those." He shuffled through a few more papers in her file, "So tell me what's been going on with you. You've lost some hair?"

Amelia showed him the spot and reiterated what she had told Sandra about her health since their last appointment. "It's been horrible - to say the least - and," Amelia took a deep breath, "I can't compromise my health because we want to have children." *There it's out... well, almost.* She looked to Jake, "We've decided that it may be better for us to look into adoption in the future since my body can't really handle any changes apparently."

Dr. Carter was quiet for a moment - not an upset or disappointed quiet, more contemplative quiet. "Well, the hair loss is localized, so that wouldn't be a thyroid problem." He said as he went into thought about what the issue could be.

"It's definitely auto-immune," Amelia interrupted, "I have the paperwork from my primary care physician right here stating so. She did blood tests right around when it was all really bad." She pointed to the results of the antibodies level indicating it was auto-immune related, "So I stopped eating dairy immediately, and some of the symptoms lightened, but my hair still hasn't grown back yet, and I still get night sweats occasionally."

"Have we talked about Lose Dose Naltrexone yet?" He pulled out a small pamphlet on it and gave it to her.

"I remembered we talked about it as one of the options that you mentioned last time, but it wasn't anything we tried yet."

He explained that Naltrexone helps the body create endorphins better. "Are you tired a lot?"

"Gee, you could say that. I'm always falling asleep. Sometimes in the car, Jake and I will be in the middle of a conversation, and one minute I'll be talking to him and the next I'll be asleep."

"Then Naltrexone might be worth a try for you." He noted that there were some side effects like vivid dreams - which Amelia already had a vivid dream life anyway - and some patients experienced nausea - but only when increasing the dose. "Overnight a person is supposed to create endorphins, and if you're not creating endorphins overnight or enough of them, then you're energy level is going to be really low, which would cause a person to be tired a lot. Someone with an auto-immune issue like you has your body fighting against itself all the time, so you're probably not creating the right level of endorphins that you need." He went on to say that the endorphins also would help calm the cells that attack the body causing the auto-immune flare ups she was experiencing. "It's up to you whether you want to try it or not." His beeper went off, and he pulled it from his belt and checked the number. "I need to take this, but I wanted to say one more thing. Adoption is a great option, and it's great that you're both thinking of that as something you may want to do, but don't give up on this process because you think that adoption is going to be the easier route. It has its own challenges and heartaches as well - just as much as this process does, but think about it and which one you want to put the time and energy into more. I'll be right back."

That was a no brainer. Of course if she was going to put time, energy, heartache into anything, it was going to be in trying to have their own children. She wasn't against adoption, but if it was going to be just as challenging why not stick with the process they had already started?

"What do you think?" She looked to Jake hoping that he was on the same page as her.

"I think it's worth you trying the Naltrexone. If that would help you, then that would be great!"

"So, we're not quitting this process then?"

He shook his head, "Nope," and they both smiled while a peace overcame them. The funeral attendants went home, and Amelia kept her heart as a renewed hope began to grow inside.

# BEES

"Your results are in from your blood work done last week at the office, and your estradial level was 146.2," Amelia's heart dropped. Jake mouthed the word, "What?" as he stood there waiting patiently to hear the results but seeing the tears well in Amelia's eyes and her mouth agape. He knew the news wasn't good.

"Ok, thank you," Amelia said calmly. "We will. Thank you." She hung up the phone.

Jake slowly approached her and embraced her as she collapsed into his arms. She cried for about five to ten minutes before she could speak any words.

"My estrogen is lower than when we started this whole process." Amelia picked her head up from his shoulder and looked him in the eyes – mascara streaming down her face. "I'm not even back to square one. I'm like minus or negative square one." Her lip started to quiver. "You know, it's supposed to be over 300, and it only came in at 146.2."

"Shhhh," Jake guided her back to his chest. "That was before you started the Naltrexone. Your results may change after you're on this for a while - only time will tell."

"How did the appointment go? Was the doctor able to help at all?" Lane asked when Amelia stopped by the next day.

Amelia explained how they had every intention of telling the doctor that they were done with the whole process because of Amelia's auto-immune issues flaring up and how they were planning on taking the adoption route. "He warned that if they were choosing that route because this process was trying that the adoption route would also have its trials. I don't think he was trying to scare us away from adoption, but he wanted to make us aware that it wasn't the easy answer out, and I'm glad he did." Amelia mentioned how he also encouraged her to follow up with an auto-immune specialist to find out if that could be interfering with her fertility. "He is still very hopeful for us though, so we left the appointment with renewed hope and decided to continue to stick it out."

Amelia traced the top of her tea cup with her index finger as she gazed at her friend's beautiful flower garden and told Lane about her low results from the blood test that was drawn when they saw the doctor, "Lane, I'm tired of trying so hard at everything in life and feeling like I'm on the road to nowhere real fast. Whether it's adoption or working

95

with the Catholic doctors through NaProTechnology, I feel so worn out... and we've only just started with this all."

Lane remained silent. She knew Amelia needed to vent a little, especially after the news of the test results.

"Take the bees, for example," Amelia continued, " they work hard at gathering all the pollen to make honey, but at least at the end of the day, they can sit back and see a job well done and know they contributed, made a difference, and are on their way to making honey. I feel like everything I do yields no results." Amelia sighed.

Lane smiled sympathetically and sipped her iced tea. "What if the bees feel the same way?"

"I don't see how they could. Every day is such an accomplishment to their task at hand."

"Exactly," Lane looked at Amelia, "exactly my point. The bees bring the pollen each day but it doesn't instantly turn into honey. There's a process- just like with everything. Some bees don't even gather the pollen – their jobs are to protect the queen, but no one bee is less important than the other. They are all working at one task and in the end they accomplish it, but I'm sure there are days they wonder what it all is for and if it's worth it."

"Yea, I guess you're right." Amelia sat deep in thought, and silence filled the air for some time while the sun played hide and seek between the passing clouds. There was a slight breeze- just enough to keep cool on a warm day.

Amelia slowly glanced at Lane with tears on the brim of her eyes, "What if the queen can't do her job? Then she is useless – everything fails." A lone tear fell from her eye.

"Then she wouldn't be the queen, would she?" Lane said matter-of-factly but not without sympathy. Amelia's countenance still sunk. "Amelia, what I mean is that she'd have some other role that would be equally as important. You're on a journey right now with all this baby stuff. I know it is hard and trying, but you can't be worried over whether you're the queen bee or the gatherer, and it may feel that you don't know your place, but you have to trust that God has you right where you should be. He knows who you are and where you are at. You need to stop trying to figure out what the end product will be. You need to be still and know that He is God."

Had anyone else but Lane said this to her, Amelia probably would have been offended. But when Lane spoke, Amelia felt whispers of heaven on her words. It had always been that way since she met Lane.

"The doctor seems so hopeful, Lane, but every time I have a low test, I feel like I'm failing the biggest test - life."

"You're not a failure, Amelia. You never will be. You care too much about everything. People that are like that cannot fail."

Amelia smiled at her, "Thanks. But what if I never become a mother? How do I feel like I haven't failed God, my husband, my family, and myself? That's what women were created for - to be able to pro-create. If that part of me is broken, what good am I to existence? To God?"

"Even if you never have children - whether your own, or if you decide to not adopt - you can still be a spiritual mother by being a 'mother' to those around, and that's the calling that God wants you to pay more attention to because in being a spiritual mother, you're called to bring life to the world - it's a different kind of life though. Actually it's the highest calling of the woman to be a spiritual mother."

Amelia sighed, "All of that sounds good, Lane, but I fear that if I don't become an actual mother, that I won't be a very good spiritual mother. It's like they're linked in my head. I don't know how to separate them, and I'm not sure how I can get to one without the other."

"Well, it may take some time to understand it, but pray about it. If you surrender fully to God, through the gift of divine union with Him, He will deliver His gift of life to the world through you - through your spiritual motherhood. All you have to do is ask Him to show you how, and ask His mother. Who better to teach you how to be a spiritual mother than Mary, the mother of our Lord? Isn't that one of the greatest ways to bring life into the world?"

Amelia wasn't shocked when Lane mentioned Mary in their conversations since Lane was Catholic, and Amelia always admired that about her because Lane always seemed grounded in her life and in her faith that Amelia could never grasp for herself. Lane also knew that Amelia and Jake were starting to question where their place was in the church because the Anglican church was feeling like it lacked something that they couldn't quite figure out. Since Amelia and Jake were always deep thinkers about faith matters, Lane had mentioned to Amelia that they should consider looking into the Catholic Church.

The idea of being a spiritual mother did seem pretty great in theory, but Amelia still needed time to process it all. Later that night, she didn't tell Jake about her conversation with Lane because she wanted time to sit with it herself, so she pulled out her journal and relaxed before bed:

*Could I really be a spiritual mother? Lane makes it sound so wonderful that I want to be a spiritual mother right now. I only have one fear though. If God can't entrust the blessing of a child to me, why would He ever consider me a spiritual mother? It doesn't make sense.*

*Honestly, I don't feel like I'm strong enough in my faith to be a spiritual mother right now. I'm having a hard enough time trying to understand all this baby stuff with my own faith, that I don't think I would be able to help anyone else in their faith.*

She closed her journal and the absence of basinet or cradle made the already quiet bedroom more deafening. Chloe stared at her from the end of the bed. Amelia didn't know how else to begin overcoming her sadness, so she looked up the prayer to Mary and began to pray, ... *Hail Mary, full of grace, The Lord is with thee...*

# BROKEN HEARTS

The phone rang at seven the next morning. Saturday was the only day Amelia and Jake had the chance to sleep in a little bit.

"Who could that be this early? Don't they know that people sleep in?" Amelia crabbed. She glanced at the caller ID. "It's William," she handed the phone to Jake.

"Hey Will," he greeted his friend from college in his usual calm, casual manner, "Oh, well congratulations. That's great." He tried to sound excited through his groggy voice. "When...?" Now Amelia was interested in what Will had to say. Will usually didn't call Jake to chat, he was usually announcing some kind of news, and then they wouldn't hear from him again until something new needed to be announced. "Are the kids excited?" She kept mouthing the word "What?" to Jake, but he kept waving his hand. "Ok, well thanks for letting me know and congratulations."

Before Amelia asked again what it was, the harsh reality hit her like a crash dummy hitting a wall in a test car. "His wife is pregnant again, isn't she?" Jake slowly nodded his head.

*And today was supposed to be a good day*, Amelia thought to herself. They had plans to eat breakfast in Gloucester at the Pleasant Street Tea Company in front of the large windows as the sun came in to light the streets while sipping white jasmine tea out of one of the artisan teapots. Then they were going to take a walk at Stage Fort Park down the street where they would feel the ocean breeze on their face and the sun on their backs. Later that evening, they were thinking of catching a movie or renting a new release from their cable provider.

But now – all Amelia could think about was how unfair life can be. She could tell by the way Jake was studying her expression that she really needed to pull herself together for him and try to focus on the day ahead. She hated how these thoughts would consume all the thoughts in her head and nag at her all day – ruining all that she had left. How she wished she could restart the day. Maybe she should have started flirting with Jake or kissing him to distract him from the phone call.

"You gonna be ok?" Jake disrupted her thoughts.

Amelia blinked back some tears that wanted to burst from her eyes and forced a smile while nodding. He leaned in and hugged her. He hated seeing how much it tore her up inside. He felt the same way though, but instead of crying, he wanted to scream at the top of his lungs and throw his fist through the wall. It wasn't fair. Will already had one child that he couldn't afford because he had a falling out with his boss about something that seemed insignificant to Jake, but Will blew out of proportion and ended up getting fired, and now he had a second child on the way without any job prospects. Will wasn't exactly the most motivated person, and he blatantly told Jake once that he would rather work the system instead of working at a job. There was no way to make sense of it – it didn't make sense how someone who clearly was doing so many wrong things in life was able to have children and yet Jake and Amelia strived so hard to do everything right, and yet they were left childless.

They prepared for the day in silence. It was the type of silence that is felt and heard when at a funeral. They both felt each other's pain without even having to speak about it. Their breakfast at Pleasant Street wasn't filled with the laughter and happiness that Amelia had imagined. It was more somber though still enjoyable – like most of their days had been. Amelia had hoped that today could have been different. Jake had suggested they stay home and find something to watch on TV because he wanted to hold Amelia, and she desperately needed the cuddle time as well. Amelia needed to breathe the fresh ocean air though, so they decided to continue their morning activities as planned and then watch TV and cuddle later.

Amelia held her cardboard tea container in her hand as she leaned on the railing of the large white gazebo at Stage Fort Park. Jake put his arm around her waist, they looked out the vast ocean. The salty damp sea air curled her hair as she pulled it down from the bun she had it in. She closed her eyes and laid her head on Jake's shoulder. The sound of the waves crashing washed her ears of the silence that had surrounded them all morning until children's laughter all of a sudden broke the serenity. She opened her eyes to see a few siblings running around playing tag with each other and their chocolate lab puppy while their parents watched from a near distant.

Jake knew what Amelia was thinking, "Ready?" She nodded her head, and they walked silently to the car. They didn't need to share any words to explain that they both felt the pain of their dream being played out in front of them while they could only ever watch from a distance.

Once they were home, every station they turned to seemed to remind them even more of their incapacity to conceive. The home and garden station they loved to watch had a couple searching for a new house because they were expecting their first child. They flipped to one of the movie stations, which had a movie on all about the antics of trying to get pregnant, so they decided to watch one of their favorite shows instead, but the episode ended up being about how the main character found out she was pregnant.

Amelia decided she'd rather have a good cry in the shower than sit and watch any more reminders of the one thing she would never experience.

"You want to put in one of our movies?" Jake tried to keep her with him.

"Nah," Amelia sighed, "I think I'm going to take a long shower and then go to bed."

"Ok, do you want to talk at all?"

Amelia shook her head, "Not really." She kissed him on the forehead. "I love you."

"Love you too," he responded as she walked down the hallway to their bedroom.

Jake turned to another favorite sitcom, and the episode was about the main couple finding out they were pregnant. *Man, is this like pregnancy night on TV or what?* Jake thought. Nevertheless, Jake still enjoyed the show for its funny antics about life and working in an office setting. On the commercials, he thought about how he wished at times like these that Amelia would open up to him more, but at the same time he knew that she needed her own time and space to breathe, think, and process everything - but he still couldn't help feeling completely incapable of comforting his wife during this time.

After the show was over, he went in the bedroom expecting to see Amelia asleep already, but her journal was lying on her side of the bed and he could hear the shower running from their ensuite bathroom. He picked up her journal and wanted to read it, but he also wanted to respect her privacy. *Would she be mad at me if I read just a little? Probably not, but then again, whose knows what it could say in there?*

Jake mulled it over for a few more minutes, and then decided to read the last entry only:

*I know what it feels like to want something so badly but know it's never going to happen. I know how it feels to see your dreams played out in*

*everyone else's life and see them destroy it. A
broken heart is not enough of a description to begin
to explain what it feels like. As I watch each dream
collapse, I sit and wonder if it will ever be a reality
– could there be a hope? And then the devastating
realization comes back around again and knocks
me right off my feet. All I can do is get back up
again so to not let myself be consumed by the
darkness that wants to overtake me, that wants to
break me, that wants me to be tormented forever. O
God, I need you more than ever!*

Tears came to his eyes as he read through her
agony. He closed the journal slowly and set it back
where he had found it. How could he make it
better? What could he do to change things? The
answer was nothing. He couldn't do anything in his
power to change the situation they were in. He
couldn't make their bodies do what their bodies
wouldn't or couldn't do naturally. He had to try and
accept it. How could he though? *God, I'm supposed
to be the provider for my family. I'm supposed to be
the one to care for Amelia and give her joy, and yet,
I can't give her the bundle of joy that we both
desire. Please help us. O, God, be with us.*

"How have you been feeling?" Lane asked as
her and Amelia sat on Lane's couch together. They
had planned a very much needed girls' night
together and decided on painting their nails and
watching a movie like they were high school
teenagers again.

"Since I started the Naltrexone a few weeks
ago, I have been doing much better. The auto-

immune stuff is subsiding, and I have so much more energy." Amelia beamed, "And best of all, my hair is starting to grow back!"

Amelia explained to Lane how the Naltrexone prescription had to be filled at Conley's Pharmacy because it was a compounded medication, and Conley's was the only pharmacy nearby that did those types of prescriptions. "Thank God!" Amelia said, "Because I have no idea what I would have done or where to go if Ipswich didn't have Conley's!" Three weeks ago, she had to start on the first dose of the medicine which was 1.5mg before bed. "I guess when you take it before bed, it makes your body think it's not making any endorphins at all, so then your body has to make more because it thinks it's low. Then when you wake up in the morning, you have a boost of endorphins like every one usually has."

"How did the doctor know you needed it? Was there a test he did? How long do you need to be on it for?" Lane was intrigued.

"Well, there isn't a test for it. There used to be, but the medical field did away with it for some reason. It won't hurt me if I don't end up having low endorphins anyway. I have to take it for six months - that's how long it takes to retrain my body to function normally, but after the first week, my dose went to 3mg, and now I'm at 4.5mg. That's where I'll stay for the next six months. Sometimes people use it forever because they need to for whatever reasons. I think I may end up being one of those people because of my auto-immune issues, but we'll have to wait and see."

"Well, I'm just glad to see my friend getting back to normal. So happy that you've started feeling better and this medication is helping. What else do you need to do in the meantime for your next appointment?"

"The usual... blood tests to check estrogen and progesterone levels."

"How are things with Claire? Have you heard from her much?"

"It's still hard knowing she's pregnant, and I'm not. She called the other day and left a message saying that they were going to start looking at buying a home. Apparently their two bedroom apartment is too small for them."

"Maybe they're expecting twins?"

"Oh my gosh, I sure hope not." Amelia felt bad for saying that, "Well, you know, it wouldn't be horrible for them to have twins, just horrible for me. Sorry - I always feel so selfish when it comes to people having children. I can only think of myself and how much I'm not experiencing that instead of being happy for the other person."

"Hey, you can tell me anything, Amelia. I understand how hard this must be for you, and I know you never mean ill will on anyone. You have such a tender heart." Lane would never lie to make someone feel better, but Amelia didn't fully believe that she had a tender heart as Lane said. "So, what do you want to watch while we paint our nails?"

"Anything without babies in it," and they both laughed.

# DIAMONDS IN THE RUFF

Now that Amelia was feeling better, she was ready to start taking on something new in the next chapter of their lives. Since buying a house was out the picture right now because they had too many stipulations on their loan requirements because they didn't have a down payment and since having a child was proving to be difficult, Amelia and Jake decided to buy a puppy. She found an ad in the newspaper for golden retriever puppies, and she remembered how her childhood dog was part golden retriever. Jake had a puppy in his childhood as well and agreed the dog may be a good addition to their family since they wanted their children to grow up with a dog someday anyway.

As they pulled up to the quaint little picturesque farm in New Hampshire with an occasional goat, chicken and cow roaming around the fenced in property, Amelia's heart started pounding faster as she let the anticipation of buying a puppy fill her with excitement. She couldn't wait to pick one out of the litter. She really wanted a girl, but she wasn't sure which one they would go home with once they started playing with all the puppies. She would have a sense on which one would be perfect for them.

After they chatted with the breeders for a few minutes, the man - whose name was Ralph - opened a sliding glass door in their home that let five golden retrievers loose into the all season porch where Amelia and Jake were waiting to greet them. The puppies rolled and tumbled over each other as they made their way to Amelia and Jake, and Amelia couldn't hold back giggling.

"Aw, look at that one," she pointed to a male puppy, who though excited, was pushed out of the way by his siblings and wobbled his way a little more slowly over to them with his tail wagging helping each back foot move forward. "I kind of like how calm he is."

Jake agreed, but as they bent down to greet him, another puppy jumped onto Amelia's leg knocking her on her bottom while the puppy incessantly licked her face. Jake laughed, "I think she likes you." Amelia gave her some attention and then tried to pay attention to the first puppy, but his sibling would not leave Amelia alone. "Looks like she wants all your attention."

"This is going to be a tough choice." She wanted to take them all home, but especially the calm boy and the enthusiastic girl, but since they could only decide on one, they decided to go with the girl. Amelia wasn't a hundred percent sure, but since she knew they wanted a girl, she figured it was something she could stick to that would help with the decision.

Once the puppy was in their apartment, Amelia quickly realized that owning a dog in an apartment was very different than owning a dog in a home. When her dog went outside, all she had to do was open the slider door to her parents' fenced in yard. In their apartment, she needed to walk down two flights of stairs hoping the puppy would be able to hold its bathroom until the bottom - not to mention she had to train the puppy to stairs because he had never been around stairs before. Dragging a puppy down the stairs while trying to make sure it didn't pee all over the place wasn't what Amelia had in mind. Also, when she had a dog in her childhood, she could shovel up the dog poop in the yard, but in the apartment community, she had to use a little bag to pick up the poop with her hand. The feel of the warm pile while trying to pull it up from the grass was a step above disgusting that Amelia didn't realize existed.

Amelia noticed Jake didn't seem as enthused about the dog either. She figured it was an adjustment period, and after a few days, things would feel normal again, but they weren't as joyous with the whole situation as she thought they would be. Instead of being so excited about owning a new puppy like most families would be, it seemed more like they bought toilet paper in bulk from a warehouse club - excited because of the great bargain, but then when once its stored away in the closet, the excitement fades and is forgotten.

After Amelia had walked the puppy once last time for the night, she put in him the crate in the spare room. She sat on the bed and noticed Jake had his eyes closed already. She wanted to talk to him about the puppy, but she didn't want to wake him.

"Is he all set?" Before Jake could finish his question, the puppy began to whine.

She didn't want to carry the load of taking care of the dog by herself. She wanted them both to be invested in this new addition to their family. "I want a baby, Jake." Amelia whispered through her tears as she turned off the light and settled herself under the covers of their bed. "I don't want a puppy."

"Couldn't you have come to this conclusion *before* we bought the puppy?" Jake sounded more than irritated with her.

"Please, please don't be mad with me." Her crying begun to take over her words and the tears flooded not only her face but also her pillow. "I wish I could give you a child more than anything in the world. I really do, Jake. I wish that the crying puppy in the other room was a baby that I could comfort and not a puppy that I have to keep crated. I'm not even upset that the puppy cries all night and keeps me up – I'm really not, but I wish more than anything though that the crying was *our* baby - not a puppy." She took a deep breath to help her from choking since her nose was filling with so much mucus she thought she would drown.

"Come here," he pulled her close to him. She felt the warmth of his body and nestled her head into his chest. She loved his embrace and imagined how perfect it would be if they could have a baby cradled between them.

"As I see all the toys on the floor, I wish they were baby toys instead. I don't want to resent the dog some day, and I already do in some sense because it's not a child. I feel crazy, Jake. I really do. I feel like everything is being ripped out of me, and there's nothing I can do to stop it. I have to sit by while I watch every part of myself fall apart. I love you so much, and I really wish we could share in making a child together, and it kills me every day that we can't."

"Me too. It kills me too, Amelia. It feels like a big part of our lives are missing, and nothing can change that, but I love you more than anything. And if it ends up only being me and you for the rest of our lives, we're still very blessed because what you and I have is very special." He rubbed her head with the arm that he had around her, "Yes, it's sad that we'll never be able to share that with our children, but we'll still have a wonderful life together regardless."

The next day brought a silent car ride as they drove back to the breeder's house where they had bought the puppy. Amelia's eyes were puffy from all the crying the night before, and the air was tense with emotion as Amelia's guilt ate at her for not being able to keep a dog while Jake's annoyance still surrounded the whole situation - buying a dog and then having to return it because she couldn't sort out her feelings about it all beforehand. She really wanted this to work out. She had visions of Jake hiking with the dog and her and the puppy cuddling on the couch. She pictured them all going to the beach and enjoying camping together. But then again... each of those scenarios were the same things she saw with them and a baby. She wanted to experience all those things first with a baby in their family and then someday with a dog. It was all backwards, but if she returned the dog, then they would be back at square one. Was that worse or better? The whole trip there - a total two hour drive to a town in New Hampshire - had her mind switching back and forth, not making the decision any easier.

Once they arrived at the breeder's home, Amelia took a deep breath and made herself toughen up in order to return the puppy without any water works on her part. The return was quick and fairly easy, and they were able to get their money back, which Jake had been really concerned about. The first twenty minutes of the ride home felt like the trip there - cold, distant, and tense. Suddenly, Jake took a left hand turn at an intersection they were supposed to stay straight at causing them to deviate from the GPS directions. Amelia skeptically looked around. She wasn't sure why Jake had abruptly went off course. She desperately wanted to ask but was afraid to say anything. She didn't want to upset the waters that were already disturbed.

They ended up at a quaint little town in about five minutes. Jake circled a couple of blocks; clearly he was looking for something in particular. After a few minutes, he pulled up a side street and parked in front of a brick building that resembled a petite strip mall. There were maybe three stores inside. Jake turned off the car and left her as he headed toward the strip mall, so Amelia followed. She figured he may have to use the bathroom or something, but she noticed the sign on the door as soon as she closed the Jeep door - chocolatier. He had brought her to a chocolate shop - her favorite. After everything she put him through with the dog stuff, he had brought her here. Now she knew everything may be ok between them, but she ignored the horrible and guilty she felt about everything.

As they entered the chocolate shop, the rich aroma of melted cocoa filled their noses. She loved that smell, and she could almost taste the chocolate just by breathing in the essence that carried in the air. They perused the many shelves, shapes, and varieties of chocolate from one end of the shop to the other. When Jake broke their silence with, "What do you want?"

She looked at him surprised, "I don't know. What were you thinking?" She couldn't control herself when it came to chocolate. She would buy the whole store if she could.

"I say we do the pound of assorted chocolates and choose whatever we want from the case."

"Are you sure?" Jake was usually a little more cautious with money especially when things were a bit more expensive, but he seemed totally unaware of his normal consciousness.

"Yes, I'm sure. Which ones do you want?" For the next few minutes, they pointed to all the chocolates they wanted to try as the woman behind the counter grabbed two of all their selections -

which was also a surprise to Amelia because they would usually share each piece, but today she was being spoiled and would have one of each all to herself! Why was he being so nice to her? Not that he wasn't usually nice to her, but after everything that happened in the last twenty-four hours, she figured she wasn't his most favorite person right now.

*Maybe he's finally snapped? What if he doesn't care about anything anymore? Was he going to leave her? He could be so upset with her but just masking it all.* She definitely needed to say something and say it soon, but then again, maybe she shouldn't upset him more if he was truly mad at her. The thoughts kept whirling around in her head as she and Jake took turns using the bathroom and ordered lunch from a little shop only a few steps from the chocolate shop. Again, they would usually share a sandwich, and today, Jake said they could both order their own.

When they were back on the road again, bellies full, Amelia opened the box of chocolates and sniffed. "Mmmm," she closed her eyes as she let the essence of chocolate tickle the senses in her nostrils.

"Which one do you want to try first?" Jake said as he smiled from her antics and love of chocolate.

"These ones?" She pointed to a truffle covered in powered sugar and supposedly full of raspberry filling.

"Good choice." Jake nodded. Amelia popped one in his mouth and one in hers. Of course, her mouth was smaller, so she always had to take two bites; whereas Jake could devour it in one.

The chocolate melted on their tongues and then the splash of raspberry bursted through and trickled down their throats. They looked at each knowing what each had just experienced. They didn't even need to exchange words because they both knew that this chocolate was one of the best they have ever tasted, though they could never remember where the best chocolate they ever tasted was really from. Amelia claimed it was some place in Vermont when they were on their honeymoon, but Jake wasn't so convinced. But this chocolate definitely came in second to the mysterious best chocolate they ever had the first time.

"Is everything ok between us?" Amelia finally mustered up the courage to ask. She really needed to know even though things seemed well between them, she had to be sure.

Jake was silent for several seconds, which felt like several minutes to Amelia. "Of course, we're ok," he said matter-of-factly. "I just need you to promise me one thing." He waited for her to respond.

"What?" What could he possibly want her to promise? She was kind of nervous to hear the answer.

"No more dogs. I don't want to go through this again."

"What do you mean by no more dogs? Like ever? I can't guarantee that I'll never want another dog, especially if we ever buy a house someday."

"I don't want you to want a dog again because of all this baby stuff. It's just crazy. People aren't going to understand why we want to take back a puppy. Plus, I'm not sure we're even dog people. I mean, I know we both love dogs, but I don't know if we're really meant to be dog owners. We love Chloe. Why do we want to bring any other animal into that? Can we just be content with her for now?"

Amelia hated feeling crazy, and that's all this baby stuff made her feel like all the time - crazy. She hated it, and yet she didn't know any other way to be. Could she guarantee that she wouldn't want another puppy ever - even when the puppy looks like a baby to her? Could she let that go? It wasn't a question, no - it couldn't be a question anymore. It had to be an answer and one that she could make continually. She had to let go. She had to promise this and let it die in her. Jake was right; they loved their cat. They didn't really need any other animal to satisfy their animal care needs, so it all really boiled down to Amelia's baby craze.

"Yes, I can promise that for now I won't ask for any more dogs, no matter how cute a puppy is or how much it may remind me of a child. I can't guarantee, though, that some day when we are in a home, and if we *both* mutually want a dog, that I won't want one then - but it will be something we mutually decide and want for actually owning a dog and not because of longing for children. Dogs and kids are a better combination anyway. I think I'm always ahead of myself with wanting the bigger picture, you know - the house, the kids, the dog - that I forget what we really are - a couple in an apartment with a cat and no children." Amelia took a deep breath in to hold back her eager tears tickling the corners of her eyes. "It's not that what we have is bad. I just so badly want a piece of the puzzle, even it's the insignificant piece - a dog - of the whole puzzle. Part of me feels like if I have a small insignificant part of the puzzle that maybe the rest will fall in place somehow."

Jake reached his hand over and grabbed hers, "Life doesn't work that way, unfortunately." He squeezed her hand gently, "Believe me, I want it all just as much as you do. But if we try to force the pieces into place, we may not get the picture that's on the box. You can't force the pieces together when they are not the ones that belong in that place."

She knew all of this to be true, but she still wished that God would miraculously drop the right puzzle pieces into her lap so she could see the finished picture. In the meantime, could she be happy with a half done puzzle? Could she be patient while trying to find the right pieces to fit? Her biggest concern was more of whether or not the right pieces would ever be found. She feared that they never would.

# FLOWER BUSHES

"You have got to hear this story," John thought telling Amelia about his odd job may brighten her day. He hated seeing her so down, so his goal was to cheer her up. "You know how dad taught me to weed-whack before mowing the lawn, right?" She shook her head. "Well the other day, I intentionally had to mow first because I was told *not* to bring my weed-whacker because I was to use their tools, and later I found out their weed-whacker was broken."

He explained how though the new family he started working for was very meticulous, they had been gracious - or maybe pre-occupied – when they addressed him about this. John still couldn't decide which it was because his interactions with them had been so strange. He told Amelia about the conversation from a few days earlier:

John knocked on the door at the end of the long hallway trimmed with beautiful white crown molding and cream-colored painted walls. The door was open by a crack only wide enough to illuminate the hallway with the beaming sunlight contained inside the room.

"Come in," a stern man's voice bellowed and fear clenched John's stomach.

He had not yet met the husband of his employer, Mrs. Beau de Fontaine. She had hired him from a phone call he received from her the previous week. The woman had addressed him in the following manner, "Hello, this is Mrs. Beau de Fontaine, and a friend of mine, Sally Whittaker, raved about your landscaping abilities. I would like you to start work on my yard tomorrow. Come to the gate – I've left your name with the butler. He will buzz you in and show you to the shed with all of our tools. No need to bring your own, I don't want a huge truck outside our house with lawn equipment on it. The butler will also see that you are paid at the end of the day. Please come every Monday, Wednesday, and Friday. How does that sound?"

"Ok," John had wanted to ask how much and what things were expected to be done, but before he could manage to say anything more, she continued on in her quick talk as though they were in a one-sided conversation.

"Fantastic! We are at 104 Lilac View Lane in Hamilton. Ciao!" and that was the end of the oddest conversation John had ever been part of.

He wondered what he had signed up for, but with a gated house, a butler on hand, and a name like Lilac View Lane, he figured he couldn't have gone wrong. It would have to pay well.

The man standing behind a very elite, studious desk motioned to one of the leather chairs facing the desk, "Please sit, Mr. Morris."

John sat down quickly, "Thank you, sir."

The man sat down slowly in his riveted winged leather desk chair and adjusted some papers on his desk, "As I understand, you have seriously offended my wife!" His tone more accusing now.

"I have?" John was completely appalled. The first time he had seen her was only minutes earlier when he was brought into the kitchen by the butler as usual because that is where his paycheck awaited him the last two times he came.

"I believe my husband would like a word with you," was the only thing Mrs. Beau de Fontaine said to him in a whisper as she covered the mouthpiece to her cell phone and motioned with her head down the hallway. She continued to walk out the sliding glass door that the butler had opened for her, "Yes, I am here, I was on hold, so can you…" her words trailed off as he had started down the hallway, and the butler closed the sliding glass door.

She was an attractive woman, but he had only seen her for a second and the butler was right there. How could they have tried to conspire something against him?

"Mr. Beau de Fontaine, I'm not sure I quite understand." John really had no other words.

"She told me that you weed whacked the lawn *after* mowing, so that when she walked on the patio, her feet had grass clippings on them, and she tracked them in the pool." His tone became more and more judicious.

John wasn't sure if he should laugh as though this was all a joke and he was on some kind of reality TV show, or if his employer was actually serious.

Mr. Beau de Fontaine continued, "You are supposed to weed whack first, then mow the lawn so it will pick up all the clippings and then sweep the patio of anything left. I shouldn't have to tell you how to do your job."

"Sir, with all due respect, I was only shown the shed of equipment and left to my own…"

"You're a landscaper, do I have to show you how to use the tools too! You should know how to do this!" He stood up and turned his back to John as he looked out the window.

"Mr. Beau de Fontaine," John tried to keep his composure after being yelled at, "I always weed whack before I mow. That's the way I do things. I searched for the weed whacker and didn't see one, so I mowed. Then on Wednesday, when I returned, I brought my own weed whacker with me because I was told not to bring my equipment before." The man turned around. "I apologize for not sweeping the patio. I was not aware that was part of my duties, but I will make a note for the future."

The man looked deep in thought, "Actually, come to think of it," a little knock happened at the door, and Mrs. Beau de Fontaine appeared again, he continued, "I think I remember that our last one broke. The other guys hit a rock with it or something."

"Oh, yes, I do remember that," the oh-so-offended woman said, who was still on the phone. "We had to replace the greenhouse window because of it." She cleared her throat, "I need you to come with me right now," she tugged at his arm.

"I will notify the butler of your need of the new equipment, and you can keep your job." His wife had him half way out the door. "I must say that I do love the way you cut the grass – the lines, they're perfect!" and with that he was absorbed into the hallway.

"Thank you," John tried to fit in before they were completely gone, "sir."

John shook his head and smiled as he recounted the silliness of the whole situation to Amelia. "I have to go in today as well. I guess I'll get paid extra since I don't usually work Saturdays. They want me to tidy up the flower bushes since their daughter is having an informal birthday party with her friends today, but I guess there is the formal birthday party tomorrow, so the flowers need to be in tip top shape and flourishing by tomorrow afternoon. Even though I just trimmed the bushes yesterday, Mrs. Beau de Fontaine claims they won't be as "perky" on Sunday unless I give them attention today."

"Well, have fun today," Amelia giggled, "and let me know if you have any more fun stories."

"Ok, catch you later." John ended the phone call. He didn't really mind going in. They paid him extra, plus he didn't have any plans other than hanging out at his bachelor pad of an apartment. He wanted to buy a house and easily could since his rent was cheap and he saved as much as he could of every paycheck, but he wanted to wait until he was married to buy a house together with his wife. His apartment was empty and lonely already anyway, so he couldn't really justify buying a house and being invested in the loneliness even more.

The thoughts occupied his mind as he finished trimming the bushes. He worked his hands in between the flower bushes to pull out any weeds, and the screaming girls from the birthday party gathered around the pool watching their friend open her birthday presents. He noticed a woman standing by the refreshment table all by herself. He studied her for a moment, but she didn't resemble any of the maids he had seen roaming around so far. He could tell she was beautiful though, even from a distance – *that's when you know she's a true beauty*, he thought to himself.

Her brown hair that held a slight curl blew softly to one side in the wind, and he wondered what shampoo she used and what it smelled like – was it flowery, or maybe it had a more organic smell like hemp or something? *She's probably already dating someone or maybe even married*, his negativity wore away at him. He tried to think of ways he could get a closer look at her hand to see a ring, though that wouldn't rule out whether she was dating someone.

He wanted to meet her though, then he could get a better sense if she was available or not – maybe? She glanced over at him, and he quickly moved his focus to the bush as though he was totally enthralled in what he was doing. Why did he do that? Then he remembered that he'd have to walk by her to pick up his paycheck in the kitchen, since that's where they would leave the check for him every time he came. Though he thought that was strange, he figured out their plot behind paying him every day he came; if they pay the worker every time, then when they want to let him go, they don't have to worry about owing him. John liked receiving the payment up front anyway. Then he didn't have to keep track of whether he received his full payment either, so it was actually a win-win situation.

He kept glancing back in the direction of the pool catching glimpses of the woman who had stole his heart. He watched as she studied the children in the pool. He could sense a longing in her eyes. *Maybe she is single?* His heart jumped. *Or maybe she can't have children - meaning she's married.* Sadness filled him. Either way his compassion for her made him want to embrace and comfort her.

Once he finished the bushes, he quickly packed up the tools in the shed. He noticed his reflection in one of the windows of the shed and wiped the sweat from his forehead onto his forearm. Then he squirted some of the water from his water bottle over his head. Even though the water splashed onto his shirt, he'd rather have her see him damp with water than drenched in sweat. He shook his arms of the excess water.

As he approached the house, he noticed the children weren't around, and worst of all, the pretty woman had gone as well. His heart began to race with panic. Had he really missed his chance with the woman who could make his dreams come true? He lost his chance before he even had it. He slowly walked into the kitchen to grab his check off the counter. As he picked up the check, he looked around, but to no avail, the place was empty. *It's such a shame to have such a beautiful place and have no one to fill it.* The white couches reflected in the glossy marble floors that flowed into the fireplace that wasn't surrounded with family photos like at his parents' house. In fact, there were no family photos hanging at all. The occasional artistic piece with shapes and colors strewn all over were the only types of hangings on the walls that he had noticed in the house.

As John turned to leave, he bumped right into the woman he was looking for, "Oh! I'm so sorry. Excuse me."

"No worries." She said quickly and their eyes met for a moment. She hurried away as quickly as she had come. He didn't even get to ask her name because he had been so enchanted by her eyes. He went outside to find where she went, but she had been so fast that she was nowhere to be found.

Later that day, John called Amelia back and before she could get a word in, his voice started, "I met the most beautiful woman today, Amelia. Well, technically I didn't actually meet her yet…formally, I kind of bumped into her, but I do hope to meet her some day! I have this feeling about her though, like she could be the one!" She listened as her brother rattled on like a teenager in love.

"I can't wait to meet her, John." She managed

to fit in between his taking a breath. Thankfully the conversation ended fairly quickly since he was headed home to make dinner, and Amelia and Jake were on their way to visit Nanette for a follow up on their charting. Even though John knew about the infertility, she was glad that he didn't ask about what she was up to for the night.

# UMBRELLAS & LEMON SLICES

Sarah Key felt as though her life was slipping away from her because all she had to show for herself was her party planning business. Party planning was the profession she chose since her first work permit allowed her to labor for an income. Before that, she would help one of her mother's friends who had a party planning business and would fold invitations, prep party and table favors, and assist with the setup and tear down that came with each event. Now she had her own business that she started after college. Yes, it kept her busy, but it didn't fulfill her desire to be a wife and a mother. She always worked more hours than she should, but she justified it because she didn't have anything else to do with her time – no one waiting for her to come home, except her cat, Leo. He loved her dearly, but mostly when she had food, so even *he* wasn't the sincerest of company.

As she sat in the window seat of her house in Georgetown, MA, she thought back to the previous day when she was at the house for a wealthy family's daughter's birthday party. She had been pulled into staying the whole time to manage the food and refreshment table, though that didn't typically fall under her duties as a party planner. She would always cater to the customer though, which made her customer rating soar but her made her personal life non-existent. She couldn't understand why the family wouldn't have one of the maids manage the food and refreshment table, but the mother had begged Sarah, "Oh, you're so much younger than our maids. I think it would make Kaityln more comfortable with a woman your age being here than one of my maids." So Sarah had agreed, plus the mother offered her additional compensation.

She thought back on how long she had to search for the bathroom in that house – there were so many doors, and they were all shut. She knocked on each one hoping it wasn't someone's bedroom. *Where is the butler when you need him?* She thought as she knocked on the next door – no answer – she slowly opened it. *Nope, the bathroom's not here either.* Before her was only one large empty room. *Why would you need such a large house if you weren't even going to use all the space?* Sarah had been a little jealous of the size of the house, but she seemed to be jealous of a lot of things these days.

After she located the bathroom, she realized she didn't have her purse and needed it because that time of the month had come for her - she was hoping it would have held off until the next day, so she left her purse in her car. When she rushed out of the bathroom in search of her purse, she bumped into a man that seemed to appear out of nowhere at the end of the hallway.

"Oh, I'm so sorry. Excuse me." He apologized.

"No worries," and her eyes met his for a moment; however she needed desperately to find her purse otherwise this meet cute wouldn't be so cute. As she hurried away, she thought, *Why couldn't my period have waited until Sunday?* She never worked on Sundays. It was one of her rules.

Once Sarah found her purse and used the bathroom again, she needed to refill the brownie and cookie tray, and she nonchalantly glanced around in search of the man she bumped into briefly. Then she switched out the lemonade and iced tea with new pitchers filled with ice and floating slices of lemons, and she thought that the fancy clear plastic cups with little umbrellas dancing on the tops of the drinks seemed a bit too much to her for an nine-year-old's birthday party, but who was she to say anything? She always presented and delivered whatever the client ordered.

Sarah stood there next to the refreshment table with her arms crossed watching the curly red-haired birthday girl chatter with her little friends, as she dissected their conversation. The little red-head, Kaitlyn, had the mannerisms of a valley girl from California with the poise of an English woman at tea time with the queen of England.

Sarah still couldn't figure out why Kaitlyn had chosen brownies and cookies instead of something more delicate and sophisticated like everything else she had requested. It didn't seem to fit altogether. *Maybe there is still a part – a small part, but a part – of an actual little girl inside her*, Sarah thought to herself.

Little yelps and screams came from the opposite side of the pool as Kaitlyn opened her gifts and all the girls fawned over each of them. Kaitlyn smiled but Sarah couldn't tell how real the smiles actually were – Kaitlyn had been trained well.

Sarah watched the gentle breeze blow the wildflowers outside her window in her small garden. She would love to have children, though Giorgio Armani sunglasses that Kaitlyn received as a present would be the last thing she would let her nine-year-old daughter receive as a gift. No, she would raise her children to appreciate and love the simple. Children these days were too independent-like mini adults. The thought made her quiver. Children should be able to enjoy their childhood – the simplicity and pureness that it can hold. Now instead of trying to protect them from it, parents allowed their children to launch full force into adulthood by age five with their cell phones and computers. The working age might as well be lowered to ten. Productivity in a company would be tremendous, but then they'd have to include nap time.

She remembered the strange interaction she had with the daughter and mother when they were telling her what they wanted for the birthday party -

or rather what the daughter wanted for her birthday party.

Kaitlyn started with, "I would like to have those puffy Chinese lanterns strewn (*yes, she used that word*) all around the pool area, but I prefer them in the pastel colors not those gaudy reds and yellows." The mother had been too distracted with her iPhone smiling and texting or emailing, maybe even liking something on FaceBook. Sarah had no idea what people did on those types of things.

"I don't mind paper napkins for this type of event," Kaitlyn went on, "but they must be that denser type of paper, not the cheap ones that fall apart with one use."

Sarah couldn't believe how the mother was completely enveloped in the cyber world when her daughter in reality sat right next to her.

"Umbrellas!" Kaitlyn paused and shoved her face into Sarah's stare, "Are you taking notes or even listening to me?"

"Yes," Sarah blinked, "sorry," she continued jotting down the girl's list.

Even the day of the party, Sarah found the mother to be absent as well. She had a feeling that her disappearance was more of the norm than not. The mother - that's what Sarah had to call her because every time she tried to ask the woman's name during the planning phase for the party, the woman's phone rang or beeped, and she'd say, "Sorry, I really need to take this," as if she was some kind of rock star or important person. When she signed her name to the paperwork, she didn't read Sarah's contract or glance it over even though she could be selling a kidney and have no idea, and her signature was so illegible that she should have been recruited to be a doctor. So Sarah had no way to figure out her name, and she remained to be the mysterious unnamed mother until Sarah received their check for payment at the end of the day noting *The Beau de Fontaine's* on the top left corner.

Sarah hated that the mother didn't seem to have any interest in what her daughter liked or did. The mother was only a monetary presence in her daughter's life. *I would definitely be a better mother than her,* Sarah thought to herself as she traced her finger traced along the boxed pane of her window.

She thought back on how terrified she had been when she thought she had lost the girls because they had disappeared in seconds when Sarah had gone into the kitchen to throw her cup away. Her heart had begun racing as she searched frantically with her eyes for the children. She wanted to start running around yelling for them when she stopped herself. *You're not their mother. They're not drowning or in danger,* her inner voice spoke to her.

Sarah wanted to cry as the feelings from that day swamped her emotions, but she blinked back the tears; her longing for being a mother broke her heart so much sometimes. She was nearly thirty – at least felt like she was thirty - even though she was only twenty-four because there was no way for her to meet anyone now. She lived her work, and at the end of a long day, she would curl up on her sofa with a soft pillow, fluffy blanket, and a pint of Ben & Jerry's to watch a movie about princesses. She sighed. In order to even try to have a child, she needed to find a man first.

She remembered the man she bumped into again. He was very handsome for the moment she held him in her eyes. *Could he be Kaitlyn's brother?* She wondered. She quickly decided that he couldn't have been because he was definitely not dressed to the family's typical aristocratic fashion. They all looked as though they stepped out of an L.L. Bean or Ralph Lauren catalog; whereas, he definitely looked rougher around the edges as if he was ready for a weekend camping trip at any moment. She kind of liked that though - it made him seem more real, more approachable.

She usually dated guys that she felt like she needed to impress because they always dressed and acted like they were part of some royal English line, but she never felt them to be hearty enough to protect her from danger. Not that men were dueling over women anymore, but Sarah was still caught up in the fairy tale land where the prince would save the damsel in distress.

*He must have been a hired worker,* she thought to herself. She had looked around the yard that day hoping to see him again. *Actually!?* She had recalled seeing a man at the flower bushes trimming them. *It must have been him!* But she never did see him again that day. Her sadness deepened as she realized that she may never see him again.

Sarah thought about how the girls filed out of the three huts alongside the pool dressed in bathing suits that were more like adult bathing suits with their tiny straps and skimpy bottoms, and they were all in bikinis. "What happened to the cute little one-piece bathing suits they used to make with polka dots and bows?" She had said to herself in a low voice only she could hear. She wasn't sure whether to be enraged at the parents for letting their children where bathing suits that better resembled underwear or if she should be saddened by the fact that the innocence of children was no longer cherished by society. Each tugged at her heart equally.

Sarah had chuckled to herself when she saw all the girls were all on floats in the pool sun tanning. They had carefully placed themselves on the rafts so that not one of them had even set foot in the water. What was more amusing to Sarah was that they all had their lemonade or iced tea – floating lemon slices, umbrella, and all – in the cup holder of their floats. *Mini adults*, she thought to herself again. *Well done, Society.*

Later that night, Amelia picked up the phone when John called, "I totally forgot to tell you that when I was at my job today for that wealthy couple in Hamilton, you know that one I had to do the extra shift for the birthday party?"

Amelia nodded her head and then realized he couldn't see her gesture, "Yea, you were quite giddy about that girl you bumped into."

John sighed, "Oh yes, I asked them who she was. Apparently, she runs her own party business, and they gave me her business information. I do hope I can find and meet her somehow, but anyways, I wanted to tell you that the wife stopped me on the way out and asked me if I'd want a tent."

"A tent? That's odd."

"Yea, but listen, she said they bought it to go camping, but they realized they are more of the Ritz-Carlton type of people and camping wasn't for them. She wanted to get it out of the basement to make room for some remodeling they'll be doing, so she gave me the tent, a cot and two chairs!"

"Well, that's great... I guess. Are you going camping?"

"No, but I took the stuff because I was wondering if you and Jake would want it. At Easter, Jake was talking to me about how much he wanted to go camping but how expensive tents can be."

Jake was sitting next to Amelia when she picked up the phone and was listening to her every word intently once she mentioned the tent. "How big is it?"

"It's an eight person Eddie Bauer Edition tent." Amelia had the phone on speaker now, so Jake could listen in, and he was practically drooling as John explained the tent. "I set it up to take a look at it, and it's in perfect condition. You can stop by to take a look at it too, if you'd like."

"I guess we'll take it. Jake is practically doing a victory dance over here just thinking about it." Amelia giggled. "Thanks for thinking of us, John!"

John asked her about how she was feeling and how things on the infertility front were doing. She was glad to report that she was feeling better. "Nothing really new to do. We're hoping to keep me in a healthy state and see how my hormone levels are doing and then reassess from there." She was still annoyed that endometriosis was the diagnosis, especially since the surgery to find out *if* she even had it was out still out of the question for her, but she refused to think about it all until it was her last option at having children.

"We are so go camping!" Jake popped up from his seat as soon as she hung up with John, and he headed over to the computer to start looking up campsites in the Vermont State Parks. "Check it out! You can see pictures of all the different tent sites at each campground!" He acted as though he was a kid in a candy store and for the next few hours they checked each of the parks that had the soonest availability in August.

# CATHEDRALS

As Sarah walked through the wide open double doors of the Catholic cathedral, all the old familiar smells, faces and gestures came back to her even though she had never attended a Catholic Church before. She grew up in the Episcopal church, and this specific architectural giant reminded her a lot of her church. She perused the order of service that she grabbed after blessing herself at the door with the holy water. The Nicene Creed, passing of the peace, offertory, Lord's prayer, Holy Communion – *check, check, check – yup all still there*, she thought as she looked through the order of service. Actually that's what made it all real to her. Why had it mattered so much to her? Why was she always drawn to it? Why did she ever leave in the first place? She wracked her brain trying to recall the reason. She counted how long it had been; three years.

Once she had settled in her pew, she looked up for the first time and allowed the majestic interior of the cavernous beauties in the front of the cathedral wrap her in its ethereal essence. It was full of articulately carved cream-colored pillars holding up the ceiling that portrayed angelic figures surrounding Jesus. It was as if the architecture was presenting an opening to heaven for all to see. Light beamed in through the stained glass windows on either side of the church presenting the most angelic light. She inhaled slowly, closed her eyes, and let the incense tickle her senses.

Peace, she began to feel peaceful again, which is exactly what she wanted - and needed - to experience. She liked how no one was bothering her as newcomer. In the Episcopal church, she would have had someone come up to her by now clearly disregarding her need for time before the service starting. They would be ornately dressed with a forced teethy smile and would ask her name and let her know about the coffee hour after church, which would sound like prompts that were well-rehearsed. Then the person would be off to another unsuspecting victim.

As the prelude began, Sarah knew it was safe to investigate her human surroundings with her eyes now that people would be mute and file into their usual seats in the pews. There seemed to be a good number of people around her age there. There was a nice balance between all the ages actually – hopefully a good indication that this church had potential of reaching people where they are at in their needs in life.

She caught a young man noticing her from the opposite side of the sanctuary, and her heart skipped a beat – not in a good way, but terror clenched her heart. *Scott*, she remembered. He broke her heart in the deepest way a heart could be broken. As she slowly glanced in his direction again, she realized that it wasn't in fact him, but something about him reminded her of Scott. *He's probably on the other side of the world with the "love of his life" and doesn't even have a single thought about me*, she thought to herself.

There was a silence in the music, and then the choir began to sing as the processional of clergy started to process down the center aisle of the church. As her eyes followed them, she spotted a young couple with the absolute most adorable little girl she had ever seen. The couple looked happy as they held each other, and the mother cuddled their child. The little girl glanced over her mother's shoulder and focused on Sarah.

Sarah blinked back the tears forming in her eyes. *That should have been me by now.* But what did she have to show for herself at her age? Nothing but an empty house given to her by her parents before they moved to South Carolina for retirement, aside from her cat, and a job that she had poured herself into after the break up with Scott. Scott had promised her the world; his words still whispered to her in the quiet moments. She remembered - *he* was the reason she left church, though not intentional.

After he broke off their engagement for another woman, she found it hard to trust anyone – especially at church, since they met there on her first Sunday attending a new church when she started college. He had the most charming smile that melted her heart. When he ran off with "Miss Right" as Sarah liked to call her, Sarah stopped attending everything. It was gradual at first, but then she had collapsed into a world of broken dreams. They had dated through her first three years at college and were engaged for her entire senior year. Their wedding date was set for the summer after graduation, but when he revealed the news to her two weeks before graduation, and what was supposed to be the most exciting time of her life, she watched everything fall apart before her eyes – her excitement, her dreams, the ability to enjoy each day – it was all gone.

She had not intended on coming to church today. She was on the area running a few errands and had been on her way to grab a quick coffee at The Atomic Cafe, which she always liked to do when she was in Beverly, but she noticed people in the streets and on the sidewalks walking to church. She had always seen this church but had never thought of actually crossing through its doors. The people were nicely dressed and were smiling – something about the scene felt comforting to Sarah. She could hear the choir signing inside through the open windows, and the whole scene brought warmth to her spirit that she couldn't quite ignore.

Sarah glanced at the date on the front of her order of service sheet – Saint Mary's Star of the Sea, August 9th – the day she was supposed to say her vows to Scott three years ago. *A good day to restart*, she thought, and something inside stirred as she felt the promise of a new beginning arise.

"Where did you go?" Amelia asked as John walked back to their pew. Amelia and Jake had been waiting for John when the service ended, but he bolted past them.

"Sorry, I swore I saw the women from the Beau de Fontaine's here. I noticed she left very quickly, so I wanted to see if I could catch her outside, but by the time I got outside, I didn't see her anywhere."

"Geesh, you really have her on the brain, don't you?" Amelia smiled thinking how cute it was to watch her brother fall in love.

He shrugged, "What can I say? I'm smitten," and they both giggled at his use of the word.

Amelia pointed to the front of the church, "The service was beautiful. Thanks for inviting us. We've seriously been considering becoming Catholic, and we needed to make the first step of actually trying a Catholic Church."

"Like I said, this church is amazing. I've been so completely satisfied after joining a couple of years ago. It's so much different than the Protestant churches that we grew up in, but different in a good way. I find it challenges me every day to be a better person and more like Christ than any other church I've ever experienced."

Amelia nodded, "Well put. I can see how the Church can do that. With the reading we've been doing, and the experience we've had with the Catholic fertility center, it's shown us an entirely different way to see Christ and how to live our lives. We're definitely considering making the change from the Anglican Church. One of the major draws for us is the Catholic's standpoint on pro-life especially in regards to fertility. And you know, it's not that people in these other denominations don't have pro-life views, but it can be all over the board. We like that the Catholic Church is bold enough to take a stand on its beliefs despite whether it's the popular opinion - just like Jesus did when He was among us."

"Well, I'm glad you guys are considering it. Let me know if you ever want to chat more about it."

"Yea, we should definitely get together sometime because I can talk about this stuff all day long." Amelia smiled.

John nudged Jake with his elbow, "So, you gearing up for the camping trip?"

"Am I ever!" Jake's smile beamed from ear to ear. "Only another week or so away. Thanks again for getting that tent for us. It's awesome!"

"No problem at all. I'm glad you guys could use it. I figured it would be too good to pass up, so I agreed to it and figured I'd find someone for it before too long. Then I remembered you had mentioned wanting to go camping." He turned to Amelia, "Though I never thought of my sister as the tent camping type." He teased.

"What! Really? I've always loved spending time outdoors. I think you're mistaken. Now if we were talking about Claire, then yes, you nailed it. She can't even look at a bug without screaming and running away." They all chuckled.

# TENTS & CAMPING

As Jake attempted to start a fire with a flint - he watched many survivor type shows and wanted to try some of the techniques of things he learned on their camping trip - Amelia decided to work on setting up the cots and sleeping bags inside the tent. She zipped up the tent door, took a deep breath, and slowly let all the air escape her lungs in an exaggerated deep sigh. She looked around the cavernous tent, and it resonated with her empty womb.

She remembered when they brought home the tent for the first time and set it up. She thought it was way too big for the two of them but had suddenly realized it would be perfect for them and a couple of kids since it was an eight person tent. But until the day they could fill the tent with children, she felt the tent seemed excessive in size for just the two of them. When they walked by other campsites on their way to the bathrooms, Amelia noticed families of four jammed in a four person tent when the tents didn't look like they'd be big enough for two people.

*Over-prepared* - that was the only word that came to her mind. She was always over-prepared, but in this case being over-prepared for children just seemed silly. The tent would  always be a reminder every time they went camping that, yet again, they were without children. She loved the big tent but felt like a bit of a city slicker when other couples crammed themselves in tents that they pretty much had to crawl into. Then she began to feel bad that she couldn't just enjoy the gift of the tent from John. It's not that she went out and purchased this huge tent for the two of them, and it would be great if they ever invited friends along. They would have plenty of space for everyone to sleep.

She hadn't heard the fire crackling yet, so she decided to check on Jake. When she stepped out of the tent, he was still leaning deep into the fire pit and looked quite agitated as he frantically rubbed the flint and striker against each other. "Not as easy as it looks," he looked at her when she approached.

"Can I try?" She put her hand out, and he handed her the flint. "Why is your finger bleeding?"

"You'll see." He pointed to the tool that needed to be struck against the flint to create a spark. "Be careful - that's sharp enough to hurt you but not sharp enough to cause a spark." She tried several times before she gave up because her fingers became raw from getting scratched on the striker as well.

They decided to use the fire starter they brought with them since the sun was starting to set, and the mosquitoes were becoming quite fierce in their attacks. Amelia pushed two large incense sticks in the ground, which they read were supposed to help ward off the mosquitoes but not negatively affect their fertility. Some products that they researched said that it would keep mosquitoes away for up to fifteen feet but warned against being in the vicinity of that fifteen feet because it could cause infertility. They didn't need anything else going against them.

She positioned the sticks behind their canvas chairs hoping that the fire would have them covered in front and the incense sticks would cover their backs. Within five minutes, Jake had the fire roaring, and the smoke from the incense sticks filled the air enough that swarms of mosquitoes diminished to about two or three every few minutes, and the mosquitoes seemed completely mellowed so that they more or less bounced off of Amelia and Jake instead of being concerned with biting them. The rest of the night they enjoyed around the campfire while eating dinner and the some S'Mores before heading into bed.

The next morning after they finished breakfast, Amelia and Jake sat around the small campfire enjoying the quietness and serenity of their surroundings. From their campsite, they could see a few other sites around them, but Amelia couldn't help notice one site where a woman had come out of the tent and started making breakfast over the campfire that her husband had started a little while earlier. A few minutes later the husband unzipped the tent and out came two little children who were very well-behaved for their young age. Amelia estimated that the children were about three or four years of age, and they ran up to their mother and hugged her around the waist. As the mother still tended to the breakfast, she reached her arm down and around both of them. Then the two children scurried off with their father to the restrooms. By the time they returned, the mother had finished making breakfast and divided up the portions on four paper plates. The children's feet swung back and forth under the picnic table as they enjoyed their breakfast.

*Will that ever be us?* She thought as she watched the family smile and enjoy each other's company. She glanced over to Jake, who had been completely oblivious to the family scene that she had been studying, and he was relaxed in his canvas fold-out chair staring at the fire embers. *I really wish I could be that relaxed right now and enjoy this peaceful setting. It looks like he doesn't have a care in the world. I want to be carefree, but every time I turn around there is either a family or an announcement of pregnancy staring me in the face and making me realize how my body is completely incompetent.*

"What's on your mind?" Jake looked at her intently, "Looks like you're in deep thought." He grabbed her hand.

"Just thinking..." she nodded her head in the direction of the family, "you know..."

He looked at the family. He had noticed them earlier as well. "I know, but can we have a good time this weekend here without thinking about all that stuff, right?"

"I'll still have a good time, but there's no way I can turn it off, Jake. It's not that easy."

"I'm not asking you to turn it off but don't let it ruin your time away on vacation."

She was able to make herself half smile, "I'll try."

After finishing breakfast, they prepared for hiking as there was a trail connected to the campground that led up to a small mountain. As they packed their bags full of necessary survival essentials like knives, first aid kit, compass, matches, water sacs, snacks, and a light lunch, Amelia felt the emptiness of not having to worry about packing for a child. "Ready?" Jake interrupted her next thoughts. She nodded her head, finished tying her shoes, and secured her pack to her back. *Focus. Be here for Jake. Just breathe.*

They were into the hike for about ten minutes when Amelia blurted out, "You know, the Native Americans had it right." Jake looked at her puzzled because he obviously had no context to what she was thinking about. "When they hiked, they would bind their babies up like a swaddle and hike miles with them that way." Amelia smiled. "I think if we ever had kids, we should do that. Then they can't get into anything you don't want them to, and they are completely safe all bound up like that." *Oh no, I'm doing it again. Hopefully he won't be upset. I just wanted to state a fact I thought was interesting.*

Jake smiled at her. He did love her enthusiasm. Amelia being part Native American Indian thought it would be a great connection to her ancestors to learn how to do something like that. Would she ever have the chance to though? That was a question she may never know the answer to, which terrified her.

They ate their light lunch of some trail mix and a peanut butter sandwich when they reached the top. The sun shined on them as a light breeze cooled their sweaty bodies. There was a small sapling tree that gave them a little bit of shade, so they enjoyed its shelter. Amelia noticed a nest that had been built in the corner of one of the tree limbs. It was empty now, but she  wondered what type of baby bird hatched out and made its first flight from it this past spring. Then a chickadee with its little black cap landed on the same limb. It shuffled a few hops closer to the nest and looked to be peering into the nest and then took a few hops back to the edge of the limb. *I know how you feel little chickadee. I know how you feel...it's empty, poor little thing,* Amelia thought to herself.

Later when they were back at their campsite, Jake said, "Do you want to shower first?"

"How about you go first? That way when I'm showering you can get a fire started, and we can do dinner when I get back?"

"Sounds like a plan." He grabbed his towel from in the tent, walked over to her, and kissed her on the forehead as she sat in her fold out canvas chair. "I like your thinking." He gently pinched her cheek the way a grandmother would do to her grandchildren, and Amelia swatted at him playfully.

She wasn't sure what to do with herself while he was gone. She looked around the site from one side to the other - so empty... quiet and peaceful, yes, but empty... lonely. She needed to vent her feelings, so she decided to grab her journal from her bag. When she was seated back in her canvas chair, she wasn't sure where to start. She put her head back and could see to the tops of the trees, and she remembered the chickadee from earlier.

*I have been in a pretty pensive mood this whole trip about families and children and such. Today I saw this chickadee overlooking a nest, and I could only imagine the chickadee wondering if there was a baby bird in it that it could help, but I also felt the disappointment the chickadee felt when the nest was empty. It's the disappointment I feel all the time when I realize yet again that someone else participated in giving life, and I'm left on the sidelines to watch it all.*

*Actually it reminded me of a beautiful poem Maya Angelou wrote about a caged bird watching the world around it while being trapped inside its cage. In "I Know Why the Cage Bird Sings," I am that bird. I am trapped by this body that doesn't do what it's supposed to, and yet I have to watch every other bird - or woman - experience the world and life the way I should be able to. But alas, my wings are clipped, and all I can do is hop from one perch to another hoping to steal a glimpse of what it is I can't have.*

*I know that she was writing about slavery, but I do feel enslaved by my body. It binds me as the caged bird's feet are bound. All I can do is sing, but it's a fearful song because even though I hope for freedom that one day my Keeper will open the door to my cage and let me fly, I wonder if I'll know how. Will my wings actually work? Will I not only be able to fly - for anyone can do that - but will I be able to soar? Is it my fearful song that keeps me trapped? Does my Keeper know my insecurity and wait for my song to change?*

*So many questions, and yet no answers. So I wait... and I watch... from inside a cage as the world changes, and I remain the same. I see families grow from two, three, four, and on. I sing a happy tune for them by day and a melancholy song for myself by night - always feeling this dichotomy of emotions becomes exhausting... will one day my song vanish as well? Then I'll only be what looks like a bird in a cage for I will have no song, and no one recognizes a bird without their song.*

After dinner, Amelia and Jake enjoyed the rest of their night around the fire as the sun slowly set behind the trees and into the forest of pines. They made sure to light the incense sticks again to keep the mosquitoes away. Once dinner had settled in their bellies, they gathered a couple of sticks and grabbed the marshmallows, graham crackers, and chocolate. Within a few minutes, they were feasting on S'mores again until their stomachs hurt from eating too many.

"Why do we always do this to ourselves?" Amelia sat back in her chair holding her stomach thinking about how they could never contain themselves with sweets.

"I don't know," Jake sighed. "But it tastes good," Amelia could see his teeth reflecting the fire light as he smiled at her. She couldn't help but giggle.

She loved their time camping. It felt like such a pure intimate time for the two of them to reconnect with each other and with life the way God meant it to be. The next day they would be traveling back home and resume with their busy lives again. Just thinking about it was starting to stress her out. They were always rushing around everywhere doing everything to keep busy because they didn't have anything tying them down. It was nice in some senses because they could take advantage of more opportunities that most couples couldn't at their age because other couples had the responsibilities of children or houses, but sometimes having the freedom to experience what others couldn't seemed meaningless without having a family - without children to share it all with. Amelia decided she didn't want these negative thoughts to rob any more of her time with Jake. She reached over and grabbed his hand. He winked at her and she leaned over and kissed him. They smiled at each other and then snuggled together as they enjoyed the warmth from their campfire as the damp, cool air moved in for the night.

# DEAR LETTERS

"Hey, hun," Jake called to Amelia from what they called the great room. It was like a second living room with couches but without a TV. Other than their computer in that room, it acted like a large sitting room.

Amelia was working on cutting up the vegetables from their farm share that they had picked up earlier that morning. Since it was nearing fall, she decided to make up a stew with some pumpkin, butternut squash, curry, carrots, potatoes, and a touch of a few other seasonings. She was consumed in the process of making the stew and wondered what the end product would taste like. She always cooked this way – a little bit of this, a little bit of that, a taste here and there and then perfecto! The only problem was that Amelia would never write her concoctions down, so to repeat the same exact taste was quite impossible - though every time it did taste phenomenal in its own unique way.

She would like to work on cooking up her own concoctions when she wanted to take her mind off something else. Amelia was thinking about the blood test she had done that morning, as she was in the time of her cycle when ovulation would be happening soon. She hoped her estrogen levels would prove to be in the healthy range as they had been the on the last reading since her progesterone levels were still on the low side - even after trying the progesterone pills for the last few months, which were supposed to increase her progesterone level. If her estrogen level was good, that would also help her progesterone level to be higher - or at least she thought she remembered the doctor saying that. The progesterone level needed to be in range for her to even sustain a pregnancy, if she ever did conceive. She hated how her body was rejecting the progesterone treatment though because she didn't want her body to reject a baby.

The nurse knew her well by now since Amelia was there practically every month or sometimes twice a month that the nurse had photocopied her lab slip so Amelia wouldn't have to give it to her every time. When she went to have the blood work done, Jake would come with her since they only had the one car - making them both a little late to work since the lab at her doctor's office didn't open until eight in the morning, which is when they both had to be to work. Luckily, they worked at the same place, and it was only a few minutes from her doctor's office; however, if were a few people in

line before her, she would be more late. She had to
remember to wear long sleeves on those days as
well to hide the wad of gauze that would be folded
up and taped to her arm.

"Hey… Amelia," Jake's voice interrupted her
thoughts again.

"Yes, Jake, what is it?" she started drying her
hands on a towel and walked through the living
room to the great room. "What do you want?" she
looked at him semi-annoyed.

"I wanted to let you know that I sent an email
blast out to everyone to view our photos from our
camping trip on our photo website." He smiled with
pride like he had accomplished a great task. He
could tell by Amelia's expression that she was
none-too-pleased. "What?"

"You called me over here to tell me that? You
could have came into the kitchen and told me. I'm
working on a stew, and I was in the middle of…"

"Oh, I'll help you!" He jumped up from the
computer chair and wrapped his arms around her.
"Why didn't you tell me? I love to help you cook."
He smiled at her with the smile that always put
Amelia in a better mood; it was a half smirk, half
sly smile that expressed he was flirting and yet
overly happy – only a look Jacob Bayberry could
pull off.

"Ok, let's go." He wrapped his arms around her
playfully as they walked into the kitchen together.
They worked at prepping all the ingredients for the
stew for the next hour and then mixed everything
together. While they waited for the stew to heat to
boiling before they turned it to simmer for two

hours, Jake decided to check the email - as was his habit - to see if anyone had responded yet.

"Hey, Amelia, we've got some email responses from the photos, want to see?" *Again with the yelling*, she thought to herself as she smirked and slowly stirred the stew.

There were a few emails from family saying things like "Awesome photos," "Looks like fun," "Great views from the mountain top," and some friends saying, "Hope we can join you sometime!" Then they saw the email from Denise Ellingworth. Denise was Amelia's best friend from high school, and they had been in each other's weddings – Denise was her maid of honor, and Amelia was Denise's matron of honor. They hadn't been in touch for so long. Amelia had been meaning to call Denise, but when they talked on the phone, the conversation lasted hours, and Amelia found herself so busy lately that she didn't make time for a lengthy conversation like that.

The email read, "Hi Amelia! The photos you posted are lovely! You and Jake definitely have a knack for capturing the beauty of nature. I wanted to update you on some news that Greg and I have. I'm pregnant and am due next month on October 23rd. We're having a girl and are extremely excited. Greg will be graduating from law school this winter, and we're in the process of moving into a rental house. Hope to hear from you soon! Love, Denise."

Jake watched Amelia's reaction. Her face told it all; her face paled and her eyes glazed over like she had seen a ghost or something frightening. Amelia couldn't process everything quick enough that she had read. It was as if a ton of bricks had fallen on her chest, and she wasn't sure if she should cry from the pain first or scream out for the shear shock of all the news. The pressure built in her chest, and she needed to escape... she needed to breathe. Jake grabbed Amelia's hand and guided her to the couch, "Here, sit down." He sat next to her and put his arm around the small of her back.

As she sat on the couch, Amelia knew Jake was beside her but she was experiencing it as though she was in a dream watching someone else's life. Though Jake was holding her, she could only see herself sitting alone in a room trying to understand all that was before her. Every emotion came upon her suddenly and intensely – anger, jealousy, sadness, fear. *Is this what a panic attack feels like?* She wasn't really sure but she could only imagine.

Finally, after about five minutes, she was able to utter words, "Why wouldn't she have told me sooner?" She looked into Jake's eyes for the answers, and her eyes welled up with tears, "Why?... How could she forget...? Did she do this on purpose? Was she *trying* to hurt me? She knew... we had the same... we..." She broke down into her full on balling. She couldn't breathe in because her chest hurt too much from the weight of all that she was baring, but she couldn't breathe out either because her throat was so tight from her trying to hold back all the emotions she was feeling, that it threatened to close.

Jake held her to himself tightly desperately trying to calm the storm raging within her.

"Amelia," he whispered, "she doesn't know." He ran his fingers through her hair and rubbed her back. "She doesn't know what we're going through right now. I don't think she did it on purpose."

Amelia's anger welled up inside and burst forth, "I don't care!" She pushed herself away from him and stood up. "I don't care that she doesn't know what I'm going through!" Tears poured down her face. "The fact that she couldn't tell me that she was pregnant until a month before she was due – that's *not* acceptable! Not to mention – she's due on my *birthday*! *MY* birthday!" She stomped her foot. "How could she not tell me?" She became weepy again, "I know that we haven't talked in a while, but if I was pregnant, she'd be one of the first people I would tell." She sat down again. She needed to be held. "I missed it all. Even though it would have been hard, I still would have liked to go to the baby shower, and be part of her experience." She placed her head on his chest, "That's all I have - other people's experiences."

They talked for the next few hours on how to respond to the email. Amelia needed to keep things simple in her response; otherwise, she would type forever. She typed, "Congratulations! Glad to hear of all the good things happening for you – the baby, house rental, and Greg's graduation. Things here are the same as usual. Love, Amelia."

Days passed, and Amelia didn't receive a response from Denise. She was hoping to receive an invitation to the baby shower or maybe an email saying they should plan a time to chat on the phone soon, but the silence ate at Amelia even more. A

few nights later, Amelia found herself still awake
after Jake had dozed off because she couldn't stop
the thoughts from swirling around her head, and she
needed to do something to stop the insanity that was
threatening to consume her. She slipped out of bed
and headed towards the great room. Her mind
couldn't release the hurt from Denise's email. She
decided that writing a letter would be best to free
her mind and to help her sleep, though she would
probably never actually send it.

*Dear Denise,*

*I apologize for responding to your email with a
short response and without much detail. I found
myself in shock from all the news that was jam-
packed in your five sentence update on your life.*

*I am really happy for you, please know this.
Greg has been working so hard at law school for so
long – it's a great accomplishment, and I'm sure
you're very proud of him and glad that he'll be the
one making the money now. It's also great that you
get to rent a house instead of an apartment, and
that will be really important especially with the
little one on the way. And again, congratulations on
being pregnant, she'll soon be here!*

*However, I do have to say that you're email
brought me to feel so many things, and if we're still
the good friends that I remembered we were, then I
need to express this to you.*

*First, I am really angry with you. Why didn't
you tell me about your pregnancy before now? You
are due in one month! You must have already had a
baby shower or are very close to having one. I*

*would have loved to be a part of that. I would have been there, Denise, you know that. Did it happen to cross your mind at all that your daughter is due on my birthday? It hurt me that you didn't even recognize that – like we've become strangers in some sense, but still close enough to share intimate news like pregnancies and graduations – it doesn't make sense to me.*

*Second, I am really jealous of you. I always have been. Everything has always seemed to come easy for you. Even when things were hard, they still always seemed to work out. You wanted to be a teacher, and you went to college for that, and you became a teacher. You did what you set out to do. When you married and thought of having children someday, you wanted to be able to stay home with them. Now that Greg is graduating, he'll be starting his career which will supply enough income so that you can be the stay at home mom you want to be. You'll soon be in a house, and I'm sure you'll be buying one shortly after that. But I'm most jealous that you can get pregnant, and I can't. We've had the same problems, Denise, but somehow you've been showered again, and I'm left in the dust. I wish I could talk with you and find out how after all the cysts you had on your ovaries, you got pregnant, and that even though I only had one cyst, that I'm left barren. You have no idea how empty that makes a woman feel – especially when her best friend tells her that she's pregnant and failed to say anything until the baby is practically born.*

*Last, I am really sad because after the email you sent, I realized that we're not as close as I had once thought we were. I thought we were the kind of friends that even if we didn't talk all the time, we would still call each other when major life events happened. Your delayed response in telling me – if you were planning on telling me at all had we not sent out an email about the photos – showed me that I wasn't important enough for you to remember to share the news with me when you first found out. You must have found out in January that you were pregnant, which means you would have recently received the Christmas card we send to you every year, and then in July, you would have received the anniversary card for you and Greg that I send every year. I would have crossed your mind at some point within the last nine months, and to know that you still didn't bother to tell me says to me that you purposely ignored me. You intentionally didn't tell me. Maybe the only reason you're telling me now is because you figured it'd be better than waiting until I bump into you one day with a three-year-old daughter.*

*If we're really not the friends that we used to be, then I wish you hadn't told me. I wish you had kept it to yourself because now I'm left wondering, and every year on my birthday, I'll know exactly how old your daughter is while I'm still left without a child. Instead of it being something happy (if I had been part of everything), it will be something that will torment me – best birthday present ever.*

*Thank you.*
*Amelia*

# PROMISES

"Oh, and Genevieve was telling me that her teacher expects the class to have read half of Shakespeare's *A Midsummer Night's Dream* by the end of the week! Can you believe that? She's only in eighth grade."

Another woman piped up and spoke about how her son's math homework was so incredibly hard to understand even though he was only in the fourth grade, "It was like trying to read Algebra."

Amelia continued to listen as all the women chattered about their children's homework while thinking that the reason for their meeting was a women's Bible study - but there was no studying going on. The cackling hens made Amelia most inferior in the midst of her own sex. What was worse is when one of them would turn to her and say, "You'll understand someday when you have children," or "Enjoy the time you have now because once you have children, you'll never have time to yourself ever again."

Amelia hated when people would make having children sound so horrible as if she should be lucky that she didn't have children right now. But she would give up her infertility and freedom in a heartbeat to be able to share in the creation of a child with her husband. It was something so precious, but because it came so easily to these women, they couldn't cherish it the way her and Jake would. *Guess the grass is always greener,* she thought as she continued to listen to the comments being passed around the room.

Amelia wasn't sure she *would* understand what these parents were talking about though because they seemed to be overly concerned with their children's homework, so much so that they practically did the homework *for* the children. How were the children ever to learn? She knew one thing for sure - that when she had children she would never do their homework for them. Yes - she would help them if they had a question, but she would encourage them to find the answers themselves as well.

She couldn't wait for the night to end. Two hours had already passed for the study, and they hadn't discussed one passage of scripture. As the time ticked on, Amelia sat back in her chair and clenched her teeth holding back frustration and tears. If anything was convincing Amelia to join the Catholic Church, it was this moment right now because sitting around a table discussing everything about children instead of discussing the Scripture was more than beginning to wear on her. She enjoyed hearing others stories and hearing what was going on in everyone's life, but when it didn't leave time to actually have time to worship God, then it really upset her. She didn't know how to explain what she felt, but it made her blood boil.

As the women continued to chatter about the hardships of having children, Amelia thought to herself, *Doesn't it say somewhere in the Bible that God won't give us more than we can handle?* She carefully studied each woman at the table. *Well, God, I don't know how much more I can handle. You must think I'm pretty strong.*

Earlier that day, she was in the bathroom at work, and two women came in discussing about how one of their sisters was having a baby. The baby was going to be a girl, and they chatted about how fun it was to have a girl. The friend admitted how she couldn't stop buying things for the baby because there was so much out there to buy that was adorable. Amelia rolled her eyes as she remained hidden behind her stall door. What was the coincidence of her being in the bathroom at the same time? It was torture, that's all she saw it as; a constant reminder wherever she went that everyone else could have children.

Of course, she wasn't the only one dealing with this torture. She knew Jake carried the burden as well, though he didn't speak of it much. He mentioned to her later that night when she was recounting what happened at the Bible study that on Saturday at the men's group he experienced the same circumstance and feelings. All the men sat around the table and discussed everything about their kids while Jake - the only man without children in the group - observed the conversation silently. "You can't let it tear you apart though, Amelia. People are going to talk about their kids just as much as you and I would if we had children."

"Oh, I know that, Jake. And I'm not saying they *shouldn't* talk about their children. I'm not upset about that. I'm upset because I feel like a freak of nature or something. I'm sitting there wondering if I'm ever going to know what they're talking about or ever understand what they mean. But in the meantime, I'm the odd person out. I'm *so* ready to be part of that world. I'm tired of sitting on the sidelines. How can you be positive about this all the time and be able to see it from different angles? I have such a hard time separating it all."

"After the group, I went for a walk. I cry out to God too, Amelia. It's hard for me as well, but life goes on, and the people around us are going to have children and want to talk about it. I figure that I can either sit around and let it bother me every moment of the day or I can go forward with my day and not let it bother me." He paused for a few moments. "You know - we can always stop this process and go through adoption." He didn't say it matter-of-factly but with the utmost care and sensitivity as he usually did, but even then Amelia didn't want to hear any quick fix solutions that he liked to interject. There wasn't anything that would make any of it easier, except time - but time was the very thing making Amelia so anxious. Every day that passed brought her closer to menopause. Even though it was over a decade away, she feared she would blink one day and suddenly those years will have passed, and she would be standing in the wake of her worst nightmare with a bucket of tears.

"I'm not looking to rush into anything that we're not ready for yet. At least *I'm* not ready for adoption yet. I still have to process the fact that I may never carry our own child. I'll never have a baby to breastfeed or see little resemblances of you and me in. It's not that easy for me to let all of that die yet because that's what I would have to do in order to move on, and I'm not ready for the funeral yet. I wish it was easy for us, and I don't understand why it can't be."

"I know. I wish it was easy as well, but unfortunately it's not. Remember our wedding day though?" He smiled at her hoping to change the mood.

"Of course," she smirked at him.

"Remember the theme of our day?"

She nodded. "Promise," she whispered.

"I promise you, Amelia, as I did then to love you and stand by you no matter what we go through. Right now we're dealing with infertility, and it totally sucks, but I will love and cherish you all the same - whether we ever have children or not. I promise." They embraced each other tightly as a few tears trickled down Amelia's face. Jake always knew the right things to say that would tickle her emotions.

Before Amelia went to bed that night, she glanced over at her journal. She was really too tired to write, but her thoughts were so heavy after all the happenings of the night. She sighed and reluctantly grabbed her journal and pen from her night stand.

*Sometimes it feels like my thoughts about all of this baby stuff will never end. I constantly think about it to no avail; there's never a break. Sometimes I want a vacation from my thoughts - from myself - but I don't think that's ever a possibility. My thoughts will always be with me. The only way I can empty them from my head is if I take some serious time in prayer... alone... away from everyone and everything, so I can be alone with Christ and cast my cares upon Him. I'll be able to weep and be comforted in an intimate setting with no one watching or waiting for me to do the next thing.*

*I envy the Carthusian monks that Jake and I saw when we went to Manchester, Vermont. Obviously, we didn't actually get to see the monks because their vows keep them in silence and away from the outside world, but we were able to drive up the mountain near their monastery and see their residence from an overlook. How wonderful would it be to live cutoff from the cares of this world? I know it must be lonely for them at times, but to have so much time given to spend moments with our Savior must be awesome.*

*Even though they may feel cut off or trapped there at times, I already know what that feels like. I'm trapped and cutoff from a world that I desperately want to be a part of, but this burden of infertility cuts me off from a large part of the world - though I don't willingly choose to be cutoff;*

*whereas, the monks willingly choose their vows, and it enriches their lives. My seclusion is forced upon me every day by a body that doesn't work properly, and I'm bound to it - trapped inside with no escape crying out for someone to hear me. My only hope is to have precious time with Jesus. I need to make that more of a priority, and I really do feel that I need a weekend away in seclusion in order to start this process to help myself.*

The next week after church, one of the women from the Bible study group came up to Amelia and said, "I've been praying for you and Jake," as she put her hand on Amelia's forearm. Amelia thanked her - she knew that the woman was referencing their infertility and was really thankful for the woman's prayers, but Amelia didn't like how such an intimate part of her life was on display for others to constantly comment on. She felt like a fish in a bowl being at the mercy of those who taped and pointed. The conversation quickly turned into where the woman asked Amelia a bunch of questions of whether she had tried this or that as remedies - usually it was some kind of natural elixir, acupuncture, or some random remedy Amelia had never heard of before - because this woman had a friend who had tried these things and that woman was able to conceive a child. Amelia tried her hardest not to bark at this woman who had clearly overstepped the bounds of polite conversation, so Amelia politely excused herself from the conversation with some kind of random excuse like having to use the bathroom. "That could be a sign!" The woman winked at her.

"Yeah, maybe..." Amelia nodded as she quickly headed toward the bathroom and hoped that woman wouldn't follow her. She rushed to the first stall and locked herself in it. She exhaled as she threw her back against the side of the stall and her head toward the ceiling. Tears streamed down the side of her face and her eyes winced as she stared at the florescent lights above her. How she hated the insensitivity of people sometimes - but she always felt sorry as well because it wasn't their fault she was infertile, they were only trying to help - but in all honesty, she didn't want their help. She didn't want their sympathy. She just wanted someone who would cry with her and feel *her* pain for just a moment; for someone to understand that what she was going through was difficult and how completely horrible it was to be helpless to change anything that was happening. She wanted someone to help carry her through this pain and not tell her that if she tried another remedy, she could solve it and all her worries would disappear. The fact of it all was that it wasn't that easy - at least not for her.

She grabbed some toilet paper to blow her nose and wipe her tears. She had this sudden realization that she wasn't even understood in her own church. There were several women she knew that used the IVF method in her church, and who now had children while she and Jake remain barren. Though no one would condemn her and Jake for choosing not to use IVF, she also sensed they didn't fully understand why her and Jake chose *not* to use it as though she and Jake were willingly putting themselves through the torture of infertility - when really it was a matter of valuing the sanctity of life.

"Do you think our major beliefs aren't really matching up with the church background we're in?" Amelia asked Jake later that night. "It's not that our church is for IVF, but they're also not against it either, and I'm not sure I can reconcile that in my mind." Jake nodded in agreement. "How can we fully be part of a community that doesn't have the same beliefs we do on major issues like this - especially one so dear to our hearts?"

"We've been going to the Catholic fertility center, and I'm feeling a slight nudge in that direction as well," Jake's response confirmed Amelia's inclinations. "I think it might be time to start attending a Catholic Church more regularly and see what pans out from there." They had really enjoyed their visit to John's church and decided that it was a good place to start.

The next few weeks only confirmed their inklings. When they were at the next charting appointment, Nanette mentioned how they would make 'great Catholics!' before they even had a chance to mention that they were already thinking about checking out the Catholic Church. Amelia enjoyed everything she learned about the Church and decided to wear a chapel veil. Amelia loved the idea of a chapel veil since she learned what it signified; the veil is a visible sign of humility before God and a public proclamation of submission to God's Will, and it's worn inside any Catholic Church where the Blessed Sacrament is reserved inside the tabernacle. They both listened to the Eternal Word Television Network (EWTN) on the internet through earphones when at work and realized how much their beliefs matched up with the Catholic Church. One of their favorite priests that had started an Anglican church split from their previous Episcopal church recently converted to Catholicism as well, so they made plans to meet with him to discuss what caused him to make the switch.

Amelia's favorite Bible verse kept popping up as well anytime she would wonder whether or not they should swim the Tiber (as many called it when converting to Catholicism) - Jeremiah 29:11, "For I know the plans I have for you," declares the Lord, "plans to prosper you and not to harm you, plans to give you a hope and a future." Anytime she doubted any change in her life, she would be reminded of this verse, so it comforted her to know that joining the Catholic Church may be the direction God was bringing them. She wasn't entirely sure why, but she was willing to check it out and see where it would lead.

# PROPHECIES & PITFALLS

Jake was at work putting in some overtime for a project with an impending deadline, so Amelia had the night to herself. She settled into the couch in their great room and listened to the prophecy they received at their friends' church in Connecticut when they last visited. They had gone to visit for a weekend in the beginning of the year. The husband was an assistant priest at the Episcopal church, so their friends weren't as available to take weekends away to visit Amelia and Jake, so Amelia and Jake went to them instead. But they enjoyed visiting and having the time away from their apartment. Their friends lived in the rectory of the church, and Amelia and Jake really enjoyed living in a house - even if it was only for a weekend.

Amelia had recorded the prophecy on her phone because the copy they received from the church was on cassette tape. Fortunately Amelia and Jake still had a cassette tape player, but Amelia felt better about having a digital copy as well.

They had visited their friends two years in a row around the same time of the year, and they received prophecies each time. There were some similarities and some differences. Amelia decided that she wanted to listen to the most recent prophecy, so she opened the app on her smartphone that contained the prophecy and closed her eyes as she listened:

*"I feel God's pleasure in you and His delight over you. I'm feeling like - I don't have the words exactly - but He's proud of you. It's as if there has been something against you - maybe words against you - the enemy has tried to take you down or discourage you or hurt you, and you've been standing strong, and this will be gone. It was a season of the enemy attacking you in this way, and the Lord is singing over you. Well done, good and faithful servant.*

*The Lord is so pleased with your faithfulness. He has you on a road of His choosing. He has a destiny for you. He just wants you to put one foot in front of the other and follow Him. It's a walk, not a sprint, it's a marathon - to keep going forward. He wants to encourage you that He's with you every step of the way. He will fulfill all His good plans. Grace - He wants to pour His grace upon you. You just need to run around with your aprons open ready to catch all of it that He has for you. I think of that song "Pennies from Heaven" but for you it's more than pennies. Something really worthwhile is being poured out for you to receive.*

*The trees of the fields will clap their hands and this sense of joy in you and around you and bringing life. God is going to bring life through you everywhere you go, and He's doing it in you too. He's bringing creation to fulfillment the joy that creation has been groaning waiting in expectation, and He's using you to bring that life.*

*Last year when you came, someone had a word for you about having a baby. I didn't say anything, but before you came in the room, the Lord told me that you would have a baby. He brought it to mind, so seeing you here this morning, it's fresh in my mind. I don't know His timing, but you will."*

Tears slowly streamed down her face as she thought about how nine months had already passed since the prophecy was given to them, and it was already October - yet still no baby. Funny that nine months later she was listening to this prophecy again. She couldn't escape the irony of anything that had to do with babies any time she encountered it throughout her day. Something always triggered her thoughts to baby things.

As she sat there in the silence, Chloe came over and jumped up on the couch next to her. Chloe blinked slowly a few times while looking at Amelia almost as if she was showing Amelia that she was being sympathetic - or at least Amelia liked to think of it that way. "Animals know when something is wrong, right?" She asked Chloe as she reached her hand out to caress the soft, fluffy black and white bundle of fur that started to purr upon her touch. Amelia smiled. She hoped that some day her soft touch would soothe a crying baby.

Thinking about the prophecy, she remembered that at the end the woman had mentioned the prophecy from the previous year. The previous year had been the first time in the prophecy room at their friends' church. The prophecy from that time was very heavy laden with baby predictions as well.

She also had that recorded on her phone. Chloe nestled into Amelia's leg, and they listened to the first year's prophecy together:

*"It's becoming very apparent in our church that couples have a greater impact for the Lord, in a sense - couples have a greater opportunity to be a prism of God's grace, and I see in you a great beauty... and peace and gentleness flowing from you.*

*The Father says to you both that He rejoices over your relationship. He rejoices over your deep love and respect for one another, and He is rejoicing over your relationship with Him and His Son, Jesus. He says that "No eye has seen nor ear heard nor heart conceived of the great and wonderful things that He has prepared for those that love Him," and He has great and wonderful things prepared for your life - things for you to do, that He has prepared for you to do so that you can walk and glorify His Son. He has great power toward you and a deep abiding love for you as well.*

*I sense the word overwhelming grace - not overwhelming in a negative fashion - almost like a great wave that is of light that is about you when you need it, and it's joyful.*

*I was just asking the Lord what is it that He holds for you - that's special for the two of you?*

*And the word I got was love, and then He showed
me that you two are going to be ministering to kids -
a lot of kids - and you're going to show them not
only love but the love of the Father. It's powerful
because of what I'm seeing is like a bunch of little
guys following you two around like you're the Pied
Piper or something. You're singing Bible songs and
telling stories - simple little stories from the Bible -
and they're hearing because however it is you're
presenting it to them, they get it - they trust it, they
believe, they trust you two, and they believe what
you're saying to them. That's what I'm seeing.*

*I can sense the love you have for each other.
People see that, and it shows them the Father's love
in some way.*

*I just keep getting over and over again - "Be
fruitful and multiply," "Be fruitful and multiply" -
over and over - "Be fruitful and multiply" - that
your relationship bring forth fruit in Jesus' name.*

*I was just pondering all the little kids around
you. I don't even know if you're in ministry, but this
sounded to me like a Christian daycare or
something like that - and that you put the word
Christian out there on the sign. I don't know that's
just what I'm seeing. Thank you, Lord."*

The phrase "Be fruitful and multiply" pounded
through Amelia's head over and over again. By this
point, Chloe had moved to the end of the couch and
had fallen asleep curled up in the corner with her
tail covering her nose. *What if I can't be fruitful -
ever?* Amelia asked herself. *Would I be failing
God? I don't think I could live with that. I can fail
myself and let down my expectations and the*

176

*expectations of my friends and family who want us to have children, but I cannot live with disappointing God.* Shame and fear began to fill her heart with a dread that felt so immensely heavy and unbearable. *Also, what if being fruitful meant some kind of work I am to do as opposed to having children?*

Amelia's thoughts were interrupted when there was a knock at the door. Chloe perked up out of her sleep and stared at the door from her position on the couch. "Who could that be?" Amelia and Chloe looked at each other. Chloe was a special kind of cat; she was almost human. Amelia's heart ached when she thought of Chloe passing away someday. There were many times that Chloe filled the void in Amelia's heart for children.

The knock tapped on the door again. Amelia wasn't even sure how the person managed to get into the building since they lived in a complex, and you either needed a key to enter or be buzzed in by someone's intercom. Without Jake home, she didn't feel comfortable answering the door. Most of the time it ended up being a cable company's salesperson, but she was currently happy with their cable provider and didn't feel much like shooing someone away. Then a text popped up on her phone, "Are you home? I thought I saw lights on." It was from John.

She quickly hurried to the door. "Hey, how'd you get in?"

"Oh, someone was leaving with their dog when I was coming up to the door. They held it for me." John stepped into her apartment and gave her a big hug. "How are you doing? Do you have a few minutes?"

"Sure, come on in." She purposely ignored answering his first question. She was tired of lying to people about how she was doing and putting on a happy face. Though she could be honest with John, she didn't feel much like talking about it.

"What's going on with you?" She motioned to her teapot and he nodded. Amelia poured water in the pot and put it on the stove to start warming.

"I was on my way back from the Beau de Fontaine's and figured I'd stop in to see how things were going. Have you talked to Claire much at all lately?"

"Nope. I can't say I have." The water whistled on the stove for attention. "Have you?"

"Well, not intentionally. I was on my way out of Zumi's the other day because I had to be in Newburyport pretty early and needed to get a coffee," Zumi's was Ipswich's local coffee shop that served some of the strongest coffee around - like a small town Starbucks but less commercialized, "and I literally bumped into her and Seth. Seth had a couple of paint cans in his hands - said their special ordered paint color for the nursery had come in and Claire couldn't wait to see what it looked it." Claire was always impatient. Amelia was surprised she was ok with waiting nine months for the baby to arrive.

"That's weird that Seth wasn't at work on a week day." Amelia poured the steaming water into a teacup as John sifted through their assorted teas.

"Maybe he took a day off?" John stirred some sugar into his tea.

Married couples having children would take days off work to prepare for the coming child. Claire already didn't work because Seth's job provided them with enough money that she could stay at home, and because Claire never went to college, she didn't have any student loan debt either that would cause any financial burden.

"Anyway," John interjected Amelia's rambling thoughts, "on my way out of Zumi's, I noticed a flyer for a Masquerade Ball up at the country club. The theme this year is black and white. I was thinking about going. You and Jake should go too!"

"I don't think I could bring myself to hide behind any more masks." Amelia heart stopped for a second. She couldn't believe she actually admitted that out loud, but she tried to play it off coolly, "Thanks for the thought though. Why are you interested in going?"

They moved into the living and sat on either end of the couch facing each other. Chloe had already moved to the back of the sofa chair - her favorite spot. "Remember how I told you about that girl I bumped into at my job back in July and thought I saw at church recently?" Amelia nodded. "I can't stop hoping I run into her. She's like Cinderella." He smiled with a fantastical twinkle in his eye. "That day at church, she was just like Cinderella with her disappearing act." Amelia chuckled. It was nice to laugh. She had forgotten how long it had been since she sincerely laughed.

She missed it. "Seriously, I checked the church stairs for a glass slipper."

Amelia couldn't contain her smile and merriment, "Sorry," she put her teacup down before she spilled it on herself. "What does all of this have to do with the ball?"

"Well, she's been at my job and my church, so I'm thinking she must live somewhere in the area. Plus, don't princesses go to balls? They can't resist, right?" He winked and smiled, and for a minute she could tell how really serious her brother was about this woman, and his smile did almost have a Prince Charming smirk to it.

"If you do find her, John, she's going to be one lucky girl, and I'm not just saying that because I'm your sister." She grabbed his hand and squeezed it gently. "You're a true romantic, and I hope you find your princess. There's only one problem though. If she does actually show up, how will you know who she is? Everyone will have masks on!"

"Amelia, I could pick her out in a crowd - mask or no mask. She's *that* beautiful." He sighed. "It's hard to explain, but when she's around, it's as if I can tell - I can sense her presence."

"Interesting - that's either creepy or cute," Amelia winked at him, "but in your case, I think it's cute."

"Where's Jake? Are you sure you two don't want to join me? I'd love for you to meet her!"

"He had a project he needed to finish at work." Amelia checked her phone quickly to see if she received any texts from Jake saying he was done yet. Since they only had one car, she would need to pick him up. "Thanks though, it was kind of you to offer us to join you at the ball, but I want you to have a special night with Cinderella. Maybe she'll even be in a white dress with a tiara!" Amelia joked with him. John knew she was teasing as well. They could always joke with each other without the other one being offended. Amelia loved that about their relationship. She loved that she could be real with him.

"Wouldn't it be good for you and Jake to have a night out though?" She knew what he was trying to get at and that he was trying to be sensitive about bringing up the baby topic.

"John, I can't. I suffer in silence every day of my life with being infertile. Jake and I do get out and do things together, but lately, it's been feeling empty... like we're missing someone, and we are. The void of a child hurts more than you can know or than I can ever explain. I know right now you yearn and long for love in your life, and all of that is exciting, but when you yearn and long with no fulfillment, it begins to tear you down instead of give you hope. Wearing a mask in a room full of strangers would make me feel the secret I hide inside more intensely. I know it sounds like a silly answer, but you just have to trust me on this."

"I do, Amelia. I wish I could do more to help though. If there ever is anything I can do, please let me know."

"Thank you, John. You're sweet, but this battle is Jake's and mine to fight. I wish there was something you *could* do, but I feel like I've fallen in a pit and though I've been given hope many times of being found and rescued, my sustenance is running low, and I've realized the only One who can save me," she pointed to the ceiling, and John knew she meant God, "has remained silent - despite my cries." She blinked back some tears that threatened to gather and form a flood from her eyes. "I want you to go and find your princess, and I want to meet her once you do."

# MASQUERADE BALLS

Sarah still couldn't remember the reason why she had decided to come to the Masquerade Ball. She would rather be home sitting on the couch under a cozy blanket sipping tea while watching some feel good girly drama movie with her electric fireplace on to capture the ambience of a being in a cottage. Then she thought how lonely that is after awhile, when she wished she could be curled up in the arms of a man she loved. That's why she forced herself to the masquerade ball – not so much to meet someone – but to make herself more social, though meeting someone would be an unexpected bonus.

She wished she at least knew someone though. Sarah was beginning to feel more and more insecure about being alone with each step she made into the mansion. The ball was held at the Turner Hill Mansion every year, and she had never been up there before since it was primarily estates and a golf club, but the main house made her feel like she was entering a fairytale ball.

She wished she had brought a friend, but she didn't have any. That was a whole other part of Sarah's life that she wished she could erase. College had not been the easiest part of life for her. Her friends had deserted her over false accusations, and they had convinced their whole circle of friends and their friends' friends that Sarah was to never be forgiven. Sarah had written letter after letter to her friends, but there was never a response. They would move if she sat down at the same lunch table, switch groups if the teachers assigned them together, and worst of all, they would act as though she didn't even exist when they passed her in the hallways.

One of Sarah's worst memories was when her best friend moved out of their dorm room and wouldn't speak to her while doing so - even the friend that helped her move wouldn't speak to Sarah. Sarah had felt like a convict, as though she committed some kind of murder and was to be punished in some kind of solitary confinement. The half empty room felt like a prison cell she had been sentenced to while waiting for death row. The lights had that institutional psych ward glow to them, and she remembered crying for hours with no one to hold her. She was alone - completely alone in the midst of a campus full of people, just like she was now at the ball. Nothing had changed. Would it ever?

She looked around into all the masked faces. Some people smiled; others walked by with unhappy scowls on their faces – not intentional scowls, but the scowls that get stuck on peoples' faces when they don't actually enjoy life. Sarah wondered if that's what her face looked like. She forced a little smile on her face. She didn't want it to look fake but didn't want it to be like a smirk either. She caught herself in a mirror at the end of the hallway and saw that she had managed a polite smile. *Ok, I can do this. Stay confident and have fun. Be the heroine in your own story for once!* She thought to herself.

As she adjusted her hair and the feathers on her mask, she heard a familiar laugh. It rang in her ears with a warm sound, yet at the same time sent irritating pulses down her spine. She looked around to find the owner of the laugh. She didn't have to look for long when she noticed him – it was Scott. Scott Carmichael, her ex-fiance. She felt all the blood rush from her face and her countenance fell - so much for her polite smile and being the heroine.

She gathered all her strength to turn around when she heard, "Sarah?" Her heart caught in her throat, *No!* "Sarah, is that you?" She felt a hand on her shoulder, and she quickly turned around making the hand slide off her skin.

"Scott!" Every part of her wished she hadn't come. "How did you know it was me?"

"I could pick you out of a crowd anywhere. What are you doing here?" He started looking around her like he wasn't really paying attention to their conversation at all. He would occasionally nod at someone or wink.

She felt so embarrassed, so humiliated. "Just came to enjoy the festivity." She rolled her eyes around trying to think of something to say. She knew now that coming was definitely a bad decision. She never wanted to leave the house again. "Uh, what brings you here?"

"Alise is a Rotarian, and she helped coordinate all of this. My company makes quite the donation every year, and as CEO," his posture straightened, "I see it as a nice gesture on my part to make an appearance." He smiled his teethy white smile as though he was posing for some presidential campaign or dental commercial. Then he waved, "Ah, here's my wife now." A beautiful woman with straight long black hair down to her hips walked over. The reflection of light off her shiny hair made Sarah squint. The woman's eyelashes had to be fake because they were entirely too long and full. She wore a tight black and white glittery gown, which kind of made her look like Cruella de Vil and made Sarah want to laugh. "Alise, this is Sarah."

"Ah, yes," she had a bit of a British accent, "well, I hope you like it." She waved her arms around the room like she was presenting the surroundings to Sarah as a prize offered on a game show or something. "We have wonderful raffles prizes – make sure you buy lots of tickets. You're probably wondering where my mask is." She giggled, "I have it over on our table. I use one on a stick! I can't stand it being on my face, plus it clogs the pores and wreaks havoc on my complexion, but I'm sure you don't worry about those things." Sarah wasn't really sure what Alise was trying to imply.

"And we can't have that. Isn't this face too beautiful to see any blemish on it?" Even though Scott seemed to be asking Sarah the question, he was looking at his wife, and she was gazing at him. Was Sarah actually supposed to answer the pathetically rehearsed line? Then they kissed, almost too romantically for such an event.

Then Scott quickly turned to Sarah, "Oh, I'm sorry. I can't keep myself away from this one." He pointed to Alise as he chuckled. Sarah felt ill and desperately needed to escape this awkward encounter. "So, where's your date? Are you here with someone?" He began looking around, and Sarah felt infinitely small and humiliated.

"I, um…" Alise stared at her, and Sarah felt herself shrinking even more in the presence of Cleopatra, "well, you see,…"

"Hey, I've been looking all around for you." A man came up and put his arm around Sarah's back. His voice was of a medium deep tone, and he felt safe, but she wasn't really sure why.

"You have?" Sarah looked at him puzzled. She couldn't see his full features because of his mask, but his eyes grabbed her heart with the most gentle kindness.

"Who are you?" Scott seemed quite taken off guard almost as if he expected Sarah to be there by herself and was waiting to embarrass her.

"I'm John. Did she forget to tell you about me?" He smiled and gently nudged his shoulder into Sarah as a playful gesture, and Sarah couldn't help but smile when she saw his sweet smile.

Sarah decided to join in, "No. I wouldn't forget to tell them about you. Actually, Scott here was just asking who I came with."

"I'm Alise," Alise said with a seductive tone as she reached out her hand to John like a viper slithering towards its prey. Scott stood in silence. His whole being had changed from his wealthy self-righteous state to a cowardly jealous figure.

"Nice to meet you," John said but didn't accept the offer of her hand and instead turned his eyes to Sarah. "Shall we?" He gestured to Sarah that they go to the dance floor. She nodded her head but didn't take her eyes off his. She would go anywhere with him, especially anywhere away from Scott.

The music played in the background with a soft classical jazz tone. The lights were dim. They stared deep into each other's eyes. Even though they didn't speak any words during the whole dance, it felt as though they communicated in the deepest way anyone could. Sarah wanted the fairytale to last forever. The moment sparkled, and she felt like Cinderella when the prince found the shoe fit her – she grew from rags to riches in a matter of moments.

After the song finished, they made their way into another room that was quieter where they could talk. John grabbed them some water from the bar, and they stood by one of tall tables that were scattered about the room. Sarah's heart started pounding as she was about to talk to her Prince Charming. She wasn't sure what to say. She'd never been in a fairytale before.

"Well, now you know my name, what's yours?" He started.

"Oh, yea, sorry," she smiled and tucked a stray piece of hair behind her ear, "it's Sarah." She wanted all of this to be real, but she was so scared to trust again especially since the man that broke her heart was in the other room.

"I like that name." He took a sip of water.

"Thank you for what did." She pointed to the other room they had been in. "It really means the world to me. How did you know though?... I mean..."

"It was quite obvious that he was trying to make you jealous - classic guy maneuvers of bringing in the sexy lady and being overly open with the public displays of affection. Plus if you had a date, he wouldn't have left your side."

Sarah blushed, "What do you mean?"

"Well, I know, if I was your date, I wouldn't leave your side." He winked.

Sarah wasn't really sure how to respond. She sipped her water. "What brought you to this event? I'm sure if you had a date, you wouldn't be your wasting your time with me."

"Actually believe it or not, I'm trying to be social, and now I have you to be social with," he smiled. "My parents keeps telling me I don't get out enough – you know, because I'm not married with children yet, but I just haven't found the right girl yet. I'm not the kind of guy that's going to date just because. I'm intentional, and unfortunately, that can be a lonely road, especially as you hit your mid-twenties. The dating scene becomes basically non-existent unless you like the bar atmosphere, but that's not my scene at all."

"Something about you seems so familiar to me, but I can't figure it out." She looked into his eyes pondering in her mind where she knew him from.

"Actually, it's funny you say that." He chuckled and then placed his hat on the table. He reached behind his head and untied his mask. Sarah couldn't wait to see his whole face. She watched intently as the mask peeled away from his face.

"Wait, I think I've seen you at church before." She pointed at him. "The first time I visited, I remember seeing you from across the room. I thought you were Scott."

"Oh, I really hope I don't remind you of him. He seems like a real jerk."

"No, I meant when I saw you looking at me from across the church, I thought for a second you looked like him, but when I looked back I realized you didn't."

He grabbed her hand, "Well, hopefully I'll prove to be much better company than he, but we have more history than that."

"We do?" She looked puzzled and began to feel a little worried. Had he been stalking her or something?

"I believe the first time I saw you was when I was trimming the flower bushes at the Beau de Fontaine's house." She thought back to that day as she listened to him, "You were around the pool watching the girls intently. You did look over at me once, but I'm not entirely sure you really saw me."

"No, I remember now, and we bumped into each other in the kitchen as well!" She smiled as she couldn't believe that somehow without her even trying their paths had crossed again.

"Yes!" He seemed as excited as she did. "Well, from that day on I have been smitten with you. I can't stop thinking about you."

Sarah laughed. "Do people still use that word?"

"I do." He chuckled. "Call me old-fashion."

"No, I like it." She squeezed his hand slightly. "I was hoping we would be able to meet again as well. What are the odds?"

Everything felt right for once in Sarah's life. Even though she barely knew John, she felt like somehow they shared this past that she couldn't explain, but it all felt right. Could this be the one God had for her? Could her prayers actually be answered that she had prayed for so long? She didn't want to feel too hopeful, but she couldn't deny the fact that it seemed as though the stars were finally aligning for her.

# COUNTY FAIRS

Every year, Amelia and Jake went to the Topsfield County Fair. Even though they went to the same exhibits and programs each year, they still had the inert need to go year after year. "It's tradition!" Jake would say with a smile and sometimes they would follow it up with the song from Fiddler on the Roof – "Trad-i-tion, tradition!" He would snap his fingers and stomp his feet as well. It always made Amelia giggle.

They enjoyed the free country concert the fair held every year as well, and the concert was always the deciding factor on which day they would choose to go. That way they could have something new to see and enjoy; however, some concerts were more impressive than others. Their favorite had been Jo Dee Messina, who had actually grown up in the area, so maybe they were a little biased too.

It was usually just the two of them, but this year John thought it would be a great opportunity for them to meet his new girlfriend, Sarah. He hadn't had a girlfriend in a while, in fact, Amelia couldn't remember the last time John had a girlfriend – maybe high school? There wasn't many places to meet girls once out of school unless you're on the party scene a lot, and since John wasn't that kind of guy, which Amelia greatly admired about her younger brother, the odds of him finding a girlfriend weren't in his favor. He would go out with some friends for drinks occasionally, but most of his socializing happened at church. However, that presented its own problems because the girls at church his age were either already married, in a serious long term relationship or engaged, or they were focusing on their relationship with God and weren't interested in the dating scene.

Amelia was grateful that she and Jake met in college. She had no idea what she would have done or where she would have ended up if they didn't, and she sure didn't want to be single after college because she would have ended up in the same boat as John. It's not that it was a bad boat to be in, just lonely sometimes. So she was excited to meet Sarah - his Cinderella, but she felt a little anxious too. She didn't want Sarah questioning them about children - though Amelia knew that was probably an unrealistic situation, she still liked to be prepared for the worst. However, she also didn't want to seem like an old boring married couple either. Even though John at age twenty-five was only three years younger than her, Amelia felt much older because she was already settled in life, and it seemed like John was still beginning his life. He hadn't been interested in going to college, and he had started his first job while he finished high school.

Amelia and Jake took a half day off work, so they could get to the fair early enough for a good parking spot and see some of the things without having to socialize. John and Sarah were going to meet up with them around four or five because Sarah was finishing up with a job at noon, and John had to work until two. John and Sarah weren't interested in the country music, so they were going to walk around when Amelia and Jake went to the concert.

As Amelia and Jake walked into the fair, all the old, familiar smells started swirling around their noses; everything from the chickens, pigs, cows and other barnyard animals along with their fragrant feces mixed with the smell of deep fried foods, popcorn, cider and pies, peoples' perfumes, flowers, leather from the cowboy hats, paint from all the airbrush stations, wood at the carving booths, trash, and cigarette smoke mixed together. The bees whirred around trash cans and food stations, and people of all kinds gathered pointing at all the things they wanted to see and do while walking into others as they kept their heads up looking at all the tall signs, games, and rides.

"I love coming to the fair with you," Jake put his arm around Amelia and kissed her on the forehead.

"Ditto," she smiled back at him. "Let's try these this year." She pointed to the deep fried vegetables, "I know we have always sworn not to because it's looks so disgusting in the vats before they fry them, but I really really want some deep fried food, and anything else we get will be fried in with chicken or other meats – at least this station is just the veggies fried in the oil."

Jake admitted she made a good point, so they decided to share a huge plate of the veggies. Everything came is huge portions at the fair, so they had agreed to share everything this year. It would also save on the budget as well.

"These are so good!" Amelia said with her first mouth full.

"They are," Jake dipped the broccoli into the ranch dressing, "do you know how much I could make these for at home though?" He licked the salt and grease from his fingers.

"A lot less then $7.50!" Amelia wiped her mouth with a napkin, and he shook his head.

After finishing the veggies, they made their way over to the pig racing. It seemed everywhere Amelia looked there was either a pregnant woman or people who had children. She noticed one woman standing in line for ice cream. Her entire neck and shoulders were covered in tattoos, and she had the protruding pregnant belly. *Can everyone in the entire world get pregnant but me?* She thought to herself. She quickly turned her head the opposite direction determined that she wasn't going to let that ruin her day – not again, not today.

They decided to stop for some iced coffee since they had some time to waste before  they were supposed to meet up with John. Right before they reached the booth for the iced coffee, Amelia saw a mother holding a tiny little baby. Before she could contain herself, she blurted out to Jake, "Can you believe that?" She nodded her head in the direction of the mother. "That baby has to only be a couple of days old. She should not have it out in public yet, for one, and for two, she shouldn't have it outside in this weather for crying out loud. It's October!"

Jake looked in the direction of the infant. "Yea, I know," he said in a sighing voice.

*Oh, no*, Amelia thought, *I did it again, and I mentioned it to Jake. I hope he doesn't think I'm not enjoying myself.* "Sorry, I just think it's wrong."

"I know." They continued their journey to the coffee stand. The truth was that it upset Jake just as much as it did Amelia, but he tried not to focus on it and took it on as his goal to try and divert Amelia's attention from it as well because it wasn't healthy for them to dwell on all the things that upset them about how other people raised children. Though Amelia could never fully tell whether bringing things up like this upset Jake too or if he was annoyed with her constantly bringing it up. She knew he had to be dealing with similar feelings, but she felt he wouldn't express them as much to her.

The more people they passed the more angry Amelia became with everyone who had children. One mother was yelling at her child to stay with her when she was walking so fast that the child couldn't even keep up with her. *Doesn't she realize children have shorter legs? They can't walk as fast. It's not the kid's fault. It's hers. She's an awful mother.* These judgments in her mind came out one right after another. *Oh God, please help me not to be bitter. I may never be a mother, but I shouldn't judge those who are, and who - in my opinion - aren't being good mothers because I don't know what it's like. I'm sorry. Please help me.*

Amelia decided to pretend like she didn't have fertility issues, so that all of the kids or babies and their parents she saw wouldn't cause her to think about her own problems, and she could stop judging others for having what she wanted because they were abusing the gift she would care for so delicately. It was different at the fair this year though. All the past years, she had thought to herself that she couldn't wait until she could be pregnant walking around the fair or show her children all the animals and everything. This year, though, she didn't once think about how wonderful the fair was going to be in the future with children. She enjoyed it for what it truly was and not some future fantasy waiting to be enjoyed.

Before Amelia and Jake knew it, the time had come to meet up with John and Sarah. They decided to sit down on a bench by the front gate. They watched the various types of people dodge each other as they entered and exited through the fair gates – there were the people that came to the fair just for their children, but every expression on their face showed that they hated every minute of it, there were the teenagers that came to hang out with their boyfriends or girlfriends, the people who really enjoyed the fair walked around with smiles on their faces and ice creams in their hands, and then the people who came to the fair just to bum around usually had backward baseball caps on.

Through the crowd, Amelia could see someone waving at her. "Is that…?" she nudged Jake's elbow, "Claire and Seth?" She watched as the couple came closer, and it did end up being her seven month pregnant sister. *Wonderful*, Amelia tried to act happy to see her, *what easier way to forget about fertility and babies than to have my pregnant sister here!* It wasn't that Amelia wasn't happy for Claire, she just really needed a break from constantly being surrounded and reminded about babies.

"John invited us," Claire said slightly out of breath while hugging Amelia as Seth and John shook hands and gave each other a man hug. "He wanted us all to meet his new girl - or I should say only girl- at the same time, I guess." Amelia tried to smile. "Can we sit? I need to take a break for a second." Claire lowered herself gently to a nearby bench. Amelia couldn't help but notice how visible pregnancy was and how invisible infertility was. The dichotomy of the two were sitting on the bench side by side - her and her sister. The only difference being that Claire could talk about her visible changes, but Amelia was kept to silence in her invisibility.

They exchanged some meaningless chatter – how the weather was, job news, baby news, etc. Soon they saw John walking towards them with whom they assumed was his new girlfriend.

"Wow, she's pretty." Claire leaned over to Amelia while eating an ice cream Seth had fetched for her. "I hope John holds on to her. We need him to join us in the married circle." She nudged Amelia with her elbow.

All the proper introductions were made, and everyone seemed to get along really well. Amelia, Claire, and Sarah ended up walking together in front of John, Seth, and Jake. Sarah was between Amelia and Claire and felt that Amelia was really distracted for some reason. She thought Amelia didn't like her, but Claire made up for Amelia's distracted state in her endless conversation even though it was pretty much one-sided as she went on about being pregnant and having children.

Though Amelia was on the other side of Sarah, she could still see Claire's belly protruding past Sarah. Amelia tried to stop herself from staring, but when she saw a pregnant woman's belly, it was really hard for her not to stare. It was as if she was drawn to it like a cat investigating something that has caught its attention or like a moth drawn to the bright light of a fire. She not only wondered what it would feel like to be pregnant, but it was so hard for her to fathom that an actual human being was growing inside there. Though she could see the physical sign of it, she wanted to feel it herself to believe it.

Amelia also realized that she'd have to buy a gift for Claire soon. Buying baby gifts was always a bittersweet endeavor for her. She'd peruse the shelves of their local children's store, The Green Elephant, and see so many things she'd want to purchase for her own baby someday, but the harsh realization always hit her that she wasn't shopping for her baby, but someone else's baby... always someone else's baby. Making the purchase would always make her so happy as she thought of the little baby using the item, but once she had the item home, she realized how void her home was of a baby's presence. She would hold the items in her hand feeling its softness and enjoying the pastel hues that tickled her eyes. Amelia blinked back tears as she brought herself back to her current reality. *Right. At the fair. Focus. Be present.* She told herself.

Sarah could hear all the guys behind them interacting so well, as though they were all *really* brothers – joking with each other and laughing. She couldn't help but think to herself how much she wanted to be part of this family. *Oh God, please, please let John be the one.* For once in her life, she felt like she could really start being a social person. She knew she had a long way to go, but she felt that John's family was a perfect starting point, and that she was ready to open herself to love again... maybe.

Sarah took a quick glance back at John, and when their eyes met for a moment, he winked at her and smiled. She loved his smile. His smile said everything she ever wanted to hear from a man without uttering any words, and she knew that he was someone she could trust even though Scott's smile had been deceptive to her. She needed to let down her wall of protection so she could completely let John in and be part of her life. She actually wanted to, which she thought would never happen again after her relationship with Scott, but something about John felt right and comfortable like being home next to a cozy fireplace. He was confident and he had a peace that seemed to surround him. She wanted to be the same way, but she wasn't sure how to go about finding that, though she knew it probably had something to do with his faith. Scott never had that peace about him. She had always felt on edge with him like she was never really good enough for him, and he proved her right in that in the end. But she didn't want to think about Scott anymore. She wanted to be in the present and enjoy what was right before her.

The couples split to do some things on their own for a while and decided to meet back up shortly before the concert. Sarah and John walked arm in arm, "You have a great family."

"Thanks, but it wasn't always easy growing up with two girls - especially when they're older than you are."

"They seem nice enough. Amelia is a little on the quiet side though, but who am I to talk? I'd like to get to know her better though."

Some sheep bleated as they passed the tent where they were being sheered. "What do you think about Claire?"John was just curious because most people didn't like Claire initially upon meeting her because she was always a little too intense, and it usually steered people away from her even though she was nice.

"Oh, she's nice, but she definitely has a lot to say, and she's really bubbly."

John chuckled. "You could say that again. You and Amelia would definitely get along better. You'll have plenty of time to get to know both of them better though." He winked at her.

The rest of the night went smoothly, though Amelia still was completely distracted as much as she tried to force herself to not notice the injustices around her - infants up past the sun setting and children without the proper layer of clothing for the cold temperatures outside. Claire and Seth had left before the concert was over because Claire was tired, and of course, she made it known that it was because of the baby growing inside of her. John and Sarah stayed to the end with Jake and Amelia but they didn't talk to each other much.

After the concert, they all grabbed a hot cider and some warm apple cider donuts to chase away the chill that had reached into their bones. "Well, it was really great meeting you, Sarah, and I hope we get to see more of you." Amelia said as they all parted ways at the gate when they were leaving. Amelia really wanted to get to know Sarah more. She wanted to trust her; she wanted them to be really good friends. Every time Amelia felt those feelings toward making friends with women, she guarded herself. She didn't want another Denise situation because the heartbreak of not having children was all she could bear right now. Amelia was glad to have Lane. Likewise, Sarah wanted to get to know Amelia as well, but she was also feeling hesitation. She didn't want to lose Amelia if things didn't work out with her and John. Plus, what if Amelia proved to be another female that would let her down like her college roommate? Either way, it was too risky for Sarah right now even though she desired that female companionship more than anything.

The next afternoon when Jake and Amelia came home from John's church, Amelia bundled up and breathed in the fresh October air while she took some time to sit on their balcony and write in her journal:

*Being around my sister yesterday was pretty rough. Every other word out of her mouth was either about being pregnant or about babies. About five minutes into her talking made me want to pull out my hair. But the second reading today at church helped me realize some things.*

*It was from 1 Peter 2:20b-25, "But when you do good and suffer, if you take it patiently, this is commendable before God. For to this you were called, because Christ also suffered for us, leaving us an example, that you should follow His steps: "Who committed no sin, Nor was deceit found in His mouth"; who, when He was reviled, did not revile in return; when He suffered, He did not threaten, but committed Himself to Him who judges righteously; who Himself bore our sins in His own body on the tree, that we, having died to sins, might live for righteousness - by whose stripes you were healed. For you were like sheep going astray, but have now returned to the Shepherd and Overseer of your souls."*

*This really resonated with me because choosing to deal with our infertility without using IVF is a type of suffering, but it is a good suffering. I'm not sure I handle it as patiently as I should, but I do try. Because Christ suffered for us, we, too, are called to suffer for good. When I think of suffering through our infertility in this way, it makes it a little easier to handle - only a little though.*

*But imagine if Christ decided it would be too hard to die on a cross for our sins and took the easier road - where would we be now? Without hope, without a future... Though my suffering is nothing like what He went through, there are times I feel I could sweat or cry blood because of the agony I feel. Yes, it would be easier to do IVF and try to solve our infertility, but we would be actively participating in the destruction of the marital union and the unborn at the hands of a doctor who we would paid thousands of dollars in hopes of achieving a pregnancy. Why not trust the great physician with our lives and our futures?*

*Children are a blessing, not a constitutional right. A blessing can be granted or withheld. Though I don't understand why God won't grant us this blessing, I'm learning to trust that He knows best, and I need to align my will with His and stop trying to make a path of my own.*

*We, as Christians, need to live in the righteousness that He died for and uphold that. I want to be part of that righteousness. I want to stand tall in the midst of this suffering and realize that I suffered for good. It bothers me so much when I hear other Christians talk about how God is blessing them through IVF. IVF is not a blessing from God! It goes completely against everything God created for man, woman, and their unity with and in Christ. I understand the frustration of infertility, but I think it's completely wrong to force*

*the creation of children because you want to ease
your suffering - meanwhile in the process of
creating some life, you're allowing other babies to
die because the embryos didn't take in the womb or
you are going to eliminate the frozen embryos
because you've decided to not do anymore
treatments. It angers me so much!*

Jake opened the slider door and peeked his
head out, "Hey, how are you doing out here?"

"Frustrated, but ok." Chloe slipped her way out
between Jake's legs. "Hey Chloe!" Chloe quickly
ran over to Amelia and jumped up to bump her head
on Amelia's hand.

"You almost done?" Amelia knew Jake had
something in mind.

"Why?"

"Want to get some ice cream at Down River?"
Down River was the only organic ice cream stand in
their area, and it had some amazingly delicious
flavors like Happy Birthday to Me, which tasted
just like the frosting on a birthday cake with
sprinkles and chunks of cake pieces.

Even though it was a little chilly, she knew the
ice cream stand wouldn't be open much longer as it
was coming to the end of their season, and they
already started having shorter hours, "Actually, ice
cream is exactly what I need." Amelia smiled.

# PICKING UP LEAVES

As the seasons changed from fall into winter, Amelia felt whatever hope she had left for having their own children slowly blew away in the wind with the leaves and spread across the ground like a colorful tapestry - if it could only feel that beautiful in her heart. When she saw the tapestry as a whole, the hope would return slightly, but as she tried to grasp it for herself and pick up one leaf at a time, it only ruined what was before her eyes. She resolved to sit and watch the hope decay on the ground and enjoy the remaining moments she had with it – the leaves turning from once vibrant reds, yellows, and oranges to a brown, dreary faded replica of their previous state. Once the colors had completely vanished, the brittle leaves curled and crumbled. Now the winter chill would come and the white snow that would bury the remains of what Amelia wanted to hold on to forever. Though spring followed the pending winter, Amelia knew that her hope for fertility would not be awakened once all the frozen and barren land thawed.

Not only did she loose her hope for fertility over the year, a storm had come through her body, and now she was left with the aftermath – except there was no help from massive amounts of people to aid her in cleaning up the mess that was left behind. Amelia was spoiled goods and had no idea where to turn to. She knew God was there, but His silence felt like a punishment, though she could never figure out the crime that caused such a stillness.

"It's bad enough dealing with the infertility, Lane, but knowing that sickness could be around the corner for me at any time since I still don't feel 100% myself yet is completely unbearable." She wiped her eyes with a tissue. "One minute I think I'm getting better, and the next minute, I'm back at square one because I keep having small flare-ups where I'm terrified that I might be going backwards again. Sometimes I wish I had never started this whole process. I want to go back to normal – back to me."

"But then you wouldn't know, Amelia. You needed to find answers - and though you don't have complete answers, you're on your way to getting them. You will get through this and some day you'll be able to say that you're glad you searched for the answers so you wouldn't be forever tormented by the "what if" syndrome."

"I know, Lane, but I don't think I realized how painful the truth would be either. It's even more painful walking past baby stuff in a department store because instead of thinking that someday I'll be able to shop in that department, I realize that it's not true. I'll never be standing there with a pregnant belly trying to decide what little outfits to pick out. Years later, I won't have my little girl pulling at my jeans pointing to the new Easter dress she wants me to buy." Her eyes filled with tears. Lane quickly grabbed a box of tissues from her counter and placed them beside Amelia. "Thank you," Amelia whispered as she dabbed her eyes.

"Maybe you should start buying the things that you want?" Amelia wasn't sure what Lane was trying to suggest. "Instead of denying yourself the experience of buying all the things you want for your child someday, why not purchase some things and put it in a chest at home?"

Amelia considered her friend's suggestion for a moment. She did like the idea of actually being able to buy the things she would love to have for a child, but would it end up being weird? Would it let her pretend for a little while longer and delay the inevitable - that they won't be able to have children? Then the chest would sit in her room - only to haunt and mock her. "Oh, Lane, I'm not so sure about that. I like the idea. I really do, but I'm not sure I have the right to be in those departments and buying those things. I'm not sure it would be *too* helpful."

"You have the right as much as anyone else does, and you'll have children someday. They may not be your own, but I know you've talked about adoption, so you could use the stuff anyway."

"I know, but right now I feel like I'm losing a child, Lane. Buying items and trying to store them in a hope chest would be like trying to keep leaves from drying out and dying. Even if I could find a way to preserve the leaves, I still won't have the tree - which is the part that holds the life. If I can't have the tree, the leaves will only be a memory of what was - the memory of all I held dear. Right now, I feel like I need to let go and not hold on." She sighed. "Yes, we may adopt some day, but if I buy clothes and other things for the child I would birth and then never have the chance to do that, and then we adopt internationally from China or something, I might want other clothes and things. I'm not sure I could bear seeing the things that were meant for my dreamed child on a different child. I think it would be a visible failure."

Even though Amelia had told Lane that she wasn't going to keep a hope chest, the idea still tugged at her heart and mind, and Amelia thought back to the last time her and Jake were over her parents' house. They offered to helped her parents clear out some bins for a tag sale her mother wanted to do in the spring. Amelia went to grab one box, and her mom quickly barked, "Not that one!" Amelia paused, and her mother came over to her and grabbed the bin. "We're keeping this one." Amelia looked through the clear plastic side and noticed some small dresses, which she knew wasn't doll clothes.

"Oh, is that my baby stuff?" Amelia went to open the lid because she wanted to show Jake some of the cute outfits she wore as a child. She couldn't believe her mom had kept them all this time.

"Not exactly," her mother pulled the bin away from Amelia's grasp.

Amelia gave a puzzled look at her mother, "Mom, why won't you let me see it?" Her mother looked ashamed and almost sad. "Oh, is it stuff you bought for Claire's baby?" Amelia tried to contain her disappointment.

"Actually..." she slowly placed the bin on the basement floor and cracked open the lid, "it's not. It's stuff I've been collecting for your baby someday." When her mother fully revealed its contents, the bin contained a myriad of baby items and clothes. There were cute little booties with little duckies on them, onesies with baby giraffes, a dress with pink ruffles at the bottom, a few plush stuffed animals, and some of the baby clothes that have been passed down in their families for generations.

"My baby?" Amelia was shocked, "But mom, I'm not pregnant... and you know..."

"I know, but a mother can hope, can't she?" Amelia could feel her mother's sadness, and Amelia realized that their infertility broke her mother's heart as much as it broke her own. "Anytime I've seen things in the stores since you told me about your infertility, I've started buying the things I would buy if you were expecting a child, and I've saved the heirlooms for you."

"But mom, Claire is pregnant. She would probably love to have this stuff." Even though Amelia didn't want Claire to have it, she did have to state the obvious and make her mom realize that her and Jake may never have kids.

"I know, but I already have stuff for Claire. These are the things I've bought for your child someday. Plus I don't think Claire would care for the things that have been handed down for generations the same way you would care for them."

Amelia wasn't sure what else to say. The box before her was like a pirate's buried treasure as her mom clutched the sides of the bin. The only problem was that even though the treasure was within grasp, she still had to take the nine month journey to get it, but she didn't even have the map where X marked the spot of where it would be hidden.

As Amelia sat in bed later that night, she thought back on the conversation between her and Lane about the hope chest and her mother's hope bin she was keeping for them in her basement. Jake walked in and pulled back the sheets on his side of the bed. "What do you think about a hope chest?"

He looked at her puzzled, "You're gonna need to give me a little more detail than that, Amelia. I have no idea what you're talking about."

"Well, remember the bin my mom is keeping of things for us when we have children?" He nodded. "Do you think we should start keeping one for ourselves? Like when we see things we'd like to buy for our children someday that we could buy them now and put them in the hope chest. Then we'll have everything we want for when we have kids."

"Or we'll end up just accumulating all this baby stuff and never be able to use it." He said matter-of-factly, which Amelia wasn't sure whether she felt hurt by his comment or agreed with it. "And then we'll have to get rid of it all - and we won't want to give it to other people because it's stuff we specifically bought for our child, and we won't want to donate it either." Jake could tell that though his comments saddened Amelia, she could also see the truth in what he was mentioning as well.

"I know. A part of me thinks it's a good idea and then another part thinks it's outright silly. I wanted to know what you thought."

"If this is something you really feel like you need to do, Amelia, then please don't only go by what I say. If you feel buying these things will help you, then I'm all for it."

"I know. I'm not sure it *will* help though. I feel like I would get the items home and want to use them right away like a kid on Christmas Day, but then I'd quickly realize that I don't have children - and can't have children." She sighed. "There's no real easy way to deal with this infertility stuff, is there? Nothing is ever going to be big enough to fill this void I feel... this emptiness in our lives."

Jake reached over and grabbed her hand. "I know." He whispered. He knew no other way to comfort his wife. He couldn't even comfort himself. It was a pain they both felt deep in their souls and lives as if someone ripped their hearts out and all they can do is stand there in shock and awe. He wished he could do more. He wished he could solve the problem, but he was helpless as she was.

Amelia picked up her journal:

*I'm not sure what to say really. Infertility sucks. It's as simple as that. I try to think of a million reasons of why me? Why us? But no answer brings me to a satisfactory conclusion. I have nothing left to give to this. Does that mean I wouldn't be a good mother because I can't withstand this pressure? No - it means that I'm a woman with a broken heart that can't stand to watch it bleed and suck the life and joy out of everything that life does have to offer and give. I'm tired of living behind this veil of unhappiness. The problem is that infertility is a prison you can never really escape, but I must learn how to enjoy the sunshine in the midst of my cage and enjoy the things I can do. Maya Angelou had it right when she wrote, "I Know Why the Caged Bird Sings." I can't let this beat me even though it binds me. I must still sing in the midst of my cage.*

The next day they passed through a department store at the mall on their way to the Catholic bookstore where they wanted to browse around to gather more information about the Catholic faith. In the department store, they passed the children's section, and Amelia stopped suddenly, "Aww.... this is so cute!" Jake turned around from about ten steps in front of her because he hadn't noticed her abrupt halt.

Amelia touched the little white ruffled dress hanging on the rack with embroidered  pink and yellow flowers around the bottom hem. The cap sleeves had a slight ruffle to them as well, and the dress came with ruffly white bloomers. "Do you want to buy it?" Jake asked, as he wasn't sure where they had left off with the conversation the night before.

"Yes, I do," Amelia placed the dress back on the rack, "but I'm not going to." She slowly walked away from the dress.

"Why not? If you want to buy it and keep it in a hope chest, we can. I don't mind."

"I know," she grabbed his hand, "but it still feels weird. It feels wrong to buy things for something - or someone - I don't have yet or doesn't exist yet. It's like buying everything for a dog but then never actually buying a dog."

They walked hand and hand through the mall quietly and solemnly - both thinking about the dress and both feeling the absence of children in their lives. Family after family passed them in the wide open hallways of the mall - some were happy and some were completely miserable, though there seemed to more of the latter than the former unfortunately. Amelia thought about how they would be one of the happy families and how sad it was that they couldn't contribute to society in this way.

"Hey!" Amelia heard someone yell, but with the crowded aisles, she didn't pay any attention. "Hey, Amelia!" She turned around to see her sister and Seth coming towards them. Of course, her sister had more of a waddle than a walk now that she was in third trimester. Once Claire and Seth caught up with them, Claire declared, "We just came out of Carter's baby clothing store, and you have got to see what we found in there!" A big smile was plastered across her face.

Amelia wished she could be more happy and less jealous of her sister, but the green monster wasn't always that easy to keep at bay. She stood by as Claire pulled out outfit after outfit and draped them across Seth's arms and her bulging belly. Amelia could almost feel her skin turning color. Seeing the array of cute outfits displayed before her made Amelia realize even more that she couldn't keep a hope chest for herself filled with these items. Just as people have to take that step to move on after grieving a loved one - whether it means taking down items around the house that remind them of that person or changing a room they've kept the same since their loved ones absence - Amelia knew that keeping a hope chest would only be a step backwards.

# WAFFLES & SPAGHETTI

*There is this person I knew I was going to be once I was pregnant and had children. How do I find that person now without those circumstances? How can I become that person when my dreams have been broken? It feels so impossible, but yet so necessary. In every area of my life, I see how I'm not fulfilling the role of me that I would have if I had children.*

*Sometimes I feel like I need to find myself all over again; a different version of myself as though kids were never in the plans for my life, so I wouldn't know I'm missing out on something. But then I feel like I'm not truly being me either because it would feel as though I would be missing an essential part of life - like someone cutting off their leg or something.*

*Though Jake is supportive and patient, I find more and more that we process these things differently. This leaks into every area of my day.*

*From the moment I open my eyes until deep into my dreams at night. For Jake, it seems like he can turn it on and off when he wants to feel it. It's so unfair because I feel like I'm tormented constantly; whereas, he only experiences the pain when he wants to. Oh, how I wish I could be more like that. Maybe it wouldn't hurt so much.*

Amelia closed her journal, as Chloe jumped up into her lap, "Oh, desperate for some love?" Jake decided to take a walk in one of the local parks as he did often early on Saturday mornings to smell the damp morning air of the day, so Amelia found herself with a few hours in the empty apartment that she wished were filled with the coos and giggles of a child. The silence pierced through her heart, and then Chloe began to purr. Amelia couldn't stop the tears from filling her eyes.

Once Jake returned from his walk, Amelia decided to take a drive to visit Lane because Lane wanted to show Amelia the progress she made on the painting. "Oh, Lane, it's beautiful!" She said as soon as Lane revealed it from behind a draped cloth, "I love how you used the colors to fade so nicely into each other. It really pulls my eyes right into the painting so smoothly that I don't even notice the darkness surrounding the wonderful yellowish-blue hues in the center. It's perfect, Lane, perfect." Lane had fully captured the essence of what Amelia's life felt like right now just as Lane had wanted to.

The scene was of Plum Island in Newburyport as the sun rose up over the horizon from across the ocean. The sand is faintly lit by the ray protruding across the water, but what was the most magnificent part for Amelia was that even though the whole painting was dark, the hue of light on the distant horizon began to bring light into that darkness that signaled the ensuing day to come. The hope and anticipation of what the day in the painting held ignited in Amelia's mind as she gazed at the painting. The light had a mesmerizing effect on the viewer the same way that gazing at Aurelius Borealis would. This awe and wonder made Amelia want to keep watching the painting until the sun actually came up in it, even though that was an impossibility.

"Thanks so much." Lane smiled, and they moved into the kitchen as the kettle began to boil. "So, how are you doing?"

"Well, I'm hanging in there the best I possibly can, but it's really hard knowing that Claire's baby shower is around the corner. I am happy for her, Lane, I really am. I just can't help feeling bad for myself, and I hate that *too* because I feel completely selfish that I can't get over myself and enjoy my sister having a baby." Amelia stirred some sugar into her tea and wished that someday she would be drinking tea with her own teenage daughter while chatting and recounting the days they had.

"Amelia, I think it's perfectly normal to feel what you're feeling. It's really hard to deal with what you're going through. Have you told Claire yet?"

"No, we still haven't told anyone except for our parents. Oh, and John knows too. He knew something was up and asked me point blank, so I didn't want to lie to him - plus he's keeping it secret as well. It's too hard to bring myself to tell everyone even though I know they already are either wondering about it or have some kind of suspicion of it since the whole family knows that Jake and I love kids and want a big family."

"Do you think you should tell Claire at some point? Since John knows, don't you think Claire will be upset that she was the last one to know in your family?"

Amelia sat in silence for a few moments as she pondered Lane's question. She heard the kitchen clock tick while Amelia removed her tea bag from her teacup. "I know she'll be mad, Lane, but I don't want her thinking about me and my sadness when this is supposed to be one of the best times of her life though. Plus, I don't think she'll totally understand what it's like. Getting pregnant came so easily for her. I don't want her trying to give me advice on ways to get pregnant. I think that would make me angry."

"Have you talked with her much since the pregnancy or seen her much?"

Amelia shook her head. "Not too much. Probably only a handful of times." She felt like the worst sister ever. Seeing Claire pregnant made Amelia feel so inferior as a woman. So much of her wanted to talk with Claire and ask her what she was feeling and what it was like to be pregnant, but she also didn't want to get into conversation about it because it would only make her want it more than ever and be more jealous than she already was. She was happy for her sister, but at the same time she felt an intense sadness for herself.

"Well, I hope the shower isn't too hard for you. I wish I could be there to support you."

"And I wish I could be there to support *you*!" Lane was having a small art show at Zumi's coffee shop. There was going to be light refreshments and her work would be on display for the entire month, but it was on the same day that Claire's baby shower was planned. Even though Lane wasn't directly invited to Claire's shower, Amelia was going to ask Claire if it would be ok to bring Lane along. Honestly, she would rather be at the art show with Lane. Though she wanted to support her sister, it was always easier to avoid situations that made her uncomfortable on the maternity front. Amelia probably wouldn't know what half the gifts were that Claire received anyway and what they would be used for. She hated feeling incompetent, and being at a baby shower was the epitome of incompetency for her since she practically needed a manual to understand what all the objects would be used for.

Later that night Amelia wrote:

*The thing that scares me the most is that I'll never know what all the little gadgets are for that women get at baby showers. I feel like I'm always going to be in the dark. I'll feel like a freak of nature forever standing there at a distance watching it all happen before my eyes but never able to participate; I'm a gawking onlooker.*

*When people have children, there is this camaraderie that instantly happens between mothers. They all of sudden enter a world that's so foreign to me, and yet I stand there on the outside looking in trying not to stare but also trying to gather as much information from the conversations I hear trying to learn as much as possible about this unknown world that I can. However, most of the time the conversation ends, and the person looks to me and says something like, "You'll understand someday when you have kids." If only I could... and I walk away in this silent shame that somehow I'm less than normal.*

*How do you began to tell people that you can't have children? How do you begin even accepting something like that about yourself enough to even utter the words to someone else? Of course, someone will offer the option of adoption right away - like I haven't thought of that. Thanks for solving all my problems - adoption, of course - duh, everything is all better now.*

*No one knows what this is like unless they have experienced it. It's like having a terminal illness that takes more away from you every day. Some days are better; some are worse. I wonder if this is going to be any easier. I keep hoping that one day I'll wake up, and being infertile won't bother me anymore and I can move on with the next chapter in my life. But that's not the case - it's always there, under the surface, and I find that my tears are only seconds away from bursting through. I am pretty good at holding them back for a while, and then one day it hits me, and the uncontrollable crying takes over.*

*I don't want to be this way. I want to be strong. I want to be able to move past this, but I don't know how. I don't know how to give this up. I don't know how to totally surrender this to God. My grip is so tight that I can see the whites of my knuckles. If you love something enough, you have to learn how to let them go, right? Even if it means they will never come back... can I let go of my desire to have children, even if God never decides to allow that blessing in our lives? I know what Sarah felt like when her and Abraham couldn't have children. I know what she felt like when Hagar was pregnant, and she remained barren. But in the end, God blessed Sarah and Abraham with children. I know how Elizabeth and Zachariah felt when they were barren, but God blessed them with John the Baptist. I know Hannah's tears all too well, but God heard her prayer, and she conceived a son. Will that be my story? Does He hear my cries? If I give this fully to Him, will He give it back? What if He doesn't? I know I can't give it with expectation either that I will be blessed because then I'm not fully surrendering it. I don't know how to get to that point.*

The next day, Jake and Amelia were off to their charting appointment with Nanette. She reviewed the charts that Jake had been keeping about Amelia's mucus cycles as they had been taught. Nanette complimented Jake on how well he did with keeping precise charts. She made some notes in their file that she had with her, and Amelia smiled at Jake as they waited in silence.

"So, how are things going with you two?" Nanette's voice erupted through the silent air.

Amelia and Jake glanced at each other almost to ask each other telepathically what Nanette was referring to and waiting for the other to answer. The silence became awkward, and Amelia finally came out with, "What do you mean?"

"How are you two coping with everything? Are you keeping communication open about it all?" Amelia wanted to answer honestly, but she didn't want Jake to feel badly. They didn't really have long conversations about children anymore. Not the same way as when they first started the process anyway. Even though Amelia thought about their infertility all the time, it didn't seem like it bothered Jake much until after they'd been around children one afternoon and then he would make some comment about his sadness of not being able to have children yet. For a moment, it would make Amelia think that Jake actually thought about their childlessness as much as she did, but then it seemed he could change the subject and move onto the next topic.

"Well, we don't really talk about it that much." Amelia finally blurted out. "It's not that we don't understand each other or ignore it. He's here to support me when I break down and such, but sometimes it feels like there's not that much more to say."

"Let me tell you something that might be helpful." Amelia was a little nervous about what Nanette thought about her and Jake not really being all that communicative lately. "Men and women process things in completely different ways. It's just the way our brains work. Men tend to compartmentalize things they think about - almost as if the thoughts never touch each other; they are all boxed off like a waffle. For example, a man could go from talking about the infertility stuff and then move onto how he needs to mow the lawn - two totally opposite ideas - and he can switch gears in an instance with no warning, but when he's done processing the infertility subject, he has closed the door to that compartment and opened the door to the next. He has moved on, and nothing from the previous compartment is brought into the new one. It helps men cope because it allows them to tuck it away until they are ready to deal with it." Nanette paused, "Actually, if you think about it, men love all things square - TV's, iPhone's, computers," then they all laughed.

She continued, "Whereas, women think about everything all at once; their thoughts form one big long stream, and sometimes the thoughts tangle around each other like spaghetti. For example, a woman can think about her infertility while thinking about what she needs to pick up at the grocery store, how she might see children at the store and that will make her heart ache which will remind her that she'll need to research some ways to change her diet to help her fertility and then her mind jumps back to the matter at hand - that she's at work while others talk about their children, and then her mind wanders again to how she cannot have children. The cycle continues over and over again - one big jumbled clump of thoughts; no beginning, no end.

"So, when men and women try to communicate on this matter of their infertility, it can become a very challenging matter because men don't understand why women can't move on from thinking about it, and women can't understand how men can shut off thinking about it and *not* let it bother them."

"Exactly!" Amelia startled herself as the words left her mouth before she realized they had. "I mean, I thought I was going crazy because I think about this all the time and could talk about it for an infinite number of hours, but sometimes it feels like Jake doesn't care that it affects me all the time."

"It's not that I don't care. I shut that part off because it's too painful to think about all the time." Jake piped into the conversation.

"Then I envy you because I can never turn it off." Amelia really meant it.

"And with this difference in processing thoughts, you two will have a better understanding of how each deals with things as female and male." Nanette interjected.

"It does help." Amelia said matter-of-factly.

"Yes, most definitely. It's nice to know why her thoughts never end when she begins talking - makes more sense now." He winked at her.

"Hey, I resent that." Amelia tapped Jake's arm playfully.

"What? I'm just saying that sometimes you get rattling, and I can't keep up." He smiled at her, and they both knew he wasn't being rude, but there was some truth to what he was saying.

The following week presented them with an appointment with Dr. Carter where they reviewed her recent blood test that resulted in her estrogen being on the lower side. Besides the test result, there wasn't much more to review besides the same options as usual - including the surgery. Dr. Carter did seem to strongly suggest that she take Letrozole or Clomid to help boost her estrogen levels and encourage a better ovulation. She had been nervous about taking it as increasing her estrogen could cause a flare-up to happen with her auto-immune issues. Though her and Jake decided they didn't want to take that risk, he was able to waffle that door shut, but for Amelia, she allowed it to spaghetti into her every thought for the next few days as though it hadn't been decided on. She would make comments like, "... and that's why I don't think Letrozole is a good idea," in which Jake would respond, "I know." Though it stayed in her mind because she felt like they hadn't done too much with the suggestions from the doctor, she also didn't want to risk her health again.

She hated constantly thinking about and wondering if she was making the right decisions all the time. She wanted it all to be easy - even if having a baby wasn't easy, she thought that getting answers from the doctor would be easy at least. She never realized that it was going to be another turn on her journey of infertility.

# THANKSGIVING

"Why can't you all come over here for Thanksgiving?" Claire begged Amelia through the phone as though she was a child begging for a toy in a toy store. "It's our first Thanksgiving in our new place, and Seth's parents plus mom and dad will be here. It would be great to have you and Jake here as well. Oh, and John - he could bring Sarah!"

"I know, Claire," Amelia cut her off before Claire could get any more excited. Honestly, Amelia didn't want to spend the holiday with her pregnant sister, as horrible as that sounded every time she thought it to herself. "I think it would be best for you and Seth to have Thanksgiving with both sets of parents. It would be a nice gesture. If you have more people over than that, it might be too much for you - you know, with the baby and all, it may be too exhausting if there is more people."

"I hadn't thought of that," Claire sounded disappointed, "but what are you and Jake going to do for Thanksgiving?"

Amelia hadn't thought of that yet either, but she blurted out, "Well, actually we were hoping to have John and Sarah over here." Amelia realized that Claire hadn't really asked John yet since she mentioned him as an excited thought to her rambling. "He mentioned to me the other day that Sarah was considering being vegetarian, so we wanted to show her what a vegetarian Thanksgiving would be like." She wasn't actually lying because John had told her that about Sarah, and Jake and Amelia had thought about having them over for Thanksgiving but never really decided on anything because Will had invited Jake and Amelia over for Thanksgiving, so that had distracted them from working out their own plans. They wanted to avoid Will's family as well since his friend's wife would be well along in her pregnancy too.

Amelia was tired of being around everyone else for their holiday festivities because her and Jake lacked having their own family and traditions. She wanted to be home and make traditions for themselves even without children because she knew that at some point she would have to face what that would be like for them without a house full of children.

"But I want you to see our new place," Claire interrupted Amelia's thoughts.

"I will at the baby shower next week." Then Amelia remembered she still needed to get a gift for the shower. She had been putting it off because it was too painful to walk into a Babies R' Us or any other type of baby store. First, she needed to get through Thanksgiving, then she could focus on buying the present. She was able to convince Claire to keep Thanksgiving at her place with the two sets of parents and that Jake and Amelia would entertain John and Sarah.

"So what's up?" Jake said as soon as Amelia hung up the phone with Claire. "Was she ok with us not coming?"

"Yes, thankfully. I know it sounds horrible, but I really can't be around her two weeks in a row when she'll be raving about her pregnancy."

"Same with my Will's wife... so it's just me and you?"

"Not exactly. I told Claire we were going to invite John and Sarah."

Jake was on board with having John and Sarah come over as it would be a nice distraction since they wouldn't be alone for the holiday or be around someone who was pregnant. Amelia called John right away as Thanksgiving was only a few days away. Their family always did things last minute, so she was hoping that John hadn't made plans for him and Sarah yet.

"We'd love to join you and Jake for Thanksgiving." John yelled through his cell phone. "We were just talking about what we were going to do for Thanksgiving actually."

"Why are you talking so loud?" Amelia held the phone away from her face slightly.

"Oh, we're at Zumi's coffee shop, and there's a lot of people here. Someone is setting up and getting ready to play some music."

"Ok, well I won't keep you long. Glad you can make it."

"Do you need us to bring anything? Sarah can make anything." He paused. "Oh, she said she can bring the potatoes, if you don't mind. I've had her potatoes, they're killer! She makes them with chives and something else that makes them light, fluffy, and creamy. She claims it's a secret ingredient." He winked at Sarah. "I'll get it out of her someday."

"Yes, that's totally fine. She's ok with a vegetarian Thanksgiving, right? If not, you guys might want to bring your own meat stuff."

"Oh, no worries at all. She likes to try new things. Got to go - looks like they are going to start. See you soon!"

That night Amelia and Jake worked on hanging up the darkening curtains in their bedroom that had finally come in the mail along with taping up any small lights with electricians tape. Though it wasn't the most ideal thing to be doing when they had to plan for the Thanksgiving holiday, they had ordered the curtains after their last appointment with Dr. Carter. He had mentioned that there was some study that showed people who had brighter rooms while sleeping had higher rates of infertility because they weren't resting as well at night. They figured it was an easy enough solution to try since they had a very bright car wash next door to them. They taped up any lights that shone from things like the fire alarm, floor fan, stereo and telephone as well- just to be sure they covered everything.

They knew it wouldn't solve their infertility over night, but Jake had that determined type of mindset that accomplished anything before him - never leaving anything for the next day. Amelia on the other hand had always been more of a procrastinator, but she tried to be more like Jake because he would actually get things done instead of letting them sit around for weeks.

As Amelia sat on the bed, she looked at the curtains that hung in their windows. She thought to herself, *What are we doing? Is this really going to work?* Jake sported a small snore. She turned back to the curtains. *Studies show this is supposed to work, but really... this seems silly. If we were to be pregnant, what am I supposed to tell our children? We couldn't get pregnant, so we hung up some special curtains?* She scooted under the covers and turned off the light. The room was so dark she couldn't even see her hand as she waved it in front of her face. She did feel more tired though with the room darker. She fell asleep minutes later to her hopeful thoughts of what a darker room could do for their fertility.

Over the next few days, Amelia busied herself with gathering all the ingredients she needed for the holiday meal. The best stuffing came from Green Meadows Farm. They sold it in buckets with all the necessary ingredients. All she would have to do is follow the instructions in the pale and mix it up together. They usually bought some type of fake chicken cutlets made by a company called Quorn, which was a substitute for their meat source. Then she grabbed some brussels sprouts and would make them with a recipe that covered them in a nice maple glaze. Jake made sure they had canned cranberry sauce, but then would claim it was never as good as he remembered when he was a kid. For rolls, Amelia bought frozen french bread so all she needed to do was pop it in the oven.

Before Amelia knew it, the places were set at their kitchen table and they were awaiting the buzz from their intercom for John and Sarah's arrival. Once they were all settled at the table and said grace for the meal, they passed around the dishes of food. "These potatoes *are* amazing, Sarah!" Amelia said as soon as they touched her tongue, and she wasn't just being polite. They were fantastic. "I didn't even add anything to them. What do you put in them?"

"It's a secret. Sorry." She smiled and looked at John because she knew it bugged him that she wouldn't share the recipe's secret ingredient.

Amelia looked at John, "I tried." She smiled.

"Thanks, I've been trying to get it out of her for a while, but she won't budge."

The rest of the holiday meal together was very pleasant. Amelia really enjoyed getting to know Sarah some more without Claire around stealing all the attention. As Amelia cleared the table to prepare it for dessert, there was a small knock on the door.

"Who could that be?" Amelia wiped the table as Jake answered the door. "Lane!" Amelia dropped her cloth and ran over to Lane.

"Happy Thanksgiving!" Lane handed Jake a bouquet of seasonal flowers that shown hues of

orange, yellows, and browns as Amelia hugged her.
"Sorry to drop by un-announced, especially on a
holiday, but I was ..."

"Nonsense," Amelia shook her head, "you're
always welcome here."

Everyone loved Amelia's first attempt at
homemade banana cream pie. She was surprised
because she wasn't much of a baker, but even Sarah
said it was awesome, so she knew it had to be good
and not just Jake and John trying to compliment her
even if it wasn't tasty. As they finished their dessert,
they took a few moments to talk about what each of
them were thankful for in life generally or within
the past year.

Amelia wasn't sure what to say when it came to
her turn. She listened to the others while they
mentioned what they were thankful for - John and
Sarah obviously said they were thankful for meeting
each other, Lane was grateful to have such
wonderful companions she could spend
Thanksgiving with, and Jake grabbed Amelia's hand
when he stated how blessed he was to have such a
beautiful wife to share his life with. With all the
eyes on her now, her mind blanked. She didn't feel
thankful for much right now - maybe if she was
pregnant, it would be a different story.

She swallowed hard and looked around the
room, "Um, well," she squeezed Jake's hand - she
knew she could be honest with everyone in the
room, and she hoped Jake would be ok with what
she was going to say next, "As all of you know,
we've been dealing with infertility for a while, and
this year we've been working with doctors to figure

out the cause." She breathed in slowly to stop herself from being too emotional. "At our last appointment with our nurse, she mentioned a story about a Garden of Crosses."

She continued as everyone's attention was on her. "A man walked into the garden with his cross and came up to Jesus complaining that it was too heavy for him to carry. Jesus told the man that he could pick any of the other crosses that he thought were lighter. So the man went around for a few minutes and tried picking up cross after cross to see which on would be the easiest for him to handle. Eventually, he chose one and went to Jesus with his selection. Jesus looked at him and said, 'That is the cross you came in with.'

"The story is meant to show that Jesus doesn't give us more than we can carry even though we may think it is impossible for us. Each of our crosses are difficult, no doubt, but they are precisely for us, and He gives us the strength to carry them, if we allow Him to help." Everyone seemed to be a little confused as to why she had mentioned the story. "I'm thankful that God has given me a husband that not only helps carrying this cross of infertility but also trusts in God for help. God has not only given me a cross suited with the precise heaviness that I can handle but also with a husband who is perfectly suited for me. I could have never asked for a better husband." They smiled at each other.

They ended the night by deciding to watch *Despicable Me*, which Amelia loved to watch, but the cuteness of the youngest child, Agnes, Gru

decides to adopt almost made Amelia cry when
Agnes started singing her "Unicorn Song" as she
sang herself to sleep in the home for girls. Amelia
wished she could scoop Agnes up and adopt her and
her sisters.

"Thanks for letting me crash your party," Lane
said at the door before she left.

"You didn't crash any party, you know that. It
was really great to have you. I'm glad you stopped
by and that we were able to catch up a bit."

"Me as well," Lane hugged Amelia, "and if you
need me to go shopping with you tomorrow to shop
for Claire's gift, let me know."

"Thanks for the offer," Amelia sighed, "but I
think it's something Jake and I need to learn how to
do unfortunately. I can't wait to see the finished
painting though. It sounds fantastic!"

"Thanks. I can't wait to show you. Let's plan on
getting together in the new year. I know between
now and then it'll be a bit crazy for you with your
sister's new baby and the holiday."

"You may find me at your doorstep in seek of a
respite from it all!" They both giggled and wished
each other a good night.

The next morning, Amelia knew the task of
buying Claire's baby shower gift was before her,
and that made it a little more difficult to get out of
bed considering the circumstances. It wasn't an easy
thing to accomplish when dealing with infertility, as
the surrounding items almost mock from the shelves
and hanging racks.

She didn't want to buy something from Claire's
registry though. Since she couldn't experience

buying anything for a baby of her own, Amelia wanted to put more thought into it than just choosing something off a pre-determined list. In fact, Amelia hated registries. They completely took the fun out of choosing a gift for someone. Plus she didn't like giving big box stores business; she'd rather buy locally or from Burt's Bees which had a great selection of baby items. She did glance at the registry list for some ideas of things Claire wanted since Amelia was pretty much clueless on what babies needed, but then she would buy something similar from The Green Elephant store in downtown Ipswich.

The first item she grabbed was a onesie by Burt's Bees before they perused the baby section at The Green Elephant. Once in the baby section, she noticed some sucky blankets that were a little larger than a washcloth and had an animal head attached to the middle. Amelia deduced that these must be the new big thing because there were so many of them, and Claire had something similar on her registry. Amelia immediately picked up the zebra one, "This is so cute!" She held it to her face and looked at Jake like she was modeling for something. Then she realized how silly she must have looked.

"Is that the one? Ready to go?" Jake was never a fan of any kind of shopping, but what guy really is? She just wanted him to take a little more interest in it since they wouldn't be picking out anything for their own child anytime soon. She took the zebra to the counter and looked at the tiny cards on the rack by the register as the clerk assisted them.

"Would you like this gift wrapped? It's free!" The clerk said with a smile.

"Sure," Jake quickly accepted.

"No," Amelia blurted but didn't want to seem rude. "I'd like to wrap it myself." Jake looked at her puzzled. "I have baby gift wrapping paper that I never get to use, so I want to wrap it in that."

"That's fine. You know me, if it's free - I'll take it." He smiled, and the clerk giggled.

"Would you like to be part of our rewards program?" The clerk asked.

Jake and Amelia looked at each other, then Jake said, "What does it do? Does it cost anything to be part of it?"

"Oh, no," she assured them, "it's free as well. Every purchase you make gains you points on your account, and then when you reach a certain number of points you get a gift certificate."

Amelia could tell Jake wasn't sure about it, but Amelia quickly said, "Sure." She turned to Jake, "We'll probably be here a lot buying things for Claire's baby, and then we have your brother as well."

When they got home, Jake went into the great room to work on their budget as he did once a week. Amelia took the zebra to the bedroom and reached under their bed to find the wrapping paper. The paper had little baby rattles and pacifiers all over that were pastel pink and baby blue. She cut the paper to the right size, made sure the price tags were off both items, and laid the zebra down on the paper first. As she saw it lay there on her bedroom floor, an emptiness filled the room and her heart -

the silence lacked the noise of a baby coo or giggle. She stared at the zebra wishing that it was on the floor from their infant playing with it, but instead she had to wrap it up for someone else to enjoy - for someone else's baby. She picked up the zebra and sniffed it - it even smelled like a new baby - and a tear formed in her right eye and trickled down her face. She took in a deep breath to stop the rush of tears that wanted to follow, and she pressure built in her throat by trying to keep her emotions from bursting out.

She quickly wrapped the two items along with her feelings. Now that they were perfectly packaged, she could relax until Claire's baby shower that weekend. She hoped she could contain her emotions at the shower, but only time would tell.

# BABY SHOWERS

Sarah asked Amelia about helping to plan Claire's baby shower when she was over for Thanksgiving. Amelia thought it nice of Sarah to offer, but let her know that Jane, who was Claire's best friend from college, had already done most of the planning. Amelia was glad that she wasn't expected to throw Claire's baby shower - not only because Claire could be really picky and hard to please, but also because it would have been too painful for Amelia to bear - though she would have needed to deal with the pain silently since she and Jake still hadn't told their extended family about their infertility.

Claire wanted her shower to be simple yet classy. Claire wanted it at her and Seth's new condo opposed to some venue - mostly because she wanted to show off their new place and have everyone ogle over the newly decorated nursery. Because Claire wanted it at their new place, the shower was pushed pretty close to Claire's due date since Claire and Seth had been busy with the move and holiday until then.

"It's getting harder and harder to hug people!" Claire enthusiastically smiled as she pointed to her belly when Amelia finished hugging her. "Here, feel this." She grabbed Amelia's hand and placed it on her belly, and Amelia could feel a little vibration coming from inside. Amelia was amazed that there was a little human being inside there. She wanted to escape the situation already, and she had only been there for a few minutes - but it was proving to be more difficult that she was imagining.

Once another person came in and distracted Claire's attention, Amelia casually made her way to the kitchen and hid there while Claire greeted woman after woman as they filed into the large living room, which was only separated from the kitchen by a small wall. As Amelia ran her finger along the edge of the dark granite countertop, she could hear the fawning over Claire's belly and how good she looked make its way around either side of the wall - how Amelia wished the time would pass quickly. Part of her wanted to gag from all the giddiness in the other room, yet she knew she probably wouldn't feel this way if she could have her own children and experience this for herself, but in the meantime she wished she could hide under a rock until it was all over.

Amelia came out of hiding once Sarah arrived, as Sarah was the least threatening of all the women and the only other woman at the baby shower who didn't already have children. Though if her and John were to marry, it did cross Amelia's mind that Sarah very well may be pregnant before her at the rate Amelia's fertility was going. Why did everything have to be a competition with her? Why couldn't she enjoy something in life without always comparing her fertility to that of other women?

The day seemed to drag on as each minute literally ticked by on the large standing pendulum clock that stood in Claire's living room. The clock was an antique that belonged to their grandparents. It was left to Claire when they passed away since she was the eldest child. Amelia watched the pendulum swing back and forth as she had many times in their grandparents living room; each tick making her more antsy to get home to Jake and each tock reminding her how her fertility was wasting away. She looked down to the trim of her shirt where three clothespin were clamped. Sometimes she couldn't stand the games played at baby showers. This particular one had everyone starting out with three clothespins clipped to their shirts or dresses and kept people from saying the word 'baby.' If anyone said that word, then the person who caught you saying it would get to steal one of your clothespins. At the end of the shower, the person with the most clothespins would win a prize.

Being a very mindful person made Amelia very good at these types of games, unlike her sister who already lost all of her clothespins. But Amelia didn't want to be good at it - yes, she would get a prize in the end - but not the prize she really longed for, so it all felt pretty pointless to her. She didn't want the prize anyway - it was probably baby related like a chocolate rattle pop or something cute like that anyway.

Finally after everyone finished their light lunch of salad and hors d'oeuvres, chocolates were handed out to everyone as they settled onto the couch and seats in the living room to watch Claire open the gifts. "Aw, that's so cute!" the group commented about the first gift bag. Claire hadn't even opened the gift yet, but they all thought the bag with baby elephants and giraffes all over it was cute. *This is going to be so painfully long if they have to not only comment on each gift but also what it's wrapped in,* Amelia thought to herself.

A few gifts later, Sarah leaned over and nudged Amelia, "I had no idea there were so many things for babies. Did you?"

"I know, right?" was all Amelia could respond with otherwise she would go on one of her rants. She thought it completely ridiculous how many things were out there to buy not only for the babies themselves but also for the safety of the baby. One of the gifts Claire opened was a safety clip for the toilet seat. *Really?* Amelia thought. *Are babies really running around like dogs with their heads in toilets?* She understood wanting your baby to be safe, but babies and families have been around since the beginning of time and safety clips weren't needed for the toilet. She thought it was an excuse for parents to be lazy because instead of watching their children, parents put up all these safety clips so they don't have to worry about anything happening to their children while they're not watching.

As each gift was opened and adored, Amelia wondered what it would be like to sit in the wood rocking chair with a huge belly in her lap being the center of attention while feeling another life move around inside. A sadness began to set behind her countenance. Each baby shower she went to only made her more sad instead of happy unlike when her and Jake attended weddings.

Weddings always reminded her of the day they were married and brought back all the fond memories. Maybe if she was still single and all her friends were getting married, weddings wouldn't have such a happy effect on her. Maybe she was sad only because she couldn't have children - or at least not yet. Or maybe she was sad because it felt like she's lost a child she never had. "Excuse me," Amelia tapped Sarah, "I'm going to grab some more snacks." She pointed to the kitchen.

She needed time out of the gift room before she burst into tears. She found a small box of tissues tucked next to the toaster on the counter and dabbed the inner corners of her eyes to stop the rush of tears that threatened the borders of her eyes. She rested against the island in the middle of kitchen while she let out an audible exhale. Amelia placed her hands on her belly as her heart ached. It was such a strange feeling to mourn for someone that never existed except for in her thoughts and dreams, but nonetheless it still felt very real and very painful. How could she love someone so much that she didn't even know yet and that didn't even exist yet? She couldn't answer that question - how she wished she could actually have that child within her in order to find out the answer though.

"My turn, my turn," Jane's squeaking interrupted her thoughts. Amelia peeked out from around the kitchen wall and noticed that Jane ran into another room and quickly returned, "Now I know you had a registry, but I wanted to give you something that signified your journey." Not only did Jane have a bouquet of sunflowers in hand, she had balloons with sunflowers on them, and all the little gifts she had purchased for the baby had little sunflowers on them as well – pacifier with sunflower, onesie with a sunflower, even a little bib that had a bunch of sunflowers with the statement "Look on the bright side!" inscribed at the bottom. "That one is to remind you that though times can be hard with an infant, that there is always something to smile about." All the women in the room did their womanly "aaawww" sighs. Amelia just felt even more incompetent - especially as a sister. She should have been the one to be this excited about Claire's pregnancy and baby shower. She should have been the one who purchased all those great gifts for her sister - but instead she was the selfish sister standing in the kitchen feeling sorry for herself in the midst of her sister's happiest moment.

Jane raised her champagne glass and toasted, "The sunflower grows towards the sun and represents optimism. That's what you and Seth have – you both have always put your mind to something and seen it to the end no matter how much sacrifice it took or how hard it was; you grow towards the sun. Though it took you a while to get pregnant and you had a lot of doctor appointments, tests, and so on, you both endured it together and have a strengthened marriage because of it, and this little one is going to be so blessed to be born to such a wonderful couple who will love and cherish her. To you – Claire – and Seth and your little one!"

"Cheers!" Everyone toasted with wine, except Claire who had grape juice.

Amelia rolled her eyes and hoped no one noticed. *Three months is nothing to the years I have been waiting*, Amelia thought herself as she remembered Claire telling her that they had only tried for a few months before getting pregnant. Maybe Claire and Seth had dealt with infertility, since Jane mentioned in the toast that Claire had several doctor appointments and tests. Amelia wasn't about to ask Claire though. It was not the time or place, and Amelia wasn't really sure she wanted to connect with her sister about infertility, as Amelia had a strong suspicion that Claire and Seth would have gone through a mainstream fertility clinic and could have even used IVF.

Amelia sat there with her thoughts thinking how her and Claire could be in the same boat and yet Claire was pregnant and Amelia wasn't. Everything about in-vitro was wrong and immoral, and Amelia knew that. She would never want to treat human life so carelessly. Who knows how many treatments Claire went through? How many babies died in those treatments that didn't take? How could Claire have been so careless? Amelia felt a little less jealous of Claire now imagining the circumstances of how she got pregnant. She could only hope that everything with the baby and Claire would end up ok. She knew from her Catholic fertility clinic the statistics that showed how unsuccessful in-vitro was even if there was a successful conception - sometimes the babies could have problems after birth or years later.

Amelia wished Claire and Seth hadn't gone down that path. It would make talking about her and Jake's infertility all that more difficult some day because Claire would probably say, "Why don't you try IVF? We did." Then Amelia would have to explain that it is wrong to create a life outside of the human body and essentially 'play God,' plus it removes the intimacy between man and wife of creating another human being and makes it a process between a woman and a doctor instead of husband and wife.

Claire wouldn't understand Amelia's explanation that infertility is a cross that some people must carry. Claire was definitely too much into everyone having rights no matter the cost to others, and many people think that having children is a right and not a blessing from God. Amelia knew that when it came time to discuss this with Claire that it would only further the already great distance in their relationship, but Amelia wasn't going to back down on what she believed about the precious gift and blessing of a human life.

Amelia couldn't help but write in her journal that night:

*Infertility isn't something new to our culture. Even women in Biblical times dealt with this - Sarah, Hannah, Elizabeth, and Anne(Mary's mother) - to name a few. Though Sarah was old, God fulfilled His promise and gave her a son. Hannah promised her son to God's service, if she ever bore a child, and God gave her Samuel. Zechariah and Elizabeth thought they would never have children, and then the angel Gabriel told Zechariah his wife was with child, and John the Baptist came into the world. Anne and Joachim wished for children but remained barren until Anne became pregnant with Mary, the Mother of God.*

    *Baby showers are some of the hardest events for me to endure as a woman dealing with infertility. Sometimes I wonder why God won't grant us a child when I know it's in His power to do so. The women in the Bible dealing with infertility were given children, yet I remain barren. Though, there could be other women that weren't mentioned that never conceived. I wish I could know what God has planned for the future. I wish an angel would tell me or Jake that we are with child.*

# LONGING

"Ready, one, two, three," the camera clicked and flashed in Sarah's hand. The three-month-old baby was one of the cutest babies Sarah had ever laid eyes on. The little infant had on a ruffly satin red dress with white tights and black shiny shoes. Her fine blonde hair was parted on the right side of her head with a green and white barrette holding back a portion of hair that was long enough to be gathered into it.

Sarah didn't usually do photo shoots, but one of her previous clients, Mrs. Beau de Fontaine, had asked her if she took photos. Sarah told her that she wasn't a professional, but she had taken some courses in college. Sarah had a portfolio that she leant to Mrs. Beau de Fontaine. Before she knew it, she received a call from Mrs. Beau de Fontaine's sister who wanted pictures of their infant done for Christmas cards.

Sarah agreed to the photo shoot because she felt it would be nice to have some extra cash as she wanted to buy John a Christmas present, and the winter season tended to be a slower time for her party planning business anyway. She wasn't sure what she was going to buy John yet, but she knew she didn't want her funds to be limited when making the decision. "Isn't she so adorable?" The mother of the child gloated over Sarah's shoulder.

"She is," Sarah agreed, "very adorable." The baby sat propped up against two white silk pillows on a beige couch. The house was immaculate - very much like Mrs. Beau de Fontaine's house. Actually both homes and women had a very Stepford Wives feel to them.

Sarah snapped a few more pictures when she heard the door bell ring. "Ah! There she is!" The woman declared as Mrs. Beau de Fontaine and Kaitlyn walked in from the adjoined kitchen by an archway. Mrs. Beau de Fontaine who was showing a slightly pregnant belly shuffled up to the baby on the couch and caressed her cheek. The baby cooed and a half smile formed on her face along with a little drool sneaking from the corner of her mouth. The mother quickly ran over with a cloth to wipe the drool before it reached the dress or any other of the fancy material that surrounded the child.

Sarah sat down on a chair as the two women started chatting and were standing in front of the baby while doing so. She tried not to listen to their conversation, but the volume of their voices almost made it seem like they wanted the whole world to know what they were talking about. Sarah could barely think to herself as Mrs. Beau de Fontaine blurted out, "Five cycles, but this one finally took!" She patted her belly. "You wouldn't believe the amount of doctor appointments, planning, and money..." It was all becoming clear to Sarah now why the mother had always been distracted and on her phone. She must have been going through IVF treatments, though Sarah couldn't help but feel like this mother was giving herself bragging rights for purchasing her baby.

She watched as Kaitlyn settled into the sofa chair - her arms crossed. "I like your dress," Sarah smiled trying to illicit some kind of conversation with the girl. The dress she wore was knee-length A-Line green satin with a black velvet shoulder cap sleeve top. Kaitlyn looked at Sarah as though she had never met her before, and then looked back at the floor as she sighed.

Sarah began to feel like she was never going to be good with kids. Had she done something wrong? Or was this a young girl caught up in high society already? Poor thing. Though she was young, the girl looked like she carried the stress and cares of a grown adult. She definitely wasn't full of smiles like she had been for her birthday party during the summer. In fact, it looked like she never cracked a smile in her entire life. Maybe she was upset by her mother's pregnancy? Sarah couldn't blame her though considering how everything out of her mother's mouth was either about the pregnancy or how difficult it was to get pregnant.

"Excuse me," Mrs. Beau de Fontaine said interrupting Sarah's thoughts, "excuse me." She waved her hand in front of Sarah's face.

"Yes, sorry." Sarah looked at the two women before her.

"We'd like to take a few photos with the two girls. Would that be ok?"

"That's fine." For the next twenty minutes Sarah ended up taking singles of each child and then a bunch of photos of the two children in different positions - one with the baby on Kaitlyn's lap, then with them side by side, one with the baby facing Kaitlyn, and another with Kaitlyn holding the baby like a mother would.

As Sarah clicked each picture her heart longed more and more for children. Though she was dating John now, the prospect of children in the future was more of a possibility, but she still longed for it now. She didn't want to have to wait any longer. She wasn't getting any younger, and she knew that the older women get the less fertile they are.

That night Sarah uploaded all the photos to her computer. On the first run through the photos, she deleted all the ones that were not viable - blurry from movement, off center, not focused, or any other imperfections that a little photo editing couldn't fix or adjust. For the second run through the photos, she started the adjustments to each photo for exposure, straightening, red eye, etc. Then on the third run through the photos, she made duplicates of her favorites that she would then change into different tones like sepia and black and white.

It was getting late; her eyes were beginning to feel heavy and her back was tight from sitting in the computer chair for so long. When the phone rang, she felt relief to have an excuse to give herself a break. "John!" There couldn't have been a better distraction.

They chatted a while about each of their days - John had a bunch of plowing and shoveling jobs to do during the winter, and Sarah told him about the strange photo shoot. "I think Mrs. Beau de Fontaine did IVF to get pregnant." They both agreed that it made sense because of how distracted she always had been when she was around.

"And she was always on the phone!" John commented.

"Right?" They both laughed.

Sarah asked John if he would ever consider doing IVF if they had any infertility problems like Amelia and Jake. John expressed that he didn't agree with that method, and Sarah became nervous that they may never have children. She didn't really agree with the IVF method either, but she also wasn't in that point of her life of being faced with that decision either. She was a little nervous that they may face the same trials as Amelia and Jake because Amelia was John's sister. Sarah wasn't sure if infertility could run in families or not, but then again his other sister did get pregnant - though at the baby shower, there was mention that Claire and Seth had a difficult time as well.

Their conversation had been going well as they discussed the topic, but before she knew it she hung up the phone after their first fight. She didn't even remember how it happened or what it was about - it was one of those fights that was over something petty and then tumbled into fighting about fighting, but she hung up the phone before the fight continued into something larger. They had managed to date for almost three months without a fight, which she thought was pretty impressive.

She hated fighting though - not that couples enjoy fighting - but she hated it more than the average person because she felt that it meant that the whole relationship was falling apart. Since Scott, she feared what it would be like to be in a relationship again. Her and Scott had never fought. Once in a while they would tease each other, but the first time they fought was when he told her he found someone else. Though the fight with John wasn't the same, she sat in her computer chair wondering if their relationship would end. She didn't want it to, but she feared about how it would affect her if it did.

John tried calling back a couple of times, but she let the voicemail take the calls. She needed to finish up working on the photos and didn't want to be distracted with her emotions anymore, so she tucked them deep inside and looked at the computer screen to the little baby's face with the green and white barrette, and tears began to form in her eyes. What if things didn't work out with John? Would she ever have children and a family? He was so perfect for her in so many ways, but what if it didn't work out? What if she ended up alone and childless?

Sarah wanted to pick up the phone to call John and smooth over everything, but then she remembered how she had always wanted Scott to make her feel special, but she always ended up being the one to go the extra mile to keep him interested in her - apparently that didn't work, so she decided she was going to wait for John. Before she finished her thought, there was a knock at her door. She was a little nervous to answer the door because it was so late, but she was glad she did when she saw John standing on her doorstep with a bouquet of flowers.

She smiled as he handed her the flowers, "Silly fight - let's not do that again."

She hugged him, "Agreed," she whispered in his ear.

Amelia thought back on the day as she sat propped up against her pillow in bed. As usual Jake was already breathing a slight snore, and Chloe was curled up on his chest sporting a full on purr - how Amelia wished Chloe was a little infant instead. She thought how Claire and Seth would have a little infant of their own soon. Amelia immediately felt jealousy rise up in her soul and injustice that she couldn't experience the same thing with Jake, which was making her feel bitter - but she didn't want to feel any of those things anymore. She was tired of having these emotions hit her every time she saw a pregnant woman in the store or heard another announcement of someone's pregnancy.

While her mind was on the topic of infants, she remembered the newborn that was brought into church that morning. The child was only a few weeks old. She was so tiny, so precious. The mother said the infant looked more like her husband than herself. Amelia really didn't think so, "She definitely has her father's nose." As the words had left the mother's mouth, tears almost poured out of Amelia's eyes at the harsh realization came that she may never hear those words from anyone.

If her and Jake adopted, the child wouldn't look anything like them. Though that's not the most important thing about having a child, it's something that was still very hard for Amelia to swallow. Tears welled up in her eyes as she felt selfish thinking that having a child that resembled her and Jake was hard to give up. She knew she could love another child... someday. She would have to give up hopes of having her own children first though. She wasn't sure she could bury them yet. It was so easy to create and imagine a life with them, but to take those wonderful made up memories and tear them apart was like allowing all the wicked in the fairy-tale land triumph and destroy all that was good and beautiful.

Amelia opened her journal. She didn't feel like scripting full sentences. Her thoughts were choppy and emotions broken, but she needed to write something. She needed to pen this out and decided to try writing in poem form.

*Longing*

*I wail, and I watch...*
*But my voice is silenced.*

*In the recesses of my heart,*
*My longing increases; my desire burns.*

*Beauty, love, creation -*
*Once it was, now it waits...*
*Time stands still - the air is thick,*
*Breathing has never been harder.*

*Who am I? Can I save this?*
*Can I change this?*
*The sky grays, and all that was*
*No longer gleams in the sun.*

*Clouds cover, and doubt rolls in.*
*Waves crash as the wind thunders,*
*The storybook is being destroyed,*
*Can I manage to move?*

*As the ache in my soul twists and turns,*
*I wonder - will I survive this?*
*And if I do...*
*Will the remains be worth the fight?*

# SUNFLOWERS

"It's time!" Claire's excited voice reverberated through Amelia's head as she blinked in the darkness on an early December morning. Amelia fumbled around for the switch to the small light on her nightstand and sat up trying to shake herself from the stupor of her sleep.

"It is? Are you sure? Sometimes there are false alarms." Amelia hated how she knew so much about something she may never experience. It felt like wasted knowledge, but she didn't want to dispose of it in case by any chance they were ever able to get pregnant.

"No, this is real, Amelia. We're on the way...." Claire took a deep painful breath while trying to finish her sentence, "to... the hospital. Meet us there when you can."

Claire hung up, and Amelia looked at the time on her phone. She figured it had to be three or later in the morning, but it was actually much earlier. It was only shortly after midnight - *no wonder why it was still so dark*, she thought to herself. Did Claire realize what time it was? Amelia felt completely selfish that she didn't want to jump out of bed right at the moment and rush to the hospital to wait for hours for the baby to arrive when she could stay comfortably in her bed and sleep and arrive at the hospital at a decent hour when she was rested and able to function and be present to the whole experience. If she left now, she would probably only end up being an emotional wreck, which she was trying to avoid considering the situation was already going to be emotionally challenging for her.

Chloe jumped up on the bed and started slowly walking towards Amelia wondering if it was time to get up and have breakfast. Amelia leaned over to Jake, "Hey," she whispered, but he didn't seem to be phased by her attempt. She nudged him a bit, "Hey, wake up, Claire's having her baby, and she wants us to go to the hospital," by this time Chloe had made her way between the two of them and began purring. Amelia figured if Jake said they could stay home, she would be off the hook of feeling guilty because it was a decision they both made instead of just herself.

"What time is it?" He looked dazed and confused - much of the same way she felt only minutes ago when Claire broke into Amelia's deep sleep.

"Twelve fifteen."

"Are you kidding me?" He sighed. "And it's not a false alarm?" Yes, Jake knew everything about pregnancy as well.

"She said it wasn't and to come as soon as we can to the hospital."

He yawned, "Well, the soonest we can be there is once the sun rises at a normal decent time." He rolled to his side and faced her, "It's not like the baby is going anywhere. It's ok to see it when it's a few hours old, plus who knows how long she'll be in labor for - it could be a while before the baby even arrives."

"I agree." Amelia clicked the light off and snuggled back under the covers next to Jake, though Chloe was thoroughly disappointed that she wasn't going to be getting breakfast anytime soon and decided to jump down from the bed.

The phone rang again what felt like only a short time later. Even though the sun had started coming up, Amelia was thoroughly annoyed that her sister was calling again. Though Claire was excited, Amelia wasn't happy to be woke up again. "Hello?" Amelia made her voice sound a bit annoyed.

"Amelia, it's Seth." His voice sounded a little shaky. "If you could come to the hospital as soon as possible," he paused, she could tell he was having a hard time finding words, "something's wrong, and Claire wanted me to call you."

"Oh, sure. What's wrong, Seth?"

"Please tell John as well. I couldn't reach him." And with that he was off the phone.

"Hey Jake," he shook him, "we need to go to the hospital now. Something is wrong, and Seth didn't give me any details." Amelia started assuming the worst, "I hope Claire's ok." She wondered if there had been complications with the delivery and wasn't sure what to expect when they arrived at the hospital.

The sunflowers on the hospital tray table caught the first morning light that shone in the window. The yellow and brown hues once held so much happiness and promise of a future to Claire, but now tear after tear dropped from her eyes at the sight of them.

Seth was out in the waiting room with the family. Claire requested that no visitors come in to see her for a few hours. He was always very attentive to her needs, and she was appreciative of that especially at times like this. She needed some time to digest all that happened in the last few hours, and though she knew Seth needed time as well, he knew he needed to be the stronger one and hold the family off while Claire took her time to breath. She felt sympathy for her husband. She wished she could be as strong as him in this, but every part of her being was falling apart.

She stared out the window and focused on a park across the street - some leaves leftover from fall danced across the freshly fallen snow and a few leaves were still hanging on to the trees. It was almost as if nature was mourning as well - not wanting to let go of the season that had passed; trying so desperately to hold onto something that had passed and gone. Though the sun shined, it seemed filtered – bright enough to see the beauty of the earth but censored enough that you didn't need to squint your eyes.

She glanced over at the sunflowers again and bit her bottom lip to stop it from quivering as more tears streamed down her face. The flowers on her tray table, though bloomed and colorful, seemed to sit there silently with sympathy instead of dancing with their normal enthusiasm. She remembered how cheerful the sunflowers made her feel when Jane had brought a bouquet of them to her baby shower only a few weeks earlier, but these ones that were delivered to her early this morning with a card from Jane saying, "Can't wait to meet the new little one!" only seemed to mock her.

Claire looked down at the little sunflower onesie in her lap. She laid it on her still swollen belly. How many times had she done this before while sitting in the nursery? The only difference now was her little baby girl was no longer inside. She gripped the onesie in her hands and brought it up to her mouth to muffle her sobs. It smelled like any other store bought piece of clothing, but to her it should have smelled like a new born infant by now. "Ah!" escaped her mouth, and she was surprised at how loud she was.

At once, Seth entered the room and ran over to the wheelchair that she sat in. Claire could hear the whispers of the nurses in the hall as the door shut behind him, "Poor woman," "Is she ok?" "It's just not fair."

"I can't, I can't, I…" Seth couldn't really understand what she was saying since her words were muffled in the onesie, but he knew his wife's pain. All he could do was hold his wife; he felt so helpless.

"I want her back, Seth." Claire looked up at Seth with bloodshot eyes and a red nose, "I just want her back!"

His heart ached as much as hers, "Me too." A tear rolled down his right cheek.

"It wasn't enough time," she said in between her sobs.

"I know," he held his wife again.

"Don't go back out there," she whispered, "don't leave me."

"I'm here. I'm not leaving." He gave her a gentle squeeze. "I love you."

"I love you too," she said softly.

Their daughter, Ashley Marie Fitzpatrick, was born only a few hours earlier without life. The doctors had no explanation to them why their daughter was still born. The only thing they kept repeating was that sometimes the trauma of the birthing experience caused it to happen in some babies. The doctors let them keep her for a while to say their goodbyes, but no time would *ever* be long enough for Claire to say goodbye to the child she had been waiting to meet for nine months.

Claire thought of Ashley's little fingers and toes. She squeezed her eyes tightly shut trying to stop the pain that radiated through them. The precious moments she spent with Ashley had been the most memorable longest and shortest lapses of time she ever experienced.

*"The sunflower grows towards the sun and represents optimism. That's what you and Seth have – you both have always put your mind to something and seen it to the end no matter how much sacrifice it took or how hard it was; you grow towards the sun."* Jane's toast from Claire's baby shower reverberated in her head.

"It's not fair," she tried to get up from the wheelchair, and Seth assisted her to the bed. "Can we still grow towards the sun?" She pointed to the sunflowers. "How can we ever see the positive in this?"

"Shhhh," he said sympathetically, "we can't think of that now." He sat on the bed beside her and stroked the hair along her face. She closed her swollen eyes and let herself escape into the touch of her husband's soothing strokes along the side of her forehead and around her face. Before she knew it, she fell asleep.

That night, Amelia couldn't fall asleep. All the emotions of the day kept running through her head. All she could think about was the grief Claire and Seth must be dealing with, much like her own. Though Amelia hadn't physically lost a child, every day she thought of the child she longed to have and every day without that child felt like a stab in her heart of pain that she couldn't stop from hurting. It had been harder lately to feel numb to the pain because of the baby shower and impending baby, but she had never wished anything like this to happen to Claire.

She sat up in bed and turned on the small light on her nightstand. It cast enough light to allow her eyes to adjust to the change in light, but it wasn't bright enough to wake up Jake. He moved slightly, but she could tell he was still deep in sleep.

Amelia couldn't help but feel completely sad and lonely for herself. The idea of Claire and Seth losing the baby made her stomach turn and only made her own grief more real - at least the feelings of it all came more alive even though she didn't have anything physical to actually mourn over. She reached for her journal and a pen and slowly slid out of bed and headed to the great room. She clicked on the floor lamp and snuggled into the corner of the couch. She was going to be there a while.

*I write this to you, my little one, tonight. I don't know who you are, or if I will ever be able to meet you, but I wanted you to know a few things. I love you very, very much. Sometimes I feel crazy because I'm not even sure how I can love someone so much whom I've never met... but I do. There is not a day that goes by where I don't think about you and the things I dream of us doing together - the laughs we share, the cuddles and hugs that we keep, and the adventures we journey on together.*

*Each day, I hope that I'm another day closer to meeting you, but then as each day passes without you in my arms, I become more and more scared that I may never have my chance to meet you. Though you may only ever be a figment of my imagination, I want you to know that you've been my best thought of creation. Part of you is inside me right now and part of you is inside your dad right now, yet I can't see you - so that's why I can only imagine how wonderful you will be someday.*

*I do hope and pray each and every day that I will be able to hold you in my womb and in my arms, but if I can't, you will forever be held in my heart. I will keep trying all the things I can to help my body be a comfortable place for you, so you will want to stay with us. Though I understand that my body may not be able to be that place for you here, I do hope that one day I can meet you in heaven among the angels - for that's where I know you will be - my little angel - and that's where I will know to look for you.*

Amelia couldn't write anymore without soaking the paper completely with her tears, so she closed her journal and grabbed some tissues. She sat in silence for a while, as she cried for herself and for Claire. Amelia determined that losing a child - whether imaginary or real - was one of the worst things a person would ever have to endure.

# SHATTERED DREAMS

The morning light peered in from the crack in the blinds and woke Claire. She was still in the hospital, but hoped it had been all a bad dream - maybe her baby was in the nursery and the nurse would come in shortly to tell her that the baby needed to breastfed. She slowly took in the room around her. There were no congratulations balloons around and the vase of sunflowers were on the window sill mourning instead of celebrating. Maybe she hadn't been dreaming...

A small knock on the door disrupted her thoughts. "Come in," she said to the unknown guest. Could it be the nurse with her baby?

Amelia peeked her head around the door, "Hi," she whispered, "Seth said you would be ok with me coming in." Claire nodded, and Amelia quietly shut the heavy hospital door that would usually keep the sound of crying babies contained in each room.

"Where is Seth?" Claire adjusted herself to a more upright position.

"Oh, he's out in the lobby getting some coffee and snacks." Amelia sat in the comfy chair that had been reclined for Seth to sleep on. She wasn't entirely sure what to say to her sister, but she knew she felt Claire's loss more than Claire would ever understand. She reached for Claire's hand and squeezed it gently. Claire too had nothing to say. They sat like this in silence for a few moments.

It was so unusual to be around a *quiet* Claire. She always had something to say. Amelia knew she would have to be the first one to speak today though. "I'm so sorry," Amelia's eyes began to well up, "but, unfortunately, I understand how you feel. Maybe not to this extent, but I do know what it feels like to experience the loss of a child."

"How so?" Claire looked intrigued but a little perturbed as well.

"Well, we haven't told the family yet but were planning on doing so soon. Jake and I have been dealing with infertility for a while now. I know I haven't physically lost a child, but I do know what it's like to emotionally lose a child month after month."

Claire released Amelia's hand and sat back against the bed. Claire stared at the ceiling as tears trickled down her cheeks and soaked into her hospital gown. Amelia let her take time to respond and clasped her hands together as the tension in the room loomed around them. The heaviness of loss almost made it impossible to breathe as it filled the room like a dense humidity in a sauna.

"Leave," Claire said quietly and calmly.

Amelia was puzzled, "What?"

"Please leave," Claire stated louder.

Amelia stood to go, but she wasn't really sure what she had done wrong. Maybe Claire needed more time. "Are you ok, Claire? I can stay..."

"No. Leave." Her voice sounded shaky. "I'm not ok, Amelia, and I'm not sure I'm ever going to be ok." Amelia hung her head down. She knew exactly how that felt.

"Ok." Amelia whispered. "I'm here if you need me." She began to walk away.

"How dare you!" Claire called out. "How dare you tell me that *you* understand! I'm sorry you've dealt with infertility, but I carried my baby for nine months, and I held my lifeless child in my arms yesterday feeling utterly helpless to save her. Until you experience that, you don't know what it's like to lose a child!"

Amelia eyes were full of tears that overflowed down her face. "I'm sorry." She turned away and started towards the door. The one time she tried to connect with her sister personally only blew up in her face, as she had always feared it would.

"Why didn't you tell me sooner?" Amelia turned away from the door to face Claire's question. "I mean I thought that the whole time I was pregnant, that you'd be happy for me. I wanted you to support me - to be around - but you weren't there. It felt like you didn't care. I had begun to think that you were mad at me or something." She sighed. "I wanted my sister around to share in my experience, but the whole time, you were distant. If I had known, I wouldn't have taken it so personally. I would have been sensitive to you. Why didn't you tell me?"

"Claire, it's not exactly something you broadcast to everyone. Jake and I had deal with it on our own first before involving others... *even* family. I know you think my loss isn't real because I didn't carry and birth a child, but you're wrong. Every day I carry the memories I've made up of our children... of the happiness they'd bring us, of the trials Jake and I would face together raising them... and each day, I have to let go of one more memory, one more hope, one more dream. Each day I experience a little death that one else even knows happens. So instead, I have to parade around with a smile on my face as I grieve each loss. And every month when I receive a clear negative that we're not pregnant again, it's as if I'm holding that lifeless child in my arms begging God to bring her back, but it's too late.

"Don't tell me that I don't know what it's like to experience loss! I've been experiencing it for seven years now! I'm sorry I wasn't there for you, but maybe someday you'll put yourself in my shoes and understand what it's like to be me in the midst of world where it seems everyone can get pregnant... except me. I do know what it's like to lose a child while trying to pick up the pieces left behind from the shattered dream you once had." Amelia slowly opened the door, "The difference between me and you though... is that you'll have another chance." She smiled through her tears at Claire from across the room. "I won't."

"I feel bad about being so harsh with Claire," Amelia and Jake sat on their couch later that evening. "She did just lose a child, but I lost it, Jake. I completely lost it. I couldn't hold it in anymore, especially since at our appointment last week with Dr. Carter when he strongly recommended the surgery for endometriosis again. I think it's because I carry this around all the time without anyone knowing that sometimes it doesn't feel real, but today when she said I didn't know what it was like, something snapped in me. I came completely unglued, and I bursted apart at the seams. I feel like it's getting to the point where people are going to start asking us questions. I know we're planning on telling people, but it's so difficult because then it's so official and makes it become more real. I don't want to be "officially" infertile."

"I know, Amelia, but I think it's a very necessary next step." He stroked her face.

"No, I know," she sighed, "but it still feels like I'm living some kind of bad dream that I wish I could shake myself awake from. The minute we send the letter to our families, it takes our very personal struggle and makes it public. It takes my bad dream and makes it a reality. I guess I was hoping it would never get this far. I never really thought that we'd be at this point. I was certain God would answer our prayers before now." She swallowed hard and sniffed, "But unfortunately, this is the reality we have to face, and it's our next step in dealing with it all." Jake nodded, and for the next couple of hours, they hand wrote each letter over tears and tea.

"Well, she's doing the best she can for having lost a child," Amelia had called Lane after they finished the letters to update her on everything with Claire since she hadn't chatted with her much since Thanksgiving because of the flurry of events. "I was jealous of her pregnancy, but I *never* wanted her to lose the baby."

"Amelia, I know you probably feel guilty or like somehow this is your fault, but it's not. You can't blame yourself." Lane stated in her usual calm, collected manner. "All you can do is pray for them during this time."

"I know, Lane, but it doesn't seem like enough. I feel bad about the fight we had, and I'm not sure we'll ever be able to mend the relationship. It was already strained, and this literally pushed it over the edge."

"Prayer is one of the strongest things you can do for her. It may not seem like you're doing much when you pray, but you really are. Let me ask you a question," Lane paused for a moment, "Do you think that cloistered monks or nuns that shut themselves away from the world to pray are doing nothing? Do you think their purpose is meaningless?" She didn't pose the question as though she was upset but as though she was truly curious to Amelia's response.

"Not at all. I think what they do is one of the highest callings because they give up their entire selves to serve God by loving and serving others through prayer. It's truly a selfless act and completely admirable."

"Well, there's your answer," Lane said matter-of-factly. "Your prayers are a gift to your sister, though she may never realize it - especially if the relationship cannot be mended - but your prayers are the best gift you can ever give her. They are selfless, Amelia. Always remember that if you ever doubt yourself by thinking you're not doing enough."

Before tucking into bed that night, Amelia grabbed her journal from her nightstand, and wrote:

*Jake and I have decided that at our next appointment with Dr. Carter, we're going to tell him that it will be our last appointment. The letter to the family and our last appointment with the doctor feels like it's making everything so official though. We're barren. I still don't know why, since the doctors have confirmed that everything is functioning properly. There is no real reason why we can't conceive. It's hard to reconcile why God wouldn't want us to have children, but I guess I have to trust that He knows more and knows best though it will definitely take time for me to truly believe it in my heart. In the meantime, I have no idea what to do with myself. Life is so wide open, and I know that most people would kill to be in my shoes - to be free. Well, I guess the grass is always greener, but I really do believe that if we ever did have children, I wouldn't regret it.*

*We've decided that adoption isn't really what we want to seek right now. Maybe someday we'll re-visit it, but right now, we don't need another process to be part of where the outcome is still waiting for a child. I've been waiting for Autumn for so long that I've forgotten what it's like to just be in the moment. I've always been looking ahead, and it's hard to stop and see what's around me in the present. I'm sure I'll be haunted by this forever, but all I can do is continually put it in God's hands and know that for now, this is my cross to bear, which is pretty insignificant considering the cross He bore for me.*

Amelia fluffed her pillow and pushed herself further into the covers. "Jake, you still awake?" He made a noise that was between a grunt and a moan. She tapped him until she saw his eyes open, "I was thinking more about the letters. Can we wait to send them until the new year after we have our next appointment with Dr. Carter and let him know that we're done?"

He brushed his hand to the side of her face, "Sure, if that makes it easier for you." He kissed her on the forehead.

"Thanks," she sighed, "it does because I feel like it will be nice to be past the appointments before we start fielding questions from our family members." She turned her light off and snuggled in next to Jake as he put his arm around her.

The next morning, Amelia woke to a small bouquet of petite red roses on Jake's pillow and a folded note next to them. A smile slightly formed across her face as she sat up slowly and grabbed the note.

*Happy Anniversary! Follow the petals to your next surprise.*

She hadn't noticed the petals on the other side of the bouquet that trickled over the side of the bed and into the hallway until after reading the note. She peeled the covers off her legs and scooted across the bed. She wrapped her light modal fabric robe around her and tied it as she stood up.

As she walked down the hallway towards the kitchen, the smell of french toast tickled her nose, and her smile widened. She stepped onto the cold tiled kitchen floor and peeked around the cabinets to see Jake squeezing oranges. "Oooo ... ," she made him look up. The instant he saw her, he smiled like he did on their wedding day when she was walking down the aisle to him - she would never forget that smile.

"Making some orange juice and using some of the pulp for an orange glaze frosting to drizzle on the french toast." He was quite proud of himself.

"And you came up with that all on your own?" She teased him.

"Of course," he winked at her and then pointed to the kitchen table. In the center stood a bouquet of Gerbera daisies mixed in with a few small orchids and wildflowers shining with rose, white, and lilac hues.

Amelia breathed in and put her hands to her mouth to cover her gasp. "They're beautiful!"

Jake scooted over to her and whispered in her ear, "Not as beautiful as you." He pushed her hair past her neck and gave her a gentle kiss on the nape of her neck.

She turned to him, "Thank you for the flowers and breakfast. Happy Anniversary!" She had a card for him in her nightstand and turned to fetch it from the bedroom.

"Thank *you* for marrying me." Jake grabbed her by the waist to pull her close and took her face in his hands and kissed her gently on her soft lips then rested his hands on the small of her back, "You know I love this nightie on you." He smiled. "You're going to distract me from making breakfast!"

"That was the plan," she winked. "But I'm hungry, so get back to work." She wiggled away and ran off to the bedroom for his card.

"Tease!" He jokingly called after her.

"Here," Amelia bounded back in the room - card in hand.

Jake opened the envelope, pulled out the card, and opened it to Amelia's handwritten part on the inside left section after reading the front of the card.

*Jake, I know by now we thought we'd have children - several children. Though we've been married eight years, and the last couple of years have been trying with our infertility, I couldn't ask for better husband, and I wouldn't have wanted to share our journey of infertility with any other man. God has truly blessed me with the best husband any woman could ask for. I'm sorry I can't give you any children - I wish I could more than anything - but I want you to know whether or not we can ever have children that you're enough for me. I love you so much! Happy Anniversary!*

"Thank you, Amelia," he held her and hugged her tightly. "I'm sorry we can't have children as well, but please don't blame yourself. The infertility is just as much my fault, in fact, it's not a fault of either of ours. For some reason, I don't know why, our bodies aren't working the way they should, but we can't blame ourselves." He pulled her away from him and looked into her eyes, "I love you so much whether or not we have children. Remember the theme of our wedding?"

She nodded, "Yes... promise." A tear of happiness rolled down her left cheek.

"That's right. We promised to love each other and care for each other no matter what comes our way. Well, infertility is in our way right now, but you know what? It hasn't changed our love for each other in a bad way at all. I think it's only made us stronger and made us love each other *more*!"

"Yes, I totally agree!" Amelia was so happy to be crying tears of happiness instead of sadness. She wished she could make this moment last forever.

# THE HIDEAWAY COTTAGE

Even though it had been eight years since the last time Amelia and Jake had been at the Hideaway Cottage, it was exactly the same as she had remembered as though it had been frozen in time from when they left it on their honeymoon. The small Christmas tree was still on the stand in the front window thoroughly dried out with the pine needles falling to the floor and also into the heater. The little wood burning stove was still the focus of the living room tucked into the corner of the room. Amelia remembered making spinach and feta cheese calzones in the tiny stove in the kitchen. The small dining table still sat in front of the bow window that was adjacent to the kitchen. She brushed her hand on the kitchen table and remembered the hours they spent playing all the games they had purchased from the Ye Olde Game Store that had been located in Dorset, Vermont but had gone out out of business the year following their honeymoon.

Amelia adjusted the heat to seventy as she had done many times before on the way to the bedrooms to set her bag down. She paused in the hallway. The bedrooms had not changed either – one with a king sized bed and the other with two twin beds. She never imagined coming to the Hideaway Cottage again without children. It was strange to be standing in the same spot that held so much of her dreams for children only now retrospectively to have the reality face her. She longed to hear the laughter of children in the twin bedroom.

She turned back to the living room and saw her and Jake when they were on their honeymoon curled up on the couch discussing how they would come back to Manchester Center, Vermont every year with "the kids" and stay at the Hideaway Cottage – heck, they may do Christmas there every year. She stood in the hallway and glanced down at her suitcase – still one suitcase – no baby bag or children's bag to unpack, only hers. Would it be this way forever?

"I am so thrilled to see snow!" She heard Jake announce from the kitchen when he finished unpacking the car and stomped his feet free of the packed snow.

"Yeah!" Amelia tried to sound enthusiastic. She didn't want to damper their time there with her thoughts. They were supposed to be taking a vacation from all of that. Amelia couldn't help but feel like it was a bad nightmare that stuck with her even upon waking – haunting her all day long. She dropped her bag in the big bedroom and met Jake in the dining room.

His smile was so wide that it was almost goofy, and she couldn't help but giggle at his giddiness. "What?" He ran over to her and scooped her up. "I'm so glad to be back here!"

"Me too!" She laughed as they twirled. "Now go take your boots off, they are getting the whole house wet!" She scolded him like a child. He was the only child she had – though she did feel that it was very unfair that he had to play two parts: husband and child. Amelia began to feel guilty because she remembered writing in Jake's card only a couple days earlier that he was enough for her, but she still doubted herself from time to time. Could she be happy with it being just the two of them forever? Would that be enough for her like she had promised? She always came to the same conclusion in the end though that it was never really a question of whether Jake was enough for her, as it was more of the fact that she had to let all of her dreams die that she and Jake had fantasized about when they were going to have children – all of the "when we have children" phrases that started those dreams all had to be put to rest. Unlike the nightmare that had become their reality, her dreams remained in their dream world – trapped – only for viewing behind glass that kept them safe as in a museum, beautiful to look at but never tactile. Eventually the glass would be so fingerprinted from her touching it, that the dream behind it would be blurred and maybe fade into existence - or she could only hope.

Amelia began to wonder if they would get pregnant while on this vacation. Even though they said they weren't going to keep actively pursuing it because they didn't want to risk her health taking a turn for the worse again since she still hadn't fully recovered from everything that happened over the summer, they also weren't going to prevent it either, of course. She still hoped that it would miraculously happen – that God would all of sudden realize that He forgot to bless them with a child. *What if I did get pregnant though?* She thought to herself. She felt utter joy flow throughout her body, and then in the next moment, she felt utter terror – *what if I did get pregnant?* Then she began to think of all the children she had ever seen misbehave and wondered if they would actually be the good parents they thought they could be. *Once I'm pregnant, that's it, there's no going back.* She began to feel really small and very unsure why she had let this weigh so much on her. Did she really even want children?

"Whatcha thinking about?" Jake wrapped his arms around Amelia from behind. She didn't want to tell him because she felt silly about her thoughts, but she did feel utterly concerned. When she didn't answer him right away, he became concerned, "Are you ok?" He shifted around her to face her and looked directly into her eyes.

"What are we doing here, Jake?" He looked puzzled. "I mean why did we come back here? We don't have kids yet. We might never have kids. Why did we come to such an empty place that carries so many empty memories? I just…" she took a deep breath in to stop the tears and looked down to the floor.

He pulled her chin back up so her gaze met his again, "We came because this is the first place where we started our lives together. It's the place where our hopes and dreams started for our future together, and even though we don't have all of the things we had hoped and dreamed for, we still have the most important thing – our love." Tears trickled one by one from her eyes. "And our love, my darling, has been able to withstand the test of time and hardships, and yet we love each other no less because of it all – in fact, I think we love each other even more."

She nodded. She knew all of that was true, but she still wrestled with the fact that she couldn't give her husband a child - that they would never share in the joy of making a child together. She didn't want to give up on trying but at the same time, she didn't like the options that were before her. She did know that she didn't want any of it ruining their vacation.

That night Amelia grabbed her journal and settled onto the couch. The embers were still glowing from the fire in the stove. She took a deep breath in and sighed.

*We're here at the Hideaway Cottage again. This place is magical and will always hold a special place in my heart as does everything in Vermont, but as I sit here, I can't help but remember back to our honeymoon where everything all began - hopes, dreams, the start of our future - there were endless possibilities. Now I sit here .... barren ... with not many hopes or dreams of our future. What we're living now is all we'll ever have, and that's not bad, it's just different and a truth that I never thought I would have to come to.*

She blinked as the tears filled her eyes. She heard a few pine needles fall from the dried out Christmas tree, which made her think about Claire and Seth. The family decided that they weren't going to do a traditional Christmas celebration because of Claire and Seth's loss was still so tender. Gifts had been bought for the baby and them, and Claire and Seth were looking forward to "Baby's First Christmas." So everyone exchanged presents on their own with each other, but there was not a big family event. Amelia hated that her and Claire still had not spoken since their fight in the hospital, but she wanted to give Claire time and space. Amelia knew she needed it as well.

*I'm so torn, and yet I have to make a major decision. I have the choice of bearing this cross of infertility or I can choose to have the surgery for endometriosis done, even though I don't believe I have it. The doctors can't confirm until they actually do the surgery, but with my auto-immune issues, I'm extremely nervous that the surgery recovery is going to be horrible. What if I'm right and don't have endometriosis? Then the surgery was for nothing, I have to go through all the pain of it, and yet there is still no explanation of why we are infertile. If I do end up having endometriosis, then they can remove it, but there is still no guarantee that it won't grow back or that I'll get pregnant. However, if I did get the surgery, then at least we'd have a few more answers ... hopefully.*

The next day they decided to go horseback riding in Danby, Vermont at Mountain View Ranch as they did every year since their honeymoon. They didn't have to pay for a private ride because they were usually the only ones that wanted to go horseback riding when the weather was freezing and the snow was falling.

As they rode through the enchanted forest - that was the part of the ride through a dense forest with trees planted almost perfectly in line with each other - Amelia took a deep breath of the fresh cold air into her lungs. The tips of her fingers were almost completely numb since they were about halfway through their ride now. The leader was in the front of the line, and she kept turning toward Jake who was in the middle. Amelia brought up the rear of the line, but she didn't mind. She really didn't care about small chat when she was out on exertions like this. She actually preferred for it to be quiet, so she could take it all in.

Halfway through the forest, Amelia felt a great sense of happiness overcome her. She loved riding horses and being outside. She realized that this was the first time in a long time that she was actually letting herself enjoy life - she hadn't really been living for the past year because she allowed all the baby stuff to act like a dark cloud over her casting a shadow on all her experiences. She decided she wasn't going to let the cloud block her sunshine anymore. She knew there would still be rainy days, but she didn't want the rain to stop her from enjoying what she had with Jake. She wanted to cherish every moment with him - with or without children. Though they may never have children, Amelia knew that she couldn't let it dictate her life. She may never get her happily ever after, but she wasn't going to stop being the admirable princess with a great heart in the meantime.

"Ready to run?" Jake's voice broke through her thoughts. They had cleared the forest, and Jake and the guide were looking back at her. "We're going to trot a little across the field. Ready?"

Amelia couldn't contain her exuberant smile, "More than ever!"

## About the Author

Neesha lives with her husband and cat in Ipswich, Massachusetts located on the North Shore of Boston. Her and her husband have dealt with unexplained infertility since they were married in 2006. The journey has not only brought them closer together as a couple but also has led them to the Catholic Church. She loves reading, writing, and spending time in monasteries for a quiet getaway. This is her first published novel but not her last. Visit her website at neeshaoliver.wordpress.com to stay current on her latest work.

www.ingramcontent.com/pod-product-compliance
Lightning Source LLC
Chambersburg PA
CBHW022026240626
47154CB00007B/2276